Call Me

BY

GILLIAN JONES

Julie!

Welcome to breathless Whispers!

Enquiries please email gillianjonesauthor@gmail.com

First print edition: 2016

Edited by Quoth the Raven Writing Co.
Cover design © Book Covers by Ashbee Designs
Formatting by Paul Salvette

About the Book

Some know me as Chanel69.
But to my friends and family, I'm simply Ellie Hughes.
A university student who's in desperate need of money. A lot of money, and fast.

I'm about to start a new job.

Three nights a week, I'll be the star of your late night fantasies, bringing your fetishes and fucked up scenarios to life.
You'll listen to my voice while you get off on your dirtiest desires.

Truth be told…this job makes me nervous. Regardless of the money, I don't know if I can do it.

But when he calls, I feel an instant connection.
Over time, he becomes my regular, my friend, and my confidant.

The problem is…he seems familiar…I think I know who he is.

And if I'm right, how will he react when he discovers that I'm Chanel69?

Dear Reader,

Although *Call Me* deals with the lighter side of the sex trade industry, it is important to note that this story is fictitious. *Call Me* portrays this situation as humorous, sexy, and sometimes fun, however, this is not always the case. As readers, we need to realize that this novel does not show the entire truth or depth of the issues that occur within the sex trade industry, or the negative experiences that many sex trade workers encounter.

In the story, Ellie Hughes is of legal age—which in Canada is eighteen—making her older than many of the workers that are forced into this trade. Ellie's age of twenty-four and ability to make her own decisions makes it somewhat more palatable for her to be working in an environment such as Breathless Whispers, where Ellie is employed. *Call Me* does not depict the often dangerous and degrading environments in which many sex trade workers find themselves. In general, most of those running this industry in the real world do not care about fair wages, working conditions, or employee health and safety, the way the owners of Breathless Whispers—the Conrads—do in this fictional account.

The sex trade industry operates worldwide, and within North America despite our opportunities, freedoms, and laws. Sexual exploitation and human trafficking are a serious problem and it is important that we all work together to raise awareness and overcome this issue so vulnerable persons are not exploited.

For more information, here are a couple of websites, which include statistics and ways you can help:

www.publicsafety.gc.ca/cnt/rsrcs/pblctns/ntnl-ctn-pln-cmbt/index-eng.aspx

www.thestar.com/news/gta/2013/10/05/inside_the_world_of_human_sex_trafficking.html

Jedi Code

There is no emotion, there is peace.
There is no ignorance, there is knowledge.
There is no passion, there is serenity.
There is no chaos, there is harmony.
There is no death, there is the Force.
—*Star Wars*, movie

"I write movies about mavericks, about people who break rules, and I don't like movies about people who are pulverized for being mavericks."
—Quentin Tarantino, director

"Phone sex isn't brain surgery. It takes a few times before you get good at it, but you'll be a Phone Sex Superhero in no time! You just have to allow yourself to play a little, too, sometimes."
—Greta, Breathless Whispers

Dedication

To my beta readers, thank you.

For the late night reads, my crazy messages, the words of encouragement you each give me, your time, and—most of all—for giving me a chance.

This one's for you!

Xox

Call Me Playlist

(Can be found on Spotify)

Bad Intentions – Niykee Heaton, Migos
Headrush – Aléatoire, Claire Ridgely
The Hills – The Weeknd
Feel It – Jacquees, Rich Homie Quan, Lloyd
Sex You – Bando Jonez
Body Party – Ciara
Rock with You – Pleasure P, Plies
All The Time – Jeremih, Lil Wayne, Natasha Mosley
Glory Box – Portishead
Pony – Ginuwine
PILLOWTALK – ZAYN
Phone Sex – Otis Marlon
Birthday Sex – Jeremih
High For This – The Weeknd
Neighbors Know My Name – Trey Songz
Smack That – Dirty – Akon, Eminem
Sexy Can I feat. Yung Berg – Ray J
I'm a Slave 4 U – Britney Spears
S&M – Rihanna
Ride – SoMo
Confident – Justin Bieber, Chance The Rapper
Nice & Slow – Usher
Tonight (Best You Ever Had) – John Legend, Ludacris
World In My Eyes – 7" Version – Depeche Mode
Is This Love – Corinne Bailey Rae
Makin' Good Love – Avant
Any Time, Any Place – Janet Jackson
Call My Name – Morgan James
Lose Control – Ledisi

Lullaby – The Cure

Strangers on a Train – Nathaniel Merriweather, Mike Patton, Jennifer Charles, Kid Koala, Dan The Automator

Je t'aime moi non plus – Serge Gainsbourg, Jane Birkin

Porn Star – August Alsina

Kisses Down Low – Kelly Rowland

Need You Tonight – INXS

Vindicated – Dashboard Confessional

Work from Home – Fifth Harmony, Ty Dolla $ign

Sex – Cheat Codes, Kris Kross Amsterdam

Don't Let Me Down – Hardwell & Sephyx Remix – The Chainsmokers, Daya, Hardwell, Sephyx

Might Not – Belly, The Weeknd

River – Bishop Briggs

Talking Body – Tove Lo

High For This – The Weeknd

In Your Room – 2006 Remastered Version Zephyr Mix – Depeche Mode

Table of Contents

Prologue

Ellie

Four years ago…

I WAKE TO my mom, Silvie, yelling from the hallway of our bungalow.

"Ellie. Ellie, honey! It's here, the mail. I see it. It's a *thick* envelope."

"Okay. Oh my God. It's thick? Are you sure?" I call back, tugging my hoodie over my head while trying to pull my arms through the holes at the same time. It's wintertime in St. Albert, Alberta, where we live, so layering is key, especially when getting out of a warm bed.

"Yes! It's definitely got to be good news."

Thank goodness. I've been waiting for this envelope for months. I didn't get early acceptance like my friend Courtney, but it looks like I've been accepted, and that's all that matters.

Racing down the stairs of our small home, I run right into my mom's open arms. Looking over her shoulder out the living room window, I think I can see snow falling off the tree branches at the sound of our happy screams.

"I'm going to miss my girl all the way out there in Toronto. The house is going to feel so empty with just me here," she says, tears forming in the corners of her eyes.

"I'll visit and you'll visit," I say, although I know we won't be able to afford that. "It's only four years, and it'll go by fast. That's if I've even received the sports scholarship. We already know we can't afford for me to go all that way without it." I give her a squeeze.

"I know, honey. I'm just being a mom. I'm so proud of you. I have a good feeling, Ellie. Open it. You'll be in and you'll get that scholarship. You're an excellent runner. You've been accepted to all of the other six universities you applied to, with athletic scholarships. There's no way the University of Toronto will let you pass them by. They'll want you."

She smiles tearfully, and hands me the heavy envelope.

Chapter 1

Ellie

IF YOU'RE A movie buff like me, you'll know the intense emotions films elicit from you as you chomp handfuls of buttery popcorn, anxiously waiting to see what's going to happen next. You'll then be able to relate to how I'm feeling during this little film clip of my life.

Think back to the last tearjerker or drama you watched. Remember when the heroine was about to be delivered life-altering news? The kind of news that would change the course of her life forever? Information which would act as a catalyst for helping Hollywood to create two hours of cinematic genius? Yeah, that movie. The one you watched with bated breath while it flickered away with conflict, tears but also triumphs, and, finally, the happily ever after you needed the star to have.

Well, I kind of feel like I'm starring in my own version of *that* movie as I sit here waiting for my doctor to seal my fate. Only I'm hoping to avoid all the drama, wanting to fast forward straight to the end for the "aw, yay!" moment known by all movie fans. *Hoping like crazy that I'll get my happy ending.*

But unlike some famous actress starring in a soon-to-be blockbuster, sure to make millions, sitting calmly while a narrator explains what's going on in an audio dub, I'm fidgeting, stressed out, and annoyed, trying my best to channel not only my inner strength but also my inner Yoda.

'Cause, unfortunately, for me this isn't a movie.

It's the rest of my life.

Tick tock, tick tock...

And that right there is why I need to be a Yoda. The incessant *tick tock* of the damn clock is driving me out of my mind. I mean, isn't it nerve-wracking enough to be sitting in a stuffy, overly-sterile room waiting to see a doctor? Did they really need to add the loudest clock ever? One which is taunting me, as I see it's now fifteen minutes past my appointment? *God, I hate waiting. What ever happened to punctuality?*

Tick tock, tick tock...

"Use the Force, Ellie," I mutter, closing my eyes and praying for Master Yoda to hear me, for him to gift me with a one-time Jedi pass. I close my eyes tight, trying my damnedest to use the Force. I need it, to make the clock crash to its demise. I'm positive there's enough distance between it and the floor that a fall would smash it into a million tiny pieces.

"Ellie, dear. Doctor Robinson will see you now. Please wait in Room 3."

Tick tock, tick tock...

Chapter 2

Ellie

"WHAT DO YOU mean, you don't think I'll be able to run again?" I yelp, like a wounded dog. *What?*

"Let me explain, Ellie," Dr. Robinson says placatingly, like he knows I'm about to go off like a firecracker.

"I'm almost positive I didn't hear you correctly." I shake my head in disbelief.

I can't accept this answer.

I won't.

"Now, I didn't say ever again, Ellie. I said competitively, and no longer for the Varsity Blues, that's for sure. No real running, not for a long while yet. You might still be able to run in the future—but more in a more leisurely fashion than you're used to, per se. Some light jogging..." Dr. Robinson says, bending my right knee backwards then forward again, causing a painful twinge.

I'm sitting in his office, which is located on the University of Toronto campus. A campus where I'm both a master's film student and star of the Varsity Blues track team. Well, I *was* a star, anyway, until almost nine months ago when my knee gave out at Nationals. Within the blink of an eye, my life changed, and apparently it was going to change again. *So much for bypassing the drama...*

I register the doctor's words while trying to mask the wincing his mobilization of my knee is causing. Of course, he catches it nonetheless. Dr. Robinson is the university's best sports medicine doctor, who holds not only my knee in his hands, but also my future.

"So, let's do the resection surgery," I plead.

"The surgery isn't a guarantee, Ellie. I'm not sure I want to risk it at this point, and it seems like your left knee might need some work too. From what I'm seeing here." He looks down, tapping away on his iPad's keyboard, scrolling between my x-rays and the Thomas test results. Results that ruled out a hip flexion contracture and psoas syndrome, whatever the hell they were. Apparently they are good things to have ruled out, but that still left me with a lot of discomfort in my hip and knees.

"So fix them both. All the stats I read said there was an eighty-four percent success rate after surgery. I say we go for it. Please, let's keep trying, at least," I huff.

I'm so angry right now, I could strangle the guy. The idea is actually appealing to me, so much so that I'm forced to keep a tight hold on the examination bed for fear I might reach out and choke the good doctor.

"You're right, Ellie. Most cases do have reasonably good success," he says, sliding his chair over to type something in my file before reaching for my leg again. "I'm sorry, but in your case, that resection surgery isn't going to fix it. There's more going on. The constant swelling, the clicking sound when I bend it—and the pain in your hip—concern me, I'm afraid. I think you're eventually going to need full knee replacements, but at twenty-four, you are way too young for that. I hate telling you this, believe me," he sighs.

"But, Doctor Robinson," I plead, "iliotibial band syndrome is supposed to be treatable. I mean, I feel like it's getting better, I—I can even jog a bit more regularly…sometimes. Please, we can't stop treatments. Let's try a few more weeks and then assess it again? I'm not taking this as the final prognosis. I won't." I cross my arms like a disgruntled toddler, staring down at my stupid right knee, the same one he's holding in his hands, feeling around like he has the right to tell me to quit. To give up my life. But it's the same prognosis my second-opinion doctor gave me too, after seeing the x-rays and the MRI. A simple surgery isn't going to cut it.

They don't get it though.

I've been a runner since forever.

Movies and running: those are the things that make me—me.

I love the feeling of my feet pounding the track, that feeling of nirvana as I cross the finish line before the others. I feel like the wind, I know no bounds when I'm running.

No. This cannot be happening.

It's what I live for, and they think they can take it away with a *snap?*

"I'm sorry, Ellie, but I don't think it's ever really going to feel much better than it does now, not until you're older and have the knee replacement. It's been months of regular treatment—I mean, we've tried NSAID's, stretching, physiotherapy, cortisone injections, and the pain isn't easing. And you're still feeling the pull in your hip and pelvis area. We still need to sort that out too," Dr. Robinson says in a slight scolding tone. I assume it's for when I tried to minimize earlier how much pain I'm feeling in my right hip.

"I can't in good conscience tell you to train, Ellie. Coach told me you can barely run a hundred metres. I'm sorry, but I can't sign off to let you compete. Hopefully, you'll be able to run recreationally one day, though. That, I am confident, will come back in time." With that, he stands, washes his hands, and offers a sympathetic smile. "I'm truly sorry, Ellie. I know how much competing means to you. If I thought surgery would fix it, I'd say 'let's do it'. How about you keep up with physiotherapy and strength training, and we'll book a follow-up appointment for six months? See how things look one last time."

"Fine," I agree, despite a heavy feeling in my heart that says he's only trying to soften the blow. He's such a nice man, and I believe this is hard for him too. *I can't imagine being a dreamcrusher is easy.*

"Will you still have access to the runners-only gym?"

"Not for too much longer, not if I can't compete," I huff, irritated that he's asking and adding salt to my open wounds.

"Well, I can give you free access to the sports medicine department's gym, but you'll be sharing it with both faculty and a mix of students with sports-related injuries. It can be busy, so it's best to go later at night, if possible. We're allowed to offer short-term passes to students with mitigating circumstances, so I'd say you qualify," he says, handing me what looks like a prescription. "Give this to Meredith at the gym's front desk. She'll give you your access card."

"Thank you. I'll work hard. I'll show you I'm not out yet," I say, determined.

"I have no doubts. But remember what I said, it's both knees and your hip. Don't go making it worse. Competitions are out, period. We're working towards leisure running here. Don't push it." With that, he gives me his serious doctor face before rubbing my arm in a reassuring manner. "Hope the rest of your day is better for you, Ellie. And I'm trusting you to follow my advice," I hear him mutter the last bit as he exits the exam room, leaving me alone to fully digest his words.

No more competing.

Might never be the same.

Leisure running, if I'm lucky.

Cue dramatic music…

I sit there in tears for what feels like forever, letting the information soak in.

Without running, I'll not only lose my right to the private runner's gym, but also my athletic housing.

And worst of all: my scholarship.

I'm royally screwed.

Chapter 3

Ellie

"NO, MOM. I'M not coming home. Not yet," I say, pushing open the door exiting the medical centre, annoyed at Dr. Robinson and also my mom, for once again wanting to give up so easily.

Ever since my dad left when I was five, it's just been her and me, and I can honestly say she isn't the most confident person. Silvie can't deal with confrontation or any type of conflict. It's a trait I thankfully didn't inherit. I'm more competitive, resilient, and I'll fight tooth and nail for what I want. And right now, what I want is for my mom to encourage me to stay and fight, not to hop on the first plane home. I had hoped after she met Tom, a man she trusted enough to let in again, it might lighten her up, but with the way this conversation is going, I'd say I was wrong.

Walking down the cobblestone path away from the athletics centre, I balance my phone between my shoulder and ear, while trying to pull my water bottle that is tangled up in the cables of my ear buds out of my messenger bag. I'm overheating in this late summer heat wave the city's currently suffering. At the end of August, the Toronto air is muggy and humid, unlike the cooler, drier air I was used to out west in Alberta this time of year. I'm drenched, and feel like I'm drowning. I shouldn't complain, though. It will be heavy sweater and boot weather before we know it. I glance at the hazy sky and the many trees surrounding the campus. The leaves flap limply like they, too, could use some water.

"Ellie, sweetie," my mom says, breaking my train of thought, "I can't afford to help you out financially right now. I honestly think it's best if you just fly home. Look for a job, save up to go back. It's not like you don't already have your bachelor's degree. You can still get a great job without a master's. Lots of people only finish their undergrad."

"Urgh. Mom. You don't get it. I want to stay here. I have to. There are more opportunities for work here than in St. Albert. What am I going to do there? Work at Tim Horton's? McDonald's? Because we both know, I can get jobs there in a second. That's not even fair. Or, what: St. Albert Centre? I could work at The Bay."

"You could do a lot worse than working at The Bay in St. Albert, young lady," she interjects.

She's right. I'm sounding spoiled and entitled, so I try harder to articulate my actual point: "Mom, you're right. It's a nice place to live, to make a life. But most of those entry-level jobs require a lot of standing, and I can't do that with my knee right now. Plus, my doctor and my physiotherapist are here on campus. But the biggest factor in my needing to stay is that there aren't any major movies being made at home, not many opportunities for me to learn or further myself in the industry like I can here, not for what I want to do, anyway. Everything I want to study is here. I need to be in Toronto."

She lets out a frustrated breath, and says sarcastically: "Oh, that's right, I forgot. All of you Easterners think Toronto's the centre of the universe. Well, fair enough. But you'll just have to go back and finish your master's degree once you make enough to cover your tuition and housing. Without the athletic scholarship, I'm afraid you don't have much of a choice. Be reasonable, Ellie, please."

"Absolutely not. I'm not giving in that easy, and you shouldn't ask me to either, Mom. You always give in. I can't."

"Ouch. I know I do, sometimes. You're right. But I'm not trying to tell you to give up, Ellie. I'm worried is all. I hate that I can't fix this for you. I'm supposed to be able to fix this for you…" she whispers, and it kills me.

"It's all right, Mom. I'll sort it out. I have a little time to figure something out. I'm covered for tuition for a few months still. I talked to Financial Aid; they're seeing if I qualify for any type of bursary or other financial help. The athletics department offered to let me stay in housing for another two weeks if I need, but I'm moving in with Courtney. Ruby moved out once she graduated, so Courtney's got an extra room and she says I can have it. It will work out perfectly; Mrs. Pierce says I don't need to pay rent until I sort school out. She says we're family and that Courtney isn't paying more than the bills anyway. I laughed and said that's because it's her daughter. She shushed me and told me not to worry about it, for now. That all I need to cover is utilities and food. So I have a bit of time to look for a job here."

"Well, I'm calling Vickie and thanking her. That's awfully nice of them. I hope they don't think I'm being cheap or that I'm unwilling to help," my mom adds, and I can hear tears starting to brew by the shake in her voice.

"Mom," I soothe, "they know you aren't." I hesitate, "They know about Dad," I swallow, telling her softly.

"Oh," she pauses. "God, Ellie. I'm so embarrassed. I'm an idiot. They must think I'm such a naïve woman."

"I'm sorry, Mom. But Vickie's your best friend. I can't believe you didn't tell her."

I hear her sniffling.

"Mom?"

"Sorry. I'm here, sweetie. I'm too mortified to talk about it, even with Vickie. I can't believe he took all the money, all of it. After all the years we've been divorced, I can't believe he'd drain the joint account we'd had for your schooling. I knew I should have put it in your name. You were just too young. It's my own fault. I'm an idiot. I never really thought about his name being on the statements. Truth be told, once you got the scholarship back in first year, I didn't bother checking on the account once I stopped the paper account statements. I hadn't looked in years. I just figured the money would be there, a wonderful starting off gift for you, a little something for you each year. I'm such a fool, Ellie. Such a fool."

"No, Mom. He is. He's the asshole here. I mean of all the low—"

"Ellie. Please. I don't want to talk about it. I know exactly what that man is. I'll deal with him, somehow. I won't let him get away with hurting us anymore. I agree he is an asshole and needs to pay. I will not roll over on this."

"Good, I'm glad, Mom. This time he's gone too far."

"I know, and I promise I will fix this. I'll call Vic, as well. I'm being silly. Of course I should have told her and Hank. I can transfer a couple hundred dollars to help you while I try to get this sorted at my end. Hopefully, I'll have more soon. This living paycheque-to-paycheque while trying to fight him in court is tough," she laughs. "I finally felt we were in a good place. I had a nice little nest egg for you, in case we needed it." I hear the tears fighting for freedom again.

"I'm okay, Mom. We're going to be okay. You're amazing and I love you, but keep the money. I've got a little left from my scholarship still. Work on making sure my sperm donor doesn't still have his name on anything else."

"Already done, honey. I promise. The lawyers are working on trying to find a loophole that might force him to give it back. Anyway, enough of all the bad, let's work on the bringing the good back."

"I love you, Mom," I sniffle, tears pinching my nose.

"You too, my girl, you too. I love you more. Keep me posted."

"I will. I'll call you in a few days. Don't be upset that I might not come home."

"Oh, I'm not, sweetie; just know it's an option. I'd love to have you home anytime. I'm hoping you'll get to come at least for a visit soon; I really want you to meet Tom. He's been such an amazing support with you gone and all this shit with your fath—"

"'Donor', Mom. Fathers don't do that shit to their kids. Besides, I haven't seen him in years. Fathers see their daughters. With this latest bullshit, I never want to see him again."

"Okay, Ellie, you got it. The Donor it is." She laughs and I smile. My mom is incredible, considering the raw deal she got when she married my father, Lawrence Sanders Hughes: asshole, cheater, and thief extraordinaire. Not only did he leave us when I was five, he lay dormant until eight months ago when he cleared out his only daughter's university fund, money in a joint account that was there for me since I was born. The account where my mom would put all the money I'd been given over the years from things like birthdays, gifts from my grandparents, and the monthly contributions she'd been making since I was two. Too bad she didn't realize he still had access to it before he completely cleaned it out.

"Love you, Mommy."

"You too, baby girl," she says, ending the call.

Now to figure out how to pay for tuition, rent, and the bazillion other things a student needs to pay for…

Chapter 4

Ellie

"HERE, ELLIE!" MY roommate—and best friend—Courtney calls over the swarm of students trying to find seats in the crowded theatre. Like a soundtrack to the hustle and bustle of the first day of school, it's a bit of a madhouse in here.

Thank goodness it's our final year. Sometimes I wonder why I had to be so ambitious, self-inflicting a one-year master's degree in cinema studies upon myself after completing four years of a bachelor's degree at U of T's Cinema Studies Institute. I hope it will help me in my career later on, but for now, at this time of the morning, it's a bit of a pain in the ass.

"Good thing hangovers make you wake up early, Courtney," I taunt, glancing at the other students as they continue to pack the place. I plop down into the seat Courtney's been saving for me, ignoring the array of evil looks I get from those still searching for good seats. I smile and nod to a few people I recognize. "Aisle seating. Nice work."

"Yeah, it's perfect, isn't it? Lucky for you, I'm amazeballs like that. Now shut it and give me the cure, woman," she retorts, her voice sickly-sweet, not a hint of sarcasm to be found, nope, not from Court. *Not.* I laugh out loud while placing what she wants most into her extended hand.

"Always so cheeky, eh?" I say.

"Yup. Cheers," she mumbles, lifting her water bottle to toast. "To

'Sexual Aesthetics and Representations in Film'. You'd better be worth my time, and be a whole lot of learning excellence, 'cause no student in their right mind takes a 9 a.m. class unless it's unfuckingbelievable." Court chugs back the water (and the Advil) I'd given her.

Shrugging off my light blue cardigan, I turn to try and appease her as I situate myself in the tight-fitting space, placing my iPad and portable keyboard on the small desktop. "I think you're in luck. I hear this course is all sexy and fun, which will be right up your alley, with lots of clips, discussions of porn versus erotica, and, best of all, you get to enjoy the pleasure of my company, you lucky whore," I whisper, nudging her and making her drop her hair tie as she is about to cinch her platinum-blonde hair into a messy topknot, her signature hangover hairstyle.

"Hey! I needed that. You're such a bully," she whispers back, rolling her eyes and pulling another band off her wrist. "Ha. Good thing I own shares in these things." She eyes me. "Anyway, friend, you're the lucky one." She gestures to our primo seats near the front of the class, and all I can do is laugh.

"Touché, I'll give you that for today, however let's not crown you 'world's best seat saver' yet. Let's see who gets the good seats for the rest of the semester." I thumb towards myself, and we both laugh, knowing it will most definitely be me.

"I hear the wait list for this class is huge," Court says, leaning in closer, the smell of beer still lingering. "I also heard the prof is a little slice too. Maybe it will be worth the ungodly hour." She raises her brows up and down mischievously.

"You really are a pest, you know that?" I laugh; reaching for her wrist. I pull off a blue hair elastic before grabbing a fistful of my own deep red hair, putting it into a low ponytail. "You really shouldn't have stayed up drinking with Brent and Susan last night, I can still smell the booze on you," I tease. "Maybe getting Netflix was a bad idea. Who knew you could make a drinking game out of so many shows?"

Brent and Susan are our neighbours; they've been best friends since elementary school and live across the hall from us. We've become quite close to them over the last four years. They're a few years older than us, and also attend grad school at the University of Toronto. They are both working on their sociology doctorates, while Court and I are working towards our master's degrees in film, not yet sure if we want to pursue even more education.

For me, my current financial situation is predicting a big fat "no" on the doctoral studies at the moment. Right now, I'm just happy to get more than an undergraduate degree. I'm hoping having my master's degree will give me that little bit more of an edge when it comes to job shopping, especially if I can get my thesis published in a few journals and film magazines. With the setback of no longer being able to run competitively, my sole focus is on my career in film moving forward. Not that I thought I'd be an Olympian, but being a star track-and-field athlete definitely helped to get my name out there a bit.

As for our friends, they're both on the way to having their dreams become reality, Brent planning to teach post-secondary sociology, while Susan has aspirations to manage social programs for migrants. Luckily, they're also both film buffs in the extreme. The four of us share a terrible addiction to Netflix, wasting copious amount of time watching old cult classics and *films noirs* together.

Being the smarter one of the group last night, with today being the first day of classes, I opted out of partaking in their game of "Let's Take a Sip" which entailed taking a sip every time someone uttered the "f-word" during *Pulp Fiction* at our place.

"It's not my fault," Courtney groans, sinking low in her chair, her over-bleached blonde hair blending in with the pallor of her skin so much more than usual today. "I knew Tarantino liked the word 'fuck', but who the hell would have thought he'd love it that much?" She pauses, and I giggle at her scrunched up face. "Yuck. I can't even think about it. Am I green? I feel green."

"Aww, poor Court-Court. No, you're more of a yellowish colour actually," I cackle, as she gives me her best cut-eye while running her thumb along her throat in a slitting motion. "Truth," I shrug, "but, yeah, there were a lot of 'fucks', sweets. I think Brent counted two hundred and seventy-one sips." I try to hide my smile as she makes a low gagging sound. "All right, all right, no more drink talk, I promise." I raise two fingers like a good Scout.

"You know where you can stick those fingers, you dirty, lying non-Scout," she says, her green eyes dancing with mirth. "Nonetheless, no more drink talk, please. I can't take it."

"Okay. Now, sit up straight. Class is going start in a few minutes. We need you to look presentable, like a good little student, not the grubby not-so-interested one you look like right now. Hopefully, the prof won't come near us this morning, 'cause you really do reek." I wave my hand in front of my nose.

"Zip it. I'll go drown my stink in the tub when this is over," she moans, taking another sip of water. "Now, let's take my mind off how shitty I feel *and* smell." She picks up her tablet, swiping it to life, the course syllabus displayed. "Let's see what's in store for us this semester. Shall we look at this fine syllabus? I can't believe summer's over." Court raises her bleary eyes to meet mine as she tries to feign some semblance of excitement. "Nope. I'm not ready for adulting yet."

Courtney Pierce has been my best friend since the fourth grade when her family moved across the street from my grandfather, my mom, and me. Her family moved to St. Albert, from Kamloops, British Columbia, for her father's job. He decided to open his own Tim Horton's franchise after coming into some money when his parents passed away. I guess he and Mrs. Pierce figured our growing bedroom community would be perfect for it and their family. My mom and Vickie became fast friends, as did Courtney and I.

Travelling to Toronto for school had been our dream since Grade 8 when we started to discover movies like *The Lost Boys*, *Star Wars*, even a few like *Dirty Dancing* or anything starring the "Brat Pack". We knew we needed to be involved in creating amazingness like that, no matter in what capacity. But as we got older, my love of movie genres changed. I became determined with my focus. I became obsessed with movies made from the books I loved, the film adaptions. Some books were adapted better than others, and I wanted to make the good—no, great!—adaptations. I'd discovered my niche and vowed I'd become the best screen adaptation writer, one who takes another's beautifully written prose and brings it to life, ensuring I gave the books the justice they deserved.

Have you ever read a book that completely blew your mind? I'm talking totally ruining you, leaving you thinking about it for months after. The book hangover you've only felt that every once upon a special time. Everything about it leaving a lasting impression, as if it were imprinting itself in your soul, heart, and memory. The characters. The storyline. The ending. Each piece of its complete package allowing you the perfect type of escapism, an escape you didn't even know you were craving at that moment in your life.

Movies give me my biggest hangovers.

More precisely, film adaptations. I'm obsessed with movies that have come from the world's greatest literature. How couldn't you be? It's seriously the best of both worlds, seeing the characters you've imagined in your mind coming to life on the big screen. Nothing can beat the feeling of a truly brilliant film adaptation, like seeing Ewan McGregor, as Mark Renton, experiencing heroin addiction in Irvine Welsh's *Trainspotting*, seeing how real the struggle is as it plays out in a two-hour film, accompanied by a soundtrack that complements it to perfection. Or better yet, Boris Pasternak's tale, *Doctor Zhivago,* one of my all-time favourites; watching a complicated story of love unfold before my eyes, confirming it is indeed as beautiful as I knew it to be in my imagination when I read the book.

Now, don't get me wrong, there are bad ones out there, ones that do not do justice to the literary geniuses that penned the tales, but I hope to be one of the greats. I will be one of the greats. One day, I will be a screenwriter like *Trainspotting*'s John Hodge or *Zhivago*'s Robert Bolt, bringing these books to life for the masses. I, Ellie Hughes, will be the person writing and creating some of the most amazing film adaptions to grace the silver screen, ones people will fall in love with, not the kind where people say: "It was awful, nothing like the book."

"Listen to these questions." Courtney sits up a bit straighter, drawing me out of my head, her tablet in hand once again. "This course sounds like it may be all right. *Is there enough of a difference between erotica and pornography? Should they be considered the same genre?* Ohhh, I like the sounds of that. Lots of fodder for rousing debate!" She taps her black-polished nail on the screen, rattling off another question: *"How much should we censor erotic films compared to pornography, especially if they are deemed similar? How does artistic freedom and censorship relate to larger issues of oppression, entrepreneurship, and technology?* Ah, and this one's even better: *How are sexual desires and identities shaped around appropriate sexual representations?* I think I'm going to like this course, Ellie."

Chapter 5

Ellie

PULLING OUT MY iPad, I open the course syllabus to read along with Court.

My eyes stall on the professor's name: *Doctor A. Ryan.*

"Oh, man. I hope the 'A' in his name doesn't stand for 'asshole'. 'Cause that would really blow." I huff the joke out a little louder than intended, my comment causing a few people around us to snicker. They laugh, and I die a little of embarrassment. "Shit." I sink down in my seat.

"Nice one, Els, good for you. Look at you all losing your scholarship and becoming a badass. Class clown on the first day. I'm so proud, sweetie," Courtney mocks, clearly thinking she's funny.

"Hardy har har. Easy on the scholarship jokes, lady. Too soon. But thanks for making the effort, I feel better already…" I shake my head at her and she mouths a "sorry". "Yeah, yeah, whatever. Now back to the issue at hand—this professor, what do we know?"

"Well, I hear the class itself is good, hence the throngs of people," she waves her hands gesturing to the packed theatre "Let's recap, shall we?"

I nod. "Go for it." I sit back up.

"So far, we know: one, there's a wait list a mile long. Two, the course load seems reasonable," she waves her tablet in the air, "And, three, the prof is new, which I think is the biggest plus if you ask me. It means we can only go up from here. We all know how Professor Dobbs was the worst. And like I said, I heard this guy is alllllllll kinds of yum—"

"Please hold that last bit, miss. I need to take my place at the front of the room, but I must admit, I'm curious to know what you were going to say about me," a deep voice booms, directly behind us.

Suddenly, there is a sinking feeling in my stomach. That pesky one, you know, the one you get whenever you *know* something isn't right.

Please be a joke. Please be a joke, I silently pray, waiting for the stranger to tell us he's only kidding!

Much to my dismay, my pleading goes unrewarded. *Code red, this is not a drill. Houston, your and Courtney's big fat motormouths have caused a major problem.* My mom's voice lovingly reminding me that sometimes I really need to "zip my lips" rings in my head as I realize this is my life right now, and not a joke.

This realization becomes painfully obvious as a large form now standing beside me in the aisle casts a shadow over Courtney and me. *How did he move so fast, like Gary Oldman skittering down the castle wall in Francis Ford Coppola's* Dracula*?* Turning my head to the side, I brace myself, averting my eyes away from his face. Instead, I choose to go from the ground up, before I have to meet the eyes of the man who will now likely target Courtney and me over the semester, surely giving us the label of "troublemakers". A label which will force us to work a lot harder to prove his first impression wrong, to prove that we aren't the assholes he no doubt thinks we are right now.

Bracing myself was right…even starting from the bottom. *Holy. F-ing. Cow.*

I start to make a mental list as I silently stare, my eyes roaming over this man from bottom to top, unable to stop myself from cataloguing and checking off said list as if I were Kris Kringle himself. As he shifts in the aisle right next to me, my eyes take in his attributes like I'm laser scanning him for 3D printing. *Naughty. Nice. Niiiice…*

I make a mental check as my eyes linger on his feet, noting his large black Doc Martens boots. *Remember what they say about big feet?* He's tall, and the looming feeling he arouses along with his shoe size makes me wonder.

His upper body is muscular, and despite being covered with a tan corduroy blazer, I see a tight-fitting T-shirt quoting: *"Anybody interested in grabbing a couple of burgers and hittin' the cemetery?"* from one of my favourite movies, Wes Anderson's *The Royal Tenenbaums*. A shirt that fits him perfectly, showcasing that he's lean and fit. Who knew mere clothing could have the capability to make a girl take notice and drool? And don't get me started on his ability to make me blush, as I feel my cheeks heating from the mere seconds he's been standing—no, looming—beside me.

I tick off the boxes for strong, sturdy-looking arms accessorized by large sexy hands graced with nice long fingers. My mind shifts, wondering what one might do with such stealthy-looking fingers as they hang at his side. *God, I'd love to know.*

The room falls silent around me as I continue my assessment…it's just his body, my list, and me.

He's got a broad build, a solid stature. One a person might be inclined to pounce upon if given the chance or invitation. *An invitation! Can you imagine?*

Check.

Check.

And motherf-ing check.

If this man's face is anything like his body then I'd say he needs to unfurl his superhero cape and let my hero-worshipping begin.

Finally, my eyes make a last venture up to his face. I hold my breath, waiting for the little bubble of perfection I've conjured up to pop.

I gasp as my eyes rake up, up, and up to Professor Holy. F-ing. My.

My sudden dirty mind.

My sandpaper-filled mouth.

My quivering loins.

My. Flipping. Goodness.

The man is absolutely the most beautiful thing I've ever set eyes upon.

And, oh jeez, he's crouching down. Coming closer. My palms begin to sweat, and there's a feeling surfacing that I've not felt in, in...well, *ever.*

Slightly curled inky black hair just reaches his collar, and forest green eyes are highlighted by the perfect pair of black Roy Orbison-ish framed glasses, all topped off, of course, by a dangerously sexy dimple! *I can't even...*

Hi, my name is Ellie Hughes and I. Am. Screwed.

Is he giving me a look which says: "my eyes are up here", or am I imagining it?

Before I can start to articulate the apology that my brain has instructed my mouth to deliver, it dies as our eyes crash into each other. Instead, the wanton brain between my legs takes over, interrupting my mouth and its apology, instead forcing me to expel a tiny gasp-like moan in its place, a moan that my actual brain tried in vain to get my mouth to clamp down on, then hoped it went unnoticed.

Silly brain, don't you know? Hot man trumps the English language, so moans and groans always win.

Next thing I know, he's not only crouching, he's down low and leaning into my space to better see Courtney and I. He smells frickin' incredible, too, of sandalwood laced with a subtle hint of earthy vetiver. The combination reaches my nose and I have to resist the impulse to snuffle the air around me like a dog in heat surely would.

A hoarse clearing of his throat brings me back to my impending doom.

A deep baritone voice plays out of his mouth. A mouth as sexy as the escaping sounds, ones that drip out of a beautifully elongated throat that I'm currently cataloging as a throat I think I'd like to maybe run my tongue along as if it were a plane on a runway. *Definitely maybe.*

"As much as I've enjoyed listening to—as well as being a part of—your conversation this morning, I do need to get things started before a riot ensues. But I do wish to hear the last part. I am literally chomping at the proverbial bit. I can't imagine two smart young women like yourselves having anything other than nice things to say about anyone, anyway. Maybe later though? I do, however, hope you'll focus on the lecture once it starts. I'm sure the rest of your conversations will be extremely exhilarating, but might I ask that you allow me to engage you for the next hour or so?" He winks, and I swear to eat all the rice in Japan that my clit was waving a "hell, yes" sign at the words, *engage*, *you* and *hour*.

Looking from me to Court, he offers a nod. "I do hope you feel better, and let me assure you both that this class will be well worth it. I promise," he adds, his mouth pulling to one side, offering a hint of a satisfied grin before he rights himself back to an upright position. He pauses in the aisle, his eyes resting on mine, and something passes between us, but I ignore it, worrying instead about being in trouble on the first day of class. This is my grad school prof, after all. I'm going to need him to take me seriously.

"I promise we won't need you to pull a Mr. Vernon and keep us a bunch of Saturdays," I finally pipe up, wondering if he'll get my *Breakfast Club* reference.

"Ah." He waits a second. "Nice reference. I take it you're a John Hughes fan?"

"Very much," I say, again not sure where my cheekiness is coming from.

"Me too. The man was a mastermind on the subject of teen angst. Oh, and may I clarify that the 'A' is most definitely not for 'Asshole'," he whispers to me before turning his back to us.

"Wow," Courtney whispers beside me.

"Er," is all I can muster back, as my eyes are trained on his deep blue stovepipe jeans. His ass is all kinds of tight, I note, as he starts to make his way down the stairs on a pair of legs that I want to bounce me up and down while he's deep inside of me.

About half way down the steps he stops, standing silently as if he's heard my thought, or is doing his own brand of contemplating. After a beat, he calls out over his shoulder: "And welcome to my class, ladies." I swear I see his shoulders moving with laughter as he resumes his way to the front.

Oh my shit. I'm in huge trouble here.

"Holy morsel of mouth-watering man," is all I hear being whispered, and I soon realize it came from me. It seems my brain has looped the saying as I sit repeating it to myself over and over under my breath as we watch Mr. A-is-Not-For-Asshole move to his podium at the head of the class.

"Welcome to FSD470B4: Sexual Aesthetics & Representations in Film. I'm Professor—or Doctor—Ryan, first initial 'A'—as in 'Ace', and not a word that rhymes with masshole." His emerald eyes find mine, and I slip further into my seat. "So, welcome." He raises his hands to the room, "I'm excited to see such a great turnout. I've enjoyed teaching this class at other universities, and seeing as it's the first year it's being offered here at U of T, space is limited, therefore I've been instructed to take a roll call. If your name is not on the list, I'm sorry, you'll have to leave and see the registrar's office about being added to a waitlist."

With that, he spends the next five or so minutes calling our names. I try to avoid getting trapped in his gaze again, but it's useless. As soon as my name falls from his lips, my body responds by shifting forward as if his voice alone were enough to pluck me from my seat and deposit me wherever he might want me. When his green eyes land on my brown ones, I feel a warmth in my chest I've never felt before.

This is gonna be trouble.

"Ah, a name to the face, nice to meet you, Ellie." He smiles and I know I blush, I feel it. His gaze settles on me a beat too long, but he's quick enough to move on that I don't think anyone else noticed. Other than Courtney, of course.

"Jesus, Els, you hot for teacher or what? You two just totally eye-boinked!"

"'Boinked'? What are we, thirteen? And we did not."

"Fine. You completely and utterly eye-fucked."

"Shhh, we did not," I whisper.

"You so totally did. Captain Obvious and you had better be careful," she clucks, all giddy.

"You're still drunk. You, my shitty friend, are hallucinating," I hiss. "Court, he looked at you just as long."

"Whatever. I might be hung-over, but I know what I saw. Complete eye-boinking."

"Please. Enough. Let's listen, he already thinks we're idiots, I bet."

"Okay. I'll drop it," she relents.

"Thank you."

"...for now," she adds.

Turning my head back to Professor Ryan, I notice that the lecture hall seems to have cleared out quite a bit.

"Great. Now that's done." He places what I assume is the registration sheet on his desk, swapping it for a remote. Plugging a USB stick into the computer and pointing the remote at the overhead projector on the ceiling, he begins: "Please follow along with your syllabus as we go over the course, the projects, and any questions you may have." He seeks my gaze one last time before pulling up a copy on the Smart-Board.

"Ha! Told ya," is whispered beside me, and I elbow Courtney in response.

Yep. I'm in big trouble.

Chapter 6

Ace

SCREWED.

Done for.

Finished.

Finito.

Fucked.

Completely fucked.

I need to get a grip.

I knew taking the job here was going be a risk; it always is when taking a job where you're the one on faculty with the least seniority. What I didn't expect was that there might be a risk I didn't foresee that could end my goddamned career. And one I'd meet on the first day of school.

It's my first year teaching at the University of Toronto. I was headhunted by the school, and finally agreed to make the move from Queen's in Kingston to Toronto this year. Having my friends Mercer and Dylan both teaching here helped with my decision, but it was the chair offering me the two courses I loved to teach most that cinched it: Sexual Aesthetics & Representations in Film and Masters Thesis Essay in Sexual Diversity in Film. Both fascinating courses, and both with the same student enrolled who has me rethinking my decision to come here.

Three words.

Ellie Raine Hughes.

They say you never get a second chance to make a first impression, and my first impression of Ellie—albeit unique—is not one I'll soon forget. I've never had quite the "meet cute" as I did this morning—she is adorable. I swear to Christ, I thought my dick was going to spring out of my jeans when she settled into the seat in front of me in my Sexual Aesthetics class.

First impression: not only is Ellie beautiful, she smells incredible, a mix of fruit and candy with a subtle vanilla twist, and I've never smelled anything quite so satisfying before. Don't get me started on my thoughts when she took her sweater off. I'm curious to see if she's actually a serious student or just the little jokester I saw glimpses of this morning. Not going to lie, I'm eager to find out.

I always like to sit back and observe the students as they make their way into class on the first day. I find it gives me a better sense of who's who, provides me with good insight for the semester; it gives an outlook as to what type of class I might have on my hands. Is there a good balance of serious and non-serious students? Are they a loud crew? Is the room full of students that think this will be a bird credit? And so on. This morning, however, I noted none of that. Sitting behind Ellie and Courtney only proved to distract me from my ritual viewing as my eyes and ears didn't make it past them. I was instead too caught up in them—in *her*.

As soon as I heard her honeyed voice make its way to my chair, my ears weren't the only things that perked up to pay attention. As I sat back, I saw that Ellie's smile was just as infectious as her laugh, and my senses zeroed in on her—and only her—during the time I was meant to be observing everyone coming in the lecture hall. Unfortunately, I honestly couldn't tell you shit about the rest of the students, only *her*.

If she's as smart as she is attractive, then she'll definitely be somebody's jackpot. From experience, though, it's never the way. It's rare that a person is ever actually blessed with the trifecta of wit, intelligence and beauty that Ellie's "Mr. Vernon" reply indicated. I just might like holding her for detention. Either way, I'll gladly accept the lovely view for the semester. I, myself, prefer brains with a more understated beauty. Not that it would matter if I were attracted to her anyway, teacher/student relations are a no-go.

However, listening to the two young women was quite entertaining. Entertaining to the point where I was almost late starting the class. Ms. Hughes seems to have a rebel streak, that whole "A for Asshole" joke piqued my curiosity. I'm very interested to see what type of student Ms. Hughes will be. Truth be told, I'd like to hear her thoughts about me more than I'd care to admit. *Did she find me intimidating? Good looking? Does she think I'll be some stuck up film guy, or did she like what she saw?*

I have a pretty good idea where Ellie's friend was going before I choose that as my point of entry into the conversation. Luckily, I managed to start class on time, while gaining two new model students, I presume. The look on both women's faces was priceless, once I'd introduced myself after I stood up from the seat behind them, shocking the hell out of them. The blush over Ellie's face was even more compelling. Now, if only I could stop trying to imagine what the rest of her would look like flushed under my perusal.

Ellie Raine Hughes could be big trouble if I'm not careful.

Chapter 7

Ellie

WALKING INTO OUR apartment, I slam the door a little harder than I'd meant to.

After two weeks of looking for a part-time job that pays enough, the rejection and lack of openings for a person with my current restrictions of school, an injury, and needing time for physio, is slowly taking its toll on not only my bank account but also on my confidence. You'd think in a university city, a job would be easy enough to find. Or maybe it would be if I didn't have so many constraints. No way can I stand for hours behind a counter serving coffee; my knee would most likely give out after the first hour and be swollen to the point of pain. Finding a desk job or a simple telemarketing job where I could sit is proving to be a hell of a lot harder than I ever expected. The one telemarketing job that I was offered turned out to be a bust, once I factored in the travelling time and cost. The pay was too low to be worth the long bus trip to Newmarket. And If I'm going to try to get back my spot on the team like I'm determined to, regardless what the doctors said, I need to be a bit picky about the job I take. I need to be close by so I can keep up with physio and the gym. "Stupid knee," I mutter, tossing a few bags on the floor and my purse on top of the kitchen table. After a few hours of bussing around the neighbourhood, my knee is throbbing again, needing an icepack and elevation.

Kicking off my shoes crankily, I hear Court calling me out.

"I take it from your mood, Rainbow Bright, that things didn't go well at the interviews?" I walk into the living room with its two-toned grey walls, where Court is sitting at our shared desk with her MacBook open. She's obviously working on some kind of film as I see Filmora is open and loaded with her current project.

I throw myself into the oversized cream armchair, swinging my legs over the side so I can nestle into the puffy cushion and sulk while I tell her about my job woes.

"Well, did you get something or what?" she asks.

"Nah," I sigh. "I didn't have enough experience to work in a kitchen as a prep staff or line cook, or even to be a hostess, according to Mr. Smythe. He wouldn't even entertain the idea of training me, or giving me a chance. Which totally pisses me off, despite me knowing these weren't the best jobs for my knee, but I'm getting desperate. And, I mean, why did he even call me in for an interview? You saw my friggin' resume, asshole. But I guess he might have seen me limping a bit when I walked in. I decided to walk the five blocks for exercise. Apparently that was a bad idea…"

"That's shitty, Els. I'm sorry. At least he wasn't some creep like at the last place."

"Funny you should say that. I was thinking along the same lines at first, but then I kinda started to get that pervy-old-man feeling when he started asking me about all the ways I knew to cook eggs. As I told him each way I knew, he kept looking at my tits, especially when he'd interrupt to tell me how much he loved yolks." I shudder at the memory.

"Ew, that's so wrong," she laughs, "funny. But so, so wrong."

"Gah, thinking about it makes me feel dirty. I need a shower"

"Maybe you oughta report him to the campus paper, the Varsity, so they won't run his ads anymore. Sounds like he could be some old dirty bastard looking for some university hottie to help fill his nightly spank bank," she jokes, but I cringe at how close she might be.

"Yeah. I probably should." I stand and move over to her computer, looking at the screen then down over her notes. Leaning over, I swat her hand off the trackpad and click a few options on the still picture she has up, the one she's been messing with the whole time we talked. "There. You need to click on the hamburger, then click the top of the still so you can tweak the angles."

"Bugger, I've been on this one forever trying to figure it out. You are a good girl," she says, reaching for the notes app on her iPad. "I need to write those steps down. This program is a trip to use."

"I promise it's easier than iMovie, you just have to play around with it. Let me shower then I can put my knee up and help you while you help me make a plan," I sigh, grabbing my stuff from the kitchen.

"Okay, hurry up, 'cause I might have a job you'd be perfect for," Court calls out.

"Oh, yeah?"

"Yes, I talked to Erica today. She has a great idea."

"Okay. As long as it doesn't involve eggs or selling myself on a corner, I'll consider anything in between."

"Well, this job will guarantee to keep you in school and in the green."

"Okay, now I'm intrigued. Let me go put my stuff away, I'll shower after." I scoop up my bags from the floor, then head down the hall to my room. I toss it all back on the floor, too excited to hear about the job that Erica, Courtney's sister, might help me get.

"NO WAY! COURT. There is absolutely no way I can do that."

"Ellie, listen. You need a job and Erica had the best paying job all through university. I think it's time to call in the big guns here. I think you need to take her up on her offer."

"Are you kidding me? I can't be a phone sex operator! I'm like two months short of having my hymen grow over, I'm seriously the poster child for born-again virgins. There is no way I'd have the capacity to be sexy or witty…and forget wild. I'm as vanilla as you can get. I'm prudish to the point that I only discovered the joys of masturbation in my first year of university! There's no way I could ever get a man off over the phone; I barely turn a man on in person. The Eggman aside, of course," I say, pacing the living room, my brain barely registering that this conversation is actually happening.

"Jesus, are you done your soliloquy there, Shakespeare?" Courtney moves from her desk to follow me into the kitchen. "It'll be fine. They train you. Erica was lame the first few times too. But now she's got some great stories and made a fortune. They loved her so much that when it was time to quit after graduation and get hired on at her law firm, the Conrads—the couple that own the agency—practically begged her to stay. Mrs. Conrad offered to allow her to work from home. No one at Breathless Whispers gets to work from home!"

"'Breathless Whispers'. *Pfft.* No. I'm sorry," I say, opening the fridge and pulling out a bottle of water and an icepack. "I can't. My mom would frickin' *kill* me."

"She doesn't need to know, Els. No one does. You don't really have any other options at this point. Do you?"

"Shit, don't we have anything stronger? Water isn't gonna cut it tonight."

"You know I'm right. You aren't having any luck, and this is perfect, really. I say you don't have much choice."

"Focus. I need alcohol, Court," I say, looking in the cupboard above the fridge. "I'll concede that you have a point. It seems I might not have many options at this point, but it doesn't mean I have to jump into a sex trade." I slam the cupboard door.

"Here," Courtney says. She produces a bottle of Crown Royal from some mystery hiding spot and slides it along the island. "Make it a double, you deserve it. And easy with the sex trade dramatics, it's not like I offered to be your pimp. It's all over the phone, Els. No one will ever know it's you."

"Thanks." I nod at the glasses, silently asking if she'd like one too.

I sigh. "*I'd* know though. But you're right. Tuition is just over eight thousand, plus living expenses, books, and whatever else I'll need. I've got about half paid from the last of my scholarship. I still need around forty-five hundred for December's final instalment or I'm out of the program, flying back to Mommy. And there's the huge issue that I need to make this money while seated, and only working a maximum of fifteen hours a week because of school and physio—"

"See? There's no way you'll find a regular job and make that kind of money in under three months. And you do not want to go back home, do you?" Courtney interrupts.

"No. I refuse to give up. Going home's not an option. Who's to say I'd even get back in the program if I left for a year to earn money, then reapplied. You know how many students apply to this program. One thing I don't get, though, is why would Erica have worked there? You guys are loaded," I say, gesturing around our apartment and taking a huge swig of the amber relaxant.

"Truth be told, she was bored." Court shrugs her shoulders like it makes total sense. "Her roommate, Ashley, dared her to apply with her. Turns out they both got hired and loved it...well, the *money*, not necessarily the actual job," she adds, pulling a Caramilk bar out of our treat drawer. "Ashley went on to write a memoir about her experiences actually. I think you can buy it online or something. Who knows? Maybe you could be the Barbara Walters of phone sex when you're older? And if that doesn't float your boat, you'll at least make enough to cover grad school this year, and maybe even your doctorate if you decide to go on?" She raises her eyebrows, knowing she's saying all the right things.

Biting my nail, I start to really contemplate this crazy idea. I mean the number of hours and flexibility of the shifts would be perfect. Best of all, I could sit and rest my knee, and would bring my schoolwork and do it between calls. *And really, how hard could it be?*

"Okay, but promise me it's classy. That it's not like one of Madonna's erotica characters—that 'My name is Mistress Dita'-type of crazy S&M shit—where I'll have some guy begging for me to dominate him while I pretend to spank then shit on him, right? No stomping on imaginary testicles with imaginary high-heeled shoes?" I exhale, reaching for a piece of her chocolate bar, my stress levels needing indulgence big time.

"Oh my God. Did you just compare phone sex to being a dominatrix? Girl, those are fetishes. Although I'm sure they'd teach you to handle those too. You might totally branch off into people's specific kinks. I bet you'd get to deal with all kinds of fetishes, freaks, lonely losers, and the hot bossy types. Erica had some sweet fetish stories," she winks.

"I hate you." I run my hand down my face. "I dunno, it feels wrong, and I really have doubts that I could pull it off." I lean on the counter, staring, willing her to agree that this whole thing is a bad idea.

"Fine, but why not at least go for an interview to check it out? What do you have to lose?"

I glare at her before popping the rest of her chocolate bar in my mouth. "I suppose."

"You know you love me." She reaches for her cell, I assume to call Erica. To give her the news and to get the details, the details about my becoming a phone sex operator. *Fuck my life.*

"*Loved,* past tense, is the word you're looking for."

"We'll see," she replies, covering the phone with her hand.

"Whatever. I'm taking a shower. I need to bang my head off the tiles for a few minutes. Let me know what Erica says."

"You got it, Dita," Court cackles.

I flip her the bird before heading for the shower.

Chapter 8

Ace

BEING THREE WEEKS into the fall semester, today is the first meeting for the students in my SDFM4328 Masters Thesis Essay in Sexual Diversity in Film class.

Along with meeting me, the students will be introduced to my team of grad students: Jax, Sam, and Joelle. Aside from us each sharing a bit about ourselves, the goal for today is to review the expectations for the thesis essay writing process, explain our roles, and to answer any questions that they may have thus far.

"Hey, Ace. You still keen on giving them another two weeks to get sorted? That will bring us to the second week of October before we meet to assign advisors," Jax says, looking over his iPad to where I'm setting up in the smaller conference room.

"Yeah," I say. "From my experience most won't have started taking this overly seriously yet. Today's meeting will be what lights the fire. Especially once I share the timeline and tell them about the five-page introduction paper they need to write and email in to me by next Wednesday on top of their expected thesis work. Most won't realize that by now they should have a topic, a solid grasp of the direction they think they want to go, and know they should be outlining a plan of attack for writing their thesis papers. So, two weeks is good." I laugh, picturing what the looks on their faces will be once I tell them what should technically be done.

My intention is to set a laid-back tone for our first Friday morning meeting, one where the students will get a sense that my teaching assistants and I are here to guide and support them, not dictate and demand or take over and babysit. I'd like the students to feel as if we are a team, all of us.

"I want them to grasp the process," Joelle adds and I agree, moving to the laptop and securing the cord to the projector. "I think that's important. Maybe I can talk about some research guidelines and give them a few starting points to check out. Stress the importance of not typing 'thesis topics' into Google. Explain how that never works. Encourage them to be unique."

"Good call, and mention to avoid anything Wikipedia says." I shake my head. I've seen too many people opt out of using traditional research methods and getting slammed by the Wiki. A site where unfortunately any Tom, Dick or Harry can add bits of info without confirming accuracy or validity. As grad students, you'd think they'd know this by now, but there's always one. "Sam, you can talk about how we'll be working together to help them achieve the end goal of completing their thesis. Tell them we know how stressful it is and how we have a lot of experience, to ask for help along the way, not to save it until they're freaking out."

"Sounds good," Sam answers. "I can definitely share my story. Thought I was going to have to drop the course, I was at such a standstill with mine."

"Perfect. They'll relate to that."

I'm hoping they'll see we are here to help along the way and actually take us up on using us as resources. The possibility of getting their papers featured in a published journal is a huge feat, one I know many fourth years bank on to pad their resumes. The film business is tough, so talent's not always enough, everyone needs that little bit extra. I want to set a positive tone, and encourage them to remain focused on the end goal and not get distracted.

However, when Ellie walks in, I zone out—*distracted*—just as I had been when I spotted her on the first day of class. And, subsequently, each one since as she takes her seat which, I might add, is right in front of me, every Monday and Wednesday morning in my Sexual Aesthetics/Representations class. *Distracting me.*

Ellie is very distracting. She's gorgeous, and from what I've seen so far, she's bright too. She's always ready to offer her opinion, and seems to have a real passion for gender equality in films, referencing the Geena Davis Institute on Gender in Media and Emma Watson as huge influences, women who've inspired her as a female wanting to work in the industry. Ellie went on about how Geena Davis is a force in the equal representation of women in film movement, sharing how Davis encourages all women to demand an equitable working environment; from actresses to grips, no woman should allow herself to be underpaid or made to feel less relevant than her male counterparts. Ellie spoke with so much conviction that I did more research into the Geena Davis Institute.

For the first time, one of my students sparked a curiosity in me so strong that I decided to immediately catch myself up on the Institute's progress. It's been a few years since I've looked into it, wanting to become more conscientious of the lack of equality that might exist for many of my students in the industry. I hadn't really revisited the topic since I included a few examples in an article on gender bias which I published in *Reel West* magazine.

I was very impressed with the work being done by these two actors. Along with Ellie's passion, the combination led me to decide this was something I needed to stay current on. I'd like to keep better informed about the issues facing women in the film industry so much that I have now liked and followed both Davis and Watson on social media.

Aside from equality, I've also come to discover that Ms. Hughes is obsessed with film adaptations. That was another tangent that I thoroughly enjoyed listening to her go on about.

"Ace, you ready, sir? Everything all right?" Jax's concerned voice asks, jolting me out of being lost in thoughts of her.

I run my hand through my hair. "Yeah, sorry. I thought I forgot my USB drive is all."

"Does *she* have it?" He nods towards where Court and Ellie are talking.

"Not sure who you mean, Jax. I was just thinking where I put it last, is all," I say, trying to deny my staring.

I'm becoming more and more convinced that Ellie Hughes is the creator of some sort of voodoo spell that has me in her clutches. She calls to me on some crazy level that I can't even begin to understand. Which is completely baffling, because she's barely my type. I prefer blondes usually; ones with light curves, a more scholarly look, and a bit older.

"Sure thing, Professor. Well, in case you missed it, the blonde and that redhead are both attractive," Jax says, smirking.

"I'm sure they are, but that's not what we're here for, right?"

"Of course not, Ace, I was only observing. And it's all in the Google Drive folder, no need for a stick anymore," he says, pulling up the folder on the laptop.

"Perfect. I forgot we uploaded it. Thanks."

Having spied her walking into the room affected me immediately. Sure, I looked like an idiot. I fumbled through the introductions, took longer to set up the PowerPoint presentation—my usual confidant self-wavering, all because some curvy redhead is messing with my head. Luckily, I don't think anyone really noticed, but I noticed all right...and I guess Jax did.

Thankfully, by the time I was ready to begin, she'd sat down with Courtney at the back where I couldn't maintain direct eye contact. Bad enough I'd been caught off guard by her presence in FSD470B4, I didn't need this again now. I don't know if I can keep my composure having her in two of my classes. I've never reacted to a student like this before, and I need to get this under control and quick.

Being thirty-two and in my first few years of teaching higher education, I need to be extra cautious, diligent even. On average, my students aren't much younger than I am, leaving me to have to be careful to uphold, follow, and stay within the strict boundaries of university policy, plus the ones I've put in place for myself. I will never cross the line of student/teacher relationship.

I've been extremely lucky to get where I am at my age, trust me I can acknowledge that, but truth be told, I'm good at what I do. I've earned the right to hold this position, and I will continue to keep the trust I've earned. I know people have taken a risk giving me this chance, so the last thing I'll do is screw it up, especially over some student. I've always been extra careful to maintain my professionalism and to make sure to never put myself in a compromising position. But with just one look at her, all thoughts went exactly there: to all the compromising positions in which I could put this beautiful girl.

Deep auburn hair, hazel brown eyes, eyes that warm my skin like the melted chocolate running in rivers in Willy Wonka's chocolate factory. Delicious-looking lips that would no doubt taste incredible. What I wouldn't give to suck on that pouty lower lip, run my tongue over it, to watch those eyes as they change from an innocent student's to ones which reflect the lust I know my touch will elicit from her. I want to test my theory but I know I shouldn't.

No, I know I can't.

But fuck if I don't want to.

Chapter 9

Ellie

DOUBLE-CHECKING MY PHONE'S Google Maps app, I'm happy to see that the address for the call centre (as I've come to refer to it when talking about my new job) is quite a bit closer to campus than I had originally thought. I can totally handle a fifteen-minute bus ride.

But walking up the steps towards a series of floor-to-ceiling glass windows, I see nothing to indicate that I'm actually in the right place. Looking around for the marker Mr. Conrad told me I'd see, I begin to wonder if I've written down the wrong address. Opening the heavy glass door, I see the security desk and offer the tall, awfully sexy, dark-skinned man behind it a shy wave. I'm just about to ask him if I'm in the right spot when I see the painting of the hockey player Mr. Conrad told me to stand under. Ken Danby's "Lacing Up" hangs on the far wall of the building. Nodding to the security guard, I make my way to stand by the painting. Not even a minute later, I hear an excited voice headed my way.

"Welcome to Breathless Whispers! I'm Destiny, you must be Ellie," the pretty blonde, blue-eyed woman with tight bouncing curls greets me.

"Uh-huh," is all I can manage, my eyes transfixed, fascinated, as she chomps incessantly on her gum, making her way to meet me in the exact spot Mr. Conrad told me I'd meet my trainer tonight. Finally, I smile, extending my hand to shake hers. "Yes, sorry, I'm Ellie. Hello, it's…er, nice to meet you."

"Pleasure to meetcha too." She pops a loud bubble, and I gawk at her again, this time taking in her pink leopard print shirt, one that matches her extremely bright pink nails perfectly. "I'm soooooo excited to train ya, you're my first little protégé. And I'm pumped!" Destiny gasps excitedly, forcing my eyes to focus back to her face while at the same time my heart rate picks up again as I question internally what the hell I'm doing here. "It'll be great. We'll be fast friends, I can feel it. Trust me, we'll be getting to know each other real good this week, eh?" she assures, and I can't hide the loss of my smile at the images her words have me imagining.

Letting out a laugh Destiny shakes her head. "Aw, you're an innocent one, aren't ya? I didn't mean anything by it, sweets. I only meant you're gonna hear me in action, and I'm gonna share my tricks of the trade with ya, nothing more. I mean you're a real knock out and all, but this isn't that kind of place, and I'm not into rugs," she winks, gesturing to the sterile office building in which we're standing. It's a smaller building located in the upscale area of Toronto's Liberty Village. I honestly expected the office to be in a shadier part of the city, but as Mr. Conrad assured me that Breathless Whispers was all about "Class, Discretion, and the Happy Ending". I can almost see the smirk I heard in his voice the other day when he interviewed me, as I think of the double meaning on that last bit. *What kind of "Happy Ending", exactly?*

Making our way over to the bank of elevators, I shift nervously on my Converse-covered feet. *This is really happening. No turning back now, I guess.*

"You ready to learn how to be a Phone Sex Superhero?" Destiny asks.

I laugh, despite my nerves being on the fritz, because she has got to be kidding. This girl is seriously something else. *Maybe we really will become friends?* "Phone Sex Superhero, eh? Is that how I should see this job?"

"Hell, yes, sweets! The shit you will do to get a client off is definitely hero work. I've coined the phrase and I'm making it stick," she laughs, licking her index finger and gesturing as if she's keeping score. The move causes me to belt out a laugh as I join her in the elevator, all the while shaking my head.

The ride is quick. Before I realize it, we're exiting onto the 7th-floor.

"Come on, let me give you the tour."

"Sounds good, I think," I say, while falling in step behind the petite blonde spitfire. She really is pretty, and I'm curious what her story is. She looks to be around my age, maybe a few years older. I want to ask her why she's here, but seeing as we've just met, I refrain, not exactly wanting to spill my beans yet, either. Maybe after tonight I'll feel comfortable to pry, seeing as we'll be besties.

Moving along the dimly lit corridor, Destiny opens a secured door with a black plastic pass the size of a credit card.

"You'll need this security pass to enter and exit. It's a bulletproof double-entry door with short-circuit cameras. We use this so we can come and go twenty-four hours a day. There isn't always someone at the desk, so this way the place is secure with the girls all holding different work hours," she tells me, waving the card as we walk through.

"We'll make sure you get yours tonight. You'll need it to get around in here. The Conrads are all about security, secrecy and selling sexy." She lifts her brows playfully.

"Huh, the four 'S's'. Mr. and Mrs. Conrad are real *scholars* to have thought up that *sassy* alliteration." I smile at my lame joke, which causes Destiny to look at me as if I'm just as lame. "Sorry. Nerves," I mutter.

"It's fine. I get it. We've all been there." She offers a reassuring smile.

"Wait." I stop. "I thought the motto was 'Class, Discretion, and the Happy Ending?'" I ask, confusion evident in my tone.

Destiny walks back my way, pausing in front of me. "Shit, you really are a bundle of nerves aren't ya, sweets? He has two mottos. That's the motto for clients; the other is for us workers. The Conrads are very good bosses; they will do almost anything to make sure we girls are happy and protected. All they ask in return is that we maintain the 'Class, Discretion, and the Happy Ending', for all clients with each phone call. Don't worry though, I'll teach you all of this, I swear. I promise, once you get the hang of it, you'll be asking yourself why you didn't do this sooner. The money that you make here is incredible. I bought a condo, go to Vegas on the regular, and even have some for my savings. Trust me," she says, opening a door simply marked "701" once we exited the glass chambered hallway.

Walking across the threshold, I'm met with vibrant walls painted a light lilac in I would describe simply as an office. Yep. A plain old, everyday-type of office, definitely not the setting I expected for a high-end phone sex service.

"This is where you'll check in." Destiny waves at a woman sitting at the desk in the centre of the room. "This," she gestures at the immaculately dressed grey-haired woman, "is Greta. She's the eyes and ears of Breathless. She deals with setting up all the new hires, arranges training, handles all the admin duties like scheduling, updating the website, and—most important—is our pay goddess. She also makes sure we all show up and aren't on drugs or drinking. She also deals with any emergencies should they arise, and best of all she's our at-work mama. Well, between the hours of 11 a.m. to 7 p.m., anyway. Unless she's pulling a late shift." Destiny smiles warmly at the older woman. "Greta's been known to work the nights with us sometimes. We all think it's so she can keep an eye on us, but she swears it's because she likes the quiet, and can get more done after hours. But, regardless, we all love her. Right, Greta?"

Greta nods, offering me a warm smile. "Aw, thanks, honey. You know I love you gals right back. Now, who do we have here?"

"This is Ellie."

"Hi, nice to meet you, Greta," I beam, because she makes me feel comfortable immediately.

"Oh yes," she claps her hands together excitedly, "you're Erica's friend. I've heard wonderful things about you, dear. I spoke to her about you the other day. No need to be nervous. It will pass. I'll keep an extra eye on you," she offers.

"I'd appreciate that, thank you. I'm super nervous. I have no idea if I can pull this off."

"Nonsense. Phone sex isn't brain surgery. It only takes a few times before you get good at it, and you'll be a Phone Sex Superhero in no time! You just have to let yourself play a little, too, sometimes. Once you get over the 'first caller', 'the shock call' and 'the make-me-hot call', it will be smooth sailing all the way to the bank." Greta gives me the "puh-lease" wave.

"The what-the-what calls?" I ask, bewildered. I feel like I caught everything she said, but I don't think I understood a word of it.

"Don't worry. I'll explain." Destiny laughs. "It's a little Superhero humour."

"Okaaay," I agree, albeit hesitantly.

Placing a stack of papers on the desktop, Greta goes through the paperwork that needs attention. "First, I need you to sign this non-disclosure form. I'll need your banking info, and here's your security pass. Your call ID will be…uh…let me see, I have it right here," she says, opening a file that's obviously mine. "Aha. Yes. Ha. How did I forget? You're lucky 69."

"69." I repeat, confused.

"Yes. Don't worry. The 69 is for the administration side of things. All the girls choose their handle but we add a number behind it, which is how we distinguish you all."

"Right, like my handle is Destiny21, but the clients only know me as Destiny. The 21 is simply for the computer system to connect our regular callers as that's our line number and employee number. You'll need to think of a sexy handle too. Better have it soon because I'm hoping to have you taking a call later this week.

"Okay. Right. Makes sense. A sexy handle. Got it." I feel my heart pounding in my chest; I really don't know if I'm going to be able to do this.

"Come on, I'll show you where the magic happens," Destiny says, pulling my arm. "Just breathe, you'll be fine. See ya, Greta," she winks again as we make our way past the desk to an adjacent hallway.

"Have fun, honey. Go with it," Greta calls, and I turn, offering a small wave.

"When she's not here, you'll check yourself in with the IT system in the call rooms. I'll show you that tonight too. It's easy and you'll need to do it when you clock in and then when you clock out."

"Okay. I brought a notebook, I'll write this all down so I don't forget."

"Perfect. That's what we all did, made a little cheat sheet. You'll find you won't need it for too long, this job really is simple once you get over the humps."

"I sure hope so," I mumble, as we enter a hallway filled with closed doors.

"How many girls work here in total, and on shift?" I ask, a bit reluctantly. I've read statistics, watched documentaries. I know most sex trade employers are not exactly exemplary. I know working in the sex trade industry can be a risk. I'd like to make sure I'm not getting myself into a situation I might soon regret. Luckily, from what I've seen and heard so far, I'm not too uncomfortable, no red flags have gone up yet. I know without a doubt that Erica would never suggest this job for me if it were one of the bad places.

"There are about twenty-five of us girls in total. All over twenty-one, so no need to worry about anyone being underage. The Conrads own and run one of the best agencies; they make sure everything is legal and go above and beyond to make sure that we are all well taken care of," Destiny assures me before stopping midway down the hall.

"Here's where the magic happens." She gestures at the doors lining the hallway. "These are our call suites. There are twelve girls working at all times. Shifts can be anywhere from four- to six-hours long. If you're busy, you'll find the time flies. If not, you can do homework or whatever and wait. The goal is to be busy. Get some regulars and make bank. Otherwise, you get minimum wage and clock out after four hours. So, really, this job is what you make it," she says, stopping in front of a door labeled Sweet 44.

"Ha! Nice pun. Like, Suite 44. Clever," I laugh.

"Oh, you get it? Most girls take a bit longer. Look at you, 69!" she says, opening the door and ushering me in.

Once inside, my nerves reach a whole new level.

Chapter 10

Ellie

"WOW, IT LOOKS like a mini hotel room in here," I say, in awe of what I see inside Sweet 44.

"Well, yeah…you can't expect a girl to get guys off while sitting behind a stuffy desk, now, can ya? Although, I find I tend to sit at the desk most of the time anyway. Weird, eh? Anyway, Mrs. Conrad figures we need variety, room to move, to properly set the stage." Destiny closes the door behind us. "Told ya they treat us right," she beams.

I move further in, and my eyes dart around the dimly-lit, deep purple-painted room: a room with a plush white area rug laid over dark hardwood, a comfy looking chaise complete with side table, a large cherry desk with two rolling chairs, a small fridge tucked into the corner beside the desk, and a large flat-screen TV mounted to the wall.

The décor is not what I expected, at all.

"I guess. I hadn't thought about it. I think I assumed it would look like a typical call centre, you know, with cubicles…" I shrug, still taken aback by how comfortable I feel standing in the room where I know I'll be using my voice to get men—and possibly women—off.

"Well, we gotta be comfortable to deliver the Happy Ending, right? Mr. and Mrs. Conrad spare no expense. You don't become the number one-rated sex line by making the workers unhappy. Look, we even have pay-per-view!"

"Wow, really?"

"Yeah, but it's only the porn stations," she deadpans, "consider it inspiration." She turns back to look at me, a wide grin in place. "Just kidding, you can watch anything you want," she laughs.

I'm glad one of us is having a good time here. "Can I ask a question?"

"Of course, ask me anything. I'm your open book to PSO superhero-ism."

"Okay, well, first off: 'PSO'?"

"Phone Sex Operator, silly."

"Oh right, that makes sense. I'm a bit slow off the mark, I guess." I laugh awkwardly.

"Relax, 69, I'm here to help. No question is stupid. Please, ask me anything."

"Thanks, I appreciate that. I guess the first thing I want to know is kind of personal."

"Honey, I get people off over the phone. Nothing you ask will phase me, trust me," she says, waving her hand.

"Okay. Well, do you…Have…er, I mean…" I trail off, unsure of how to ask what I really want to know.

"Have I what? Ever gotten off with a caller? Shit, yeah, many times. Sometimes you're so deep into the role-play you can't help it. Trust me, we all have, and you will too, regardless how hard you try to convince yourself that you're different," she says, pulling out the chairs at the desk. I see a phone with a super-long cord, a cordless headset, and a computer.

"Come have a seat," she taps the leather roller chair, "and I'll go over the CALLRIGHT system, the main types of callers, and…" she hums, contemplating, looking at the clock, "…yeah, I think that will be enough for tonight. I don't want you overwhelmed."

"Sounds good. I like the idea of easing into all this, seems like it might be a lot." I say. Destiny seems oblivious to my reluctance. I think she's too much of a happy-go-lucky person to recognize if I were completely freaking the hell out. Which I'm not, of course. *Of course not.*

"Perfect. Then next shift, we'll review everything from tonight again, I'll have you listen to a few calls, answer any more questions you have, then I'll support you on a call of your own. And then, my little protégé, you'll be all on your own!" she says, clapping her hands excitedly, the excitement actually becoming a bit contagious when she makes it sound so easy and breezy like that. I guess the training isn't all that involved, which makes sense, since you'll never know what type of role you'll be playing until you're in the moment.

Being on my own is my goal.

I need to prove I can do this.

The sooner I clock in, the sooner I can make the money I need for my tuition.

Chapter 11

Ellie

"I CAN'T BELIEVE I'm about to admit it, but I'm starting to feel a bit excited," I say, as I roll up beside Destiny in the training chair, reaching into my bag for my handy-dandy Hello Kitty notebook. I have a feeling I'm going to need to jot notes, seeing as I still can't fully believe I'm doing this.

"Okay, I'm ready," I say, opening to a blank page, scribbling *Computer, Possible Callers, and Tricks from Destiny* as my heading, while she boots the computer to life.

"First thing is, make sure you log into the CALLRIGHT app on the computer."

I watch as she moves the cursor to the small red rotary phone icon.

"This is where you'll find all your caller log info, and where you'll track your callers. It even lets you see who and how many are waiting in your call queue. If you're lucky, you'll also see what type of caller they might be, that is, if they decide to share that information."

"Wow, the system tells me all that?" I ask impressed.

"Yeah, it's genius. The automated service gives clients the option to say if they're looking for a specific fetish scene, dom/sub, or whatever type of call; there's a prompt system that gives them options to be as detailed as they want to be, or not. Once it gathers the details, it will direct them to the girls whose profiles match what the caller is requesting...if they are available, of course. If not, it bounces the caller to the next free line. In a few weeks, you'll update your profile, stating which types of calls you prefer. You might find you excel with the dom/sub calls and want to service only those clients over, say, companion calls and so on. Most of us are like me, I'll take any type of caller. It keeps it new and fresh."

Listening to Destiny, I try to jot down as much of this useful information as possible. Who would have thought so much planning went into running a phone sex line?

"Now. To make the most money, you should accept every call. You don't have to accept every call that pops up, but, personally, I recommend that you do. More calls means more money, the longer the calls, the more money, and the more you answer, the better chance you have of building a call back list of regulars, which means…"

"…more money."

"Right. And that's the big windfall, your regulars. Some of my regulars call three times a week—trust me that's a good chunk of change—and over time, you'll find them the easiest calls to get through because they're predictable and you'll know how to get them off. Make sense?"

"Actually it does. So, think 'more, more, more', and know my goal is to be so good that they'll want to call me again and again."

"You're getting it, 69! You're a-gettin' it."

"I feel like this is an easier-said-than-done situation. This is all straightforward so far, but the actual calls are freaking me out a bit," I share honestly.

"You'll deal just fine. Think money. It's all about the money," Destiny says. "Now, back to the calls. The system will track everything for you, every single call, dropped call, lost call and each call's length. The system will display a profile based on their responses, along with whether it's a new caller to your line or a repeat caller. The system is great for regulars, they can punch in our names when prompted ensuring they end up on our line. Just be sure to give them your number, which for you is 69. It's honestly this, like, crazy entity of a system that scares me with its abilities. Truthfully, I just log in, hit accept and make the magic happen. I don't bother trying to figure the system out," she says, laughing, then has me log in, making sure my password works.

"How do we feel about that? Easy enough?" She looks at me, waiting for a reply.

"I think so. Seems pretty straight forward, but I'm with you, I'm not even going to try to understand the system," I shake my head.

"All right then, let's talk caller types." Destiny logs back into the CALLRIGHT icon, finding her name. "I'm going to put my colour on yellow. You use yellow when you need to pause your line, so, to use the washroom, or if you need to leave your suite for a few minutes to grab food or whatever. Just be sure you put it back on green when you're done. It'll be on red, indicating you're off-line until you log in and move it to either yellow or green."

"Got it—green, go; yellow, no. Red, off-line completely."

"Yep." She moves to face me. "Really, there are probably four main types of callers you'll experience most often. First, there are The Regulars. These are the whales to the phone sex operator, these are the ones who will call anywhere between two- to four times a week, looking to talk to only you every time. These are the callers looking to get off and fast. They are sometimes shy men who have a ton of crazy scenes they'll want to role-play with you. Anything from a threesome to mutual masturbation to anal, it all depends on what they're in the mood for. In my experience, these calls usually last anywhere between five to fifteen minutes. The longer you can keep them on the phone, the better, seeing as they call so much. The Regulars will be your bread and butter. They're fun and love to play and they vary between all genres of caller types. You might even find one you'll apply your discount to."

"My discount?"

"Never mind for now, Greta will tell you about it, my job is to focus on teaching you the good stuff. And we only have about an hour left tonight."

I make a note to ask Greta about the discount that Destiny mentioned rather hastily.

"The second type of callers are what I like to call the Either/Or situations. These callers are either the *Bossy Bastard,* where they want you to submit to their every command *or* they will be the complete opposite and be all *Pansy Wansy,* getting off completely by being at your mercy, allowing you to take complete control of the scene. Those ones go off like lit fireworks at submitting to a powerful woman. These calls tend to be the longest and sometimes require a very vivid imagination. Dominatrixes do not get enough credit, if you ask me. That gig is tough." She cracks her gum. "You still with me?"

"Yup." I scribble the last of the notes, circling my reminder to look up various dom/sub scenarios on Google.

"The third type are *The Needy Babies*, as I like to call them. The easiest of the lot if you ask me. They tend to call in the evenings, mostly first-time callers who are unsure and need complete guiding, and are unsure if they even want to get off. They might be the nerdy guy or the shy guy who just wants some companionship and aren't looking for any hanky-panky. They may just want someone to talk to, to simply listen to them."

"So they don't want to get off?" I ask, a bit confused. "Why pay for us when they could go to a social group, or counselling for that matter?"

"I think they like the possibility of getting off, but they might be so shy that they may not even want to admit they're horny. Experience tells me they do get off, they just aren't as vocal about it. Except for the chatter boxes. Those guys will seriously talk your ear off and that's it, they could care less about coming."

"Jeez, maybe I need to mark that type on my preference sheet," I joke.

"Naw, they get boring, trust me. You'll want the exciting calls, makes the job fun. Anyway, the fourth type is what I like to call *The Picky Fucker*. This is your fetish caller, the one we tend to get the most. They are seriously the most unique of the bunch, but also require the most work and creativity. You'll want to laugh at some of the things they'll want you to say or pretend to do. And you will not believe some of the shit that turns them on. This is where you'll use your props the most. That being said, they happen to be my favourite callers because it is seriously never a dull moment with them."

"What sorts of things are we taking about?" I ask, turning the page, ready to make a list of other things I might want to google.

"Well, there are the common ones, like feet, water, thunder and lightning, and furries." I want to ask her to explain them all, because, honestly, I don't have a clue what the hell she means by furries, or thunder, and, frankly, I don't think I'm ready to hear it just yet. So once again, I circle those terms for later. Double circles.

"Then there are the more obscure ones like tripsolagnia, coulrophilia and—"

"Hold it, wait. What the heck is that? Tripso—*what*? Coul—*what*?"

She laughs at what I assume is the face I must be giving her. "How about this? I explain these two fetishes and we call your first day of training done? I don't think you can handle listening to a call tonight," she giggles.

"I think you might be right," I nod. "Okay. I'm all ears, so please share, the suspense is kind of killing me."

"Okay. The first one, tripsolagnia, is the act of getting off while getting your hair shampooed by someone else. And coulrophilia…that's a clown fetish. People who get off fantasizing about sexual acts with a clown. I've never had these ones, but Cinnamon and Ruby have."

Oh. My. God. Did I mention that clowns scare the bejeezus out of me? There is no effin' way I will be pretending to be a clown. Nope. No way, no how. I'm silent, letting the information settle before opening my mouth. "Remember that small tinge of excitement I had mentioned feeling earlier?"

"Yeah," she laughs.

"I think my nerves just ate it!"

Gulp.

Chapter 12

Ace

SHE'S TOO SMART.

She's too fucking beautiful.

"I shouldn't do it." I try to talk myself out of doing what I'm about to do, like some sort of crazy person. "You're asking for trouble," I mutter, my hand on my laptop's track pad where I keep moving *her* name under the column where my own name sits in bold type as a thesis advisor. The column in which I know she should not be placed.

I'm sitting at The Froth House, the local coffee shop on campus, waiting for my buddy Mercer to meet me for our usual morning coffee. It's a trendy spot with a large fireplace in the centre that is surrounded by a dozen small tables and chairs and a perimeter lined with booths, and always packed. The coffee is good and the staff is great. I'm a big fan, coming here to work between classes rather than my office or professor's lounge.

It's been three weeks since classes started, and so far everything has been going smoothly. Except for my current predicament: that is, do I or do I not assign myself as Ellie's advisor? Here's the thing: the idea of her working intensely with Jax, or Sam, or hell, even Joelle—my teaching assistants this year—irks the hell out of me. Especially after hearing her in class, and reading her intro paper. I learned a lot about all the students and have based the pairings on those intro papers. It's clear that Ellie is bright. Her introduction paper was well-written, conscientious and was dripping with her passion for film.

Needless to say, I'm very interested in hearing her thesis plans now, along with whatever else she may want to discuss. *Hell. I'd listen to this girl drone on about anything at this point.* On top of being eye-catchingly gorgeous, she's got the brains too, and that intrigues me. A lot. I'm not sure what it is, but something compels me to her, despite not having had any further close encounters like that first day. It's been weeks of stolen glances, lingering stares and subtle smiles. I sense her interest has been piqued about me just as much as mine for her. I see it in the way her chest rises then falls when I catch her watching me, and how her mouth lifts to the side when I reciprocate and it's her catching me staring a bit too long. I'm going to get myself in trouble here. I can feel the pull to the dark side already.

"See? She's too distracting," I scold myself, hitting save one last time, but leaving her in my column, of course. *Piss it. I can do this.* I've got five other students to help too; she's the same as them, a student needing support and guidance. Besides, I'm a professional. *Yeah, pep talks are good. That was a good one, Ace.* "Right. I can do this. And I will not allow myself to cross any lines. She's my student. I am her professor."

Lying bastard.

I shake my head while powering down my laptop. Looking up, I'm in time to catch my buddy Mercer entering behind a small crowd. *Thank Christ.* I need his distraction. Mercer waves an imaginary mug, offering to grab me another. I nod, mouthing my thanks as he joins the long line of coffee-seeking enthusiasts.

Mercer Reynolds and I have been friends since our first day of university. Having been assigned as roommates at the University of Western Ontario, we hit it off immediately and have stayed in touch since. He'd been trying to get me to transfer to U of T since he started teaching here four years ago. Mercer has his Ph.D., and is head of the kinesiology department.

Dr. Reynolds has been a big help in getting me settled here. I managed to rent an apartment in the same building as he and his sister, Chelsea, in Toronto's Annex neighbourhood, which turned out to be the perfect location because it's close to both work and enough places to eat, shop, and have an active social life when I choose. Not one for serious relationships, living in Toronto will be great for casual dating and hooking up when the urge hits.

Between my job and my own filmmaking, I've not had time to pursue any kind of long-term relationship in years, despite my grandparents' wishes. Growing up as an only child, I was raised by my grandparents after both of my parents died in an avalanche while heliskiing at British Columbia's Blue River. Being my only remaining living relatives, they raised me from the age of twelve on. It took a long time to adjust to life with my Grandma Lily and Grandpa Paul, but we all survived in the end and I wouldn't be where I was today without them. We didn't always have a lot, but they loved and supported me regardless.

Mercer pulls me from my thoughts, placing a steaming mug of coffee and some cream pods in front of me. "Hey, big guy. How's it hanging this fine morning?"

"So far, so good. I finished assigning advisor groups for my master's thesis students. I need to get the preliminary meeting started next week to make sure everyone's on track, knows his or her direction. I need to weed out the idiots, save the ones with potential, you know…the norm".

"Sounds fun. I still can't believe you wanted that class. Seems like way too many extra hours, if you ask me. Sports medicine is where it's at, brother. I get to workout anytime I want, and I personally keep our national teams fit and safe."

I laugh, "Yeah, you're a regular Dr. Feelgood." We both chuckle.

"How goes the documentary? Now, that's the real question," Mercer asks, taking a sip of what I assume is his usual, a triple-shot latte.

"It's good. I've got a few more interviews lined up, and I met with Alice and her pimp, Sly, last week. We wrapped up their interviews, and I was able to shoot a couple of vignettes about the life of an illegal prostitute here in the city. So, yeah, it's going really well. Thankfully, I've not run into anything too dangerous or involving the police thus far."

"That's…awesome. I can't imagine following a pimp and ho downtown at night, though. Must have been scary, even for a big boy like you. Maybe we need to buy you some pepper spray?" he teases, striking a nerve with the "ho" comment.

"Hey, man. I'm tough, downtown is my playground at night." We both laugh, "But be nice, shithead. Alice is a sweet lady; don't call her a 'ho'. She's doing what she needs to get by, and no little girl grows up wishing she might one day be a prostitute. You wouldn't believe the desperate shit these women have to do to support themselves, or the ones they love. Alice isn't like Chloe, the other prostitute I interviewed. Alice isn't doing this to support a heroin addiction, she's doing it to keep a roof over her and her daughter's heads. It's mind blowing when you go behind the scenes; everyone really does have a story. And we shouldn't judge so harshly."

He raises his hands in mock surrender. "Easy man, I didn't mean any offence, I was playing. Besides, I know how it is, trust me."

He's right, he does know. His sister, Chelsea, used to work at a pretty lucrative phone sex line while paying her way through medical school. Growing up just the two of them, she didn't have much choice when not wanting to accrue a shit ton of student loans once medical school was done. Chels was determined to find a job that would leave her debt free. In the end, she became some super hoity-toity phone sex operator and succeeded in paying her own way. Having worked in the sex industry, she's been helping a lot with this project of mine whenever I need. So, I know he isn't as judgmental a dick as he sounded.

"Sorry. I know you didn't mean it in a negative way. I'm overthinking it. The end of filming is getting closer, and then I start the submission process. What the hell am I thinking about, entering such a huge competition?"

"Stop. You're an incredible filmmaker, and this piece is important. You're shedding light on the realities of the sex trades. Opening people's eyes to the diseases that infiltrate the lives of these women: Hep C, HIV/AIDS. Women, who—for whatever reason—feel they have no choice. Women who often deal with a manipulative pimp, or some other asshole that steals from them and beats the shit out of them. I bet by the time I see the final version, I'll be praying the digital age allows some of these women to find a safer way to do business, if they must. You have every right to enter that competition, you need to enter, and I'm proud of you, Ace. I'm happy you're finally pursuing your dream. It's about time."

I nod my head. "Thanks, that means a lot," I smile, lifting my coffee mug. "Cheers. Whoever would have thought I'd be entering a film in TIFF, though?"

Mercer smiles and raises his mug before taking a sip. "Me. Cheers, man."

Ever since I was a kid, I loved filming versions of what I later came to learn were documentaries. I'd film myself in the backyard explaining the life of a bumblebee along with its importance as a living thing that needed respect. Everywhere I went, I'd record images or scenes and do voice-overs explaining the "slice of life", and the reality of what was being seen on the film. My parents were still pretty young when they passed away, so it wasn't like they had a ton of money to leave my grandparents to help raise me. I had to get a job as soon as I was of age, and I worked a string of odd jobs, saving every dime to buy equipment and chase my dream of attending film school. My grandfather, also my biggest supporter, worked like a dog and bled his life savings to help send me from Kingston, where we lived, out west to Simon Fraser University where I studied for four years, then to Western in London, Ontario, where I got my master's and my doctorate. I'd always been in love with the power of documentary films, and in the end I wrote my thesis on the importance of not letting the genre die, and how a more narrative approach was needed to help their sustainability with new generations. My paper was so well-received it was featured in three academic film journals. Now, here I am, years later, almost finished creating my first full-length documentary, one I plan on entering in the Toronto International Film Festival (TIFF).

My film, *Sex for Sale,* showcases how the digital age is forcing the sex industry to reevaluate and update itself to keep up with the times, and takes a closer look at how said changes are impacting business, the internet, anthropology and life in general. It questions whether the digital age is making it easier for human trafficking to occur, and for seedy businesses to hire underage workers and pay them less in today's sex trade industry, all while asking if one-on-one contact is becoming obsolete. With the increases in technology, will there still be any requirement for the traditional prostitute and pimp? The stripper? Are webcam operations and phone sex lines the new go-to? Will apps like Tinder and Grindr finally make the government regulate an industry that has no signs of slowing down, which the digital age is only helping to grow? I'm hoping my documentary will make viewers question the need for government intervention, that people will see that we need to protect these workers as we do all other dangerous occupations, how regulating the sex trades may create less opportunity for violence, human trafficking, and a slew of other issues that stem from non-governmental involvement.

"What's left to cover before you start editing?" Mercer asks, bringing me back to the conversation.

"I've got all the stripper clips and interviews edited, as well as the three porn stars. I have an interview set up with Trina, a webcam actor, for next Wednesday night and I've got a couple of phone interviews with some underage workers I found who refused to meet me in person, but I'm going to keep at it. If I can convince one to meet with me, I might be able to help her out. I hate the things she's told me so far. I've been in contact with the police and am waiting to hear about any next steps which I can help with, if they need. Besides that, it leaves me with the phone sex operators and male prostitutes to find and film. Then I'll be done. So, I might need to hit up Chelsea for some help. She offered, and I'm thinking I might take her up on it, I need a list of good lines to call."

"Whatever you need. You know we'll both help with anything. I'll let her know to expect to hear from you. How underage are we talking here, Ace?"

"Young enough to know that I need to try and get the place shut down. Young."

"Jesus. Well, if you ever need any help, ask."

"Thanks, that means a lot. You never know what your research might uncover."

"Fucking sick bastards out there…I hope you can convince her to come in for an interview, and to accept some help."

Mercer glances down at his watch after about an hour of discussion. "I'd better get moving. I have a seminar in twenty, across campus," he says, grabbing his brown leather messenger bag and jacket off the chair.

"Thanks for the chat," I say. "And, so you know, I'm thankful the new technology is making it safer for some of the women in the industry, 'cause, yeah, honestly, I looked over my shoulder a few times the other night with Alice. I even asked Sly if he was packing at one point."

With that, Mercer barks out a laugh. "Pansy ass film types," he mutters, walking away.

"Drinks next Thursday. Don't forget," I call out after him.

"Yeah, I'll meet you and Dyl there. He better have shaved off what Chelsea calls his 'flavour saver' by then. I'm bringing a razor, in case. No way will I listen to my sister call it that again," he chuckles, waving two fingers over his shoulder.

Our friend Dylan is currently sporting a crazy thick moustache as a result of a hockey bet between he and Mercer involving the Maple Leafs, one Dyl lost. But since growing the thing, he's fallen in love with it, claiming it's a "chick magnet", telling us repeatedly how "chicks actually dig it". Mercer retorts that it's nothing but an eyesore and needs removal ASAP, that no "chick" will ever "dig it".

Before heading to class, I decide to grab a cappuccino to go (I don't usually have this much caffeine, but I was up late editing). Stepping in line, my Spidey sense immediately perk ups when a familiar scent begins to infiltrate my space, and it's not coffee.

Ellie.

Turning sideways, I try to see if I'm hallucinating or if I'm just scent-scarred for life by the distinctive aroma belonging to one off-limits student. I'm trying to casually pull off that move where you make it look as if you're not looking out of your peripheral vision, but like an ass you totally are, and that's when I spot her. Right behind me, all 5'3" of her, and she's looking directly at me, a subtle smirk pulling at her lips. She clearly knows exactly what I'm doing.

"Hey, Professor Ryan," she beams, obviously not trying to be at all covert about acknowledging me, as I am with her.

"Ms. Hughes," I nod, moving up to place my order with the blue-eyed barista named Tracey, who flirts with me now as she always does.

Ignoring her, I turn to Ellie. "What are you having?"

She hesitates, eyeing me like I'm the horse's head in the bed in *The Godfather*. "Ellie. It's a coffee. It's the least I can do for being a side-eyed creeper just now," I say, having leaned in close to her ear so only she can hear. A sharp intake of breath confirms I've caught her off guard, and I sure as shit like knowing I've just affected her.

"Uh...I'll have a...medium chocolate raspberry, please. And thank you." Her voice is low.

Paying, I grab my coffee, and lean in once more. "See you around, Ellie," I say, before leaving her to wait for her coffee.

Chapter 13

Ellie

WALKING INTO THE kitchen, groceries in hand, Courtney and I move about the small, sage-coloured galley kitchen putting everything away. We continue the discussion I'd brought up in the car, about needing to figure out the perfect name for me for my new job. I'd finally built up the nerve to ask her for help with creating my persona. All I can think about are ridiculous handles that make me giggle rather than feel confident and sexy.

"Destiny says it needs to be a sexy yet simple name," I tell her.

"Of course. It is your *dessstiny…*!" hisses Courtney.

"Shut up. I'm dying of embarrassment here just talking about this with you. But I'm just as bad. I keep coming up with stupid shit that makes me laugh." I put the carton of eggs in the fridge, followed by the bags of milk. I huff the hair out of my eyes in frustration.

"Well, this should be easy. What have you come up with so far?" Court asks, putting Triscuit crackers in the cupboard.

"'Mary Underwear' was the first one that popped into my head. See what I did there?" Courtney bursts out laughing.

"Oh my God. Dude. You'll be fired for lameness before you even start."

"Right. It's tough. Then I thought of 'Kitten'. But that creeped me out. Way too close to pussy and pussy jokes. I'd laugh at myself for sure. 'Hi, I'm *Kitten*. I'm happy to be your pussy tonight'." I say in my lowest, sexiest voice.

"*Meow*," Court mews, causing us both to howl.

"I keep thinking of silly stuff. It's like my brain can't be serious."

"'Debbie Dick Rider'?" Court says.

"'Rideanne'?" I tilt my head, dumping apples into the fruit bowl.

"'Mia Muff'?" Court replies. "This is hard."

"See? I suck. Maybe I won't be able to do this. I most definitely can't take it seriously. Imagine how I'll be at caller training tomorrow night." *Oh man.* I smack my forehead with my hand. "I'm too lame for this. I've only ever had sex with two people!"

"Maybe you should be 'Miss Missionary', then?" Court laughs. "Or, ooh! Wait! How about 'Mrs. Mia Wallace', from that Pulp Fiction movie you like so much?"

"It's a *film*, not a 'movie'. Not helping." I toss some cut-eye her way.

"You could always hook up with Doctor Ryan and get a little more experience. I bet that man could teach you a few things. I see the way you two eye each other. I bet he'd be totally game to help you out." She raises her eyebrows up and down.

"No way! Like that would ever happen." Immediately, memories of him leaning in close to me at The Froth House surface from the other day. God, he smelled and looked so flippin' good. I wish I *could* experience that man. Not that I'd ever tell Courtney.

"Court, be serious. He barely knows who I am. Besides have you seen him? He is not looking for someone like me," I wave a hand down the length of me, "a starving student. Most likely not his type. Not that I'd be interested, anyway."

"Yeah, okay, liar. I bet he'd be very interested in you and the newly-created sexy phone operator too. I'm more than positive he'd dig both versions," she retorts.

"Shhh! No one can *ever* know I work at a sex line! Don't tell *any-*

one." I give her my most serious face. "Ugh, and I don't have a name yet. I can't even start until I have a perfect handle and there is no way in hell I'm using 'Ellie'," I sigh, exasperated.

"Relax, you'll be fine. We'll find the perfect name. We just need to do some research and channel your sexy-inner-whore-dirty-talking-fetish-loving-fantasy-making self. Maybe there's an essential oil blend for that? An app?" She keels over, laughing at herself.

"Oh, you got jokes, eh? Miss Oh-You-Can-Do-This-Ellie, Miss I'll-Help-You-Ellie…nice. Good friend. Especially when my staying here depends on this. You're not helping, bestie," I mock scold.

"I'm sorry. I had to. I couldn't resist. You know I love your oil-loving hippy ass. And that I'll do whatever I can to help."

"Yeah, yeah, I can tell," I smile.

"Seriously, now. A name. One that's sexy, yet simple and unique. Okay, I'm thinking, I'm thinking," she says, rubbing her temples in a circular motion. "What about…'Cinnamon'? Or 'Cherry'?" she asks, looking up at me.

"Nope, there's a really sexy Indian girl who goes by 'Cinnamon'. And 'Cherry' is used too."

"Damn. Okay, what about 'Honey'?"

"Imagine the comments I'd get on that?" I shake my head.

"'Candy'?"

"Lame." I roll my eyes.

"'Wendy Pantscomeoff?'" she tries.

"A mouthful."

"'Vee Gina'?"

I laugh. "Clever, but no."

"'Moonlight Desires'?"

"From the Gowan song? No," I sigh.

"'Twat Waffler'?"

"'Henrietta Hard-On'?"

"'P. Onmee?'"

"*Courtney!* Not helping. Sexy. Simple yet unique," I repeat.

"Okay. There must be one of those meme-thingy's about 'What's Your Phone Sex Name'. Let's Google this shit," she says, putting all the empty bags in the closet before reaching for her iPad. "And wine. We need wine for this. Wine, and a little meme search, and a list of movies with phone sex operators so we can see what the hell you've gotten yourself into. Sound good? Nothing says Sunday like sex, booze and a few movies to perv on with your best girl," she winks.

I nod, laughing. "And this is why I love you. I'm with you. Let's do this." I grab the wine glasses and a bottle, trailing behind her.

"Found a meme thingy: 'What's Your Phone Sex Name?' Perfect. This might work: you use your first and last initials then your date of birth."

"Awesome, let's give it a try." I plop down beside her on the couch, immediately filling our glasses with Shiraz.

"Ready?" She takes the wine glass I've offered.

"Yep, hit me," I say, putting my feet up on the distressed-style coffee table.

"Well, using the month you were born, the first letter of your name and the first letter of your last name, your new name shall be, drum roll…'Enchantress Sexy Swivel Hips'." She cocks her head as if she's even surprised herself at how terrible the name is. "Or maybe not."

"We're gonna need more wine." I reach for the bottle. "Well, let's try yours, maybe yours'll make a better one. There is no way I can use mine," I laugh.

"Okay, okay," she takes a gulp of her own wine, "what about…'Cunty Whiplash Pussyface?'"

"Oh God, this is hopeless." I do a facepalm. "Did I mention that, on top of a name, I need to pack a travel case with a bunch of sex-simulating props?"

"Oh, I cannot wait to hear this shit. I don't think I'll ever look at you the same way again once you start this job. We need to sidebar back to this shoebox o' supplies. I'm dying to hear what we need to stock you with."

Pulling out my phone, I swipe it, opening the Notes app where I keyed in all the things Destiny told me I'd need for props. "So, I need a bunch of elastics to simulate the smacking of flesh, a leather belt to whip my bitches into shape, lollipops and or popsicles for sucking instruments, a vibrator, a heavy book to slam as if it were a headboa—"

"Holy shit!" Court giggles, interrupting me. "That's amazing. Who would have thought? You might need a tote, not a shoe box though."

"Right. It's crazy, and there are about ten more things she suggested I grab too."

After Courtney gets over her wonder of my sex-simulation materials list, we spend some more time sharing useless meme-generated names.

"It's hopeless," I sigh, defeated. After two bottles of wine, a pizza, and no name to show for the afternoon, I'm spent.

"Wanna walk to Shopper's Drug Mart with me?" Court asks, after we've finished watching Meg Ryan performing a fake orgasm in *When Harry Met Sally,* and Anne Hathaway pulling off a sexy phone operator in *Valentine's Day.*

"Yeah, I need a break, this shit's overwhelming. But I can get started on "the box" there. Plus, I'm out of samples of Coco Chanel, Pink Sugar, and Light Blue. I need to swindle more from the cosmetics counter," I say, stretching as I rise from the couch.

"Holy shit, Els. That's it! It's bloody perfect. It fits you to a tee. How did we not think of that?" Courtney says, jumping up and down.

"Uh, care to fill me in, crazy lady?"

"'Chanel'. It's the perfect handle. It's sexy and tasteful, and it goes well with 69! Therefore, from this moment forth, I shall crown you

'Chanel69', phone sex operator extraordinaire!" She takes a bow and I smile, a huge stress-releasing smile, because she's right, Chanel69 is a brilliant name for me.

"I love it. I am Chanel69." *Now, if I could only build the confidence to live up to my sexy name.*

"Aww, Coco would be so proud, boo!" Court laughs, as we make our way to the elevator.

Chapter 14

Ellie

"69! I WASN'T too sure we'd see you again. I'm excited you're here, though; I know you can do this. I swear, you're gonna slip into the role in no time. It really is the easiest money you'll ever make," Destiny says, swivelling her chair to meet my gaze as I walk in the room.

"Honestly, I wasn't too sure I'd be back, either. But here I am, and I'd like to officially introduce myself," I say, closing the door to Sweet 44 behind me. "Hello, I'm Chanel, it's nice to meet you." I smile, proud of the name Court and I finally decided upon.

Hopping up from her chair, Destiny jumps up and down, clearly excited.

"I love it! It's perfect for you. I knew you'd think of a good one. It's super sexy, Ellie. Here, come sit," she says, pulling out the rolling chair beside hers. "I was just about to log on. For tonight, I thought we could go over possible voice tones that would work for you. I can also show you the voice adapter and how it works if you want. If you're keen on using it to disguise your own voice, it's an option. A lot of the girls use them, but it's up to you. I thought you could listen in on a call or two of mine tonight, then you can try one on your own, if you feel up to it. I'll be right close if you need an SOS."

"That sounds good. I'm interested in seeing how the adapter will change my voice. I'm not sure I can pull off sexy without computer assistance," I say, holding up the black phone piece and inspecting it.

"You must sound good. Trust me, Mr. Conrad is all about voice appeal. That's why he does all his interviews over the phone first, then in person. Mrs. Conrad is the one who makes sure we are paid well and are happy, but Mr. Conrad does the interviews, so if your voice is shit, you're an immediate no hire. Obviously, you passed his test. Either way, you can always use it if you want to switch it up or be incognito."

"True," I agree, putting the adapter back down and grabbing my notebook.

"You ready to listen to a call?"

Taking a deep breath, I tell her: "Yes." God, I hope I can do this. Other than seeing Anne Hathaway in *Valentine's Day* and everything Destiny has told me, I have no clue what to expect. I wasn't brave enough to let Erica share her stories with me when she called to congratulate me last week, either. I didn't want to be more worked up then I already was. I did, however, tell her she'd most likely be hearing from me sometime in the near future. "Ready as I'll ever be."

"Let's do this," Destiny says, touching the trackpad and bringing the computer screen to life, switching her colour to green from yellow. "When we have a caller in queue, you'll hear a *beep*, that way you can be wherever you like in the room and not have to sit by the computer all night, waiting. Once you hear it, read the info, then hit 'accept' or 'reject'. But we try to never hit reject. Remember the goal."

"Yes. Getting and keeping regulars. Wanting them to want me, again and again."

"Perfect. So be careful you don't reject too many, or lose calls. The Conrads get awfully grumpy when we have too many dropped or rejected calls. Sometimes it happens, just make sure it's not often, and that you can justify why it happened, and reflect on what you might do different the next time, if you get a caller hanging up on you. More than three rejects in a month, then we have to have a meeting with management. Girls have lost their jobs for not having valid reasons why they didn't take the calls. Always try," she says, tucking a curl behind her ear. "If you happen to get a bad call, most times they'll hang up before you get the chance. Some of the callers can be little pissy pants. There might come a time when the call becomes too much, like super violent, threatening or majorly creepy. Just hang up, and if it's a caller you feel needs to be flagged for the security team to look into, then write it in the comments beside the caller's details."

"Okay. That makes sense, and I'll try to take them all, I promise. I'm sure I'll feel better once I watch you a few times. I mean, it's not like they can see me or anything. I'll pretend I'm an actor—or better yet, a director. Yeah, I'll think of it as if I'm directing some major hot sex scenes in a huge motion picture." I smile at the genius of the idea. It will completely help to put me at ease to see this job like that.

"Whatever works to help keep them on the line, girlie," she says, scrolling through the list of calls in the queue. "Perfect, Daddy's calling."

"Oh my God, your dad knows you work here?" I ask in shock as Destiny picks up the line, putting her feet up on the desk in front of her.

"Hello, Daddy," she whispers, and I wonder if I should leave and let her talk to her father. I didn't realize you could give your family members a direct number to your line.

I'm about to stand when I hear a thundering voice come through the line, and realize she's got it on speaker.

"Kitten. That you? You there?"

"Kitten"?!

"Yes, sir. It's me."

He calls her "Kitten"? She calls her dad "sir"? He's okay with her working here?

"Good girl. You ready for me to make your pussy purr?"

Holy crap, it's not her real dad. I'm an idiot.

I stifle my giggle by clapping a hand over my mouth. *Jesus, I'm naïve.*

"Yeah, Daddy, I'm ready," Destiny replies without skipping a beat, despite the daggers she's pointing in my direction. "I'm more than ready. It's been so long since you've called me," she pouts. "Kitten misses her daddy's touch. I wanna come. I've been holding it like the good girl you asked me to be."

Oh. My. God.

Destiny gives me a sly smile and I know—I just know—that I'm staring wide-eyed at her with mouth agape.

"Oh my God. I don't think I can do this..." I mouth at her.

"Yes, you can," she whispers, covering the phone, "you watch. Three more minutes," she mouths back to me before opening the mini-fridge and reaching into the freezer to grab a popsicle. She unwraps it carefully while she listens to "Daddy" telling her to get on her knees.

"Oh God, how I've missed your big, hard cock. My pussy is dripping at the thought of slipping you in my hot, wet mouth," she pants, taking a lick of the cherry-pink treat. "Please, Daddy, take out that big strong cock of yours for me. I want it so bad, Daddy. I need it in my mouth."

"Fuck, yeah, Kitten, you know what I like. Take it. Fuck, take it all." We listen to the sound of a belt followed by the sound of a zipper which I assume is him getting ready for Destiny-Kitten.

"Ready for me now, Daddy?" She shoots me a smile, taking another lick.

"More than ready, Kitten."

"Watch this," she whispers to me.

I'm pretty much sitting on the edge of my seat to see how she fakes a blow job over the phone.

"Put it in your mouth now, Kitten. Suck my cock. Better yet, let me hear you choke on it. Fuck, babe, let me hear you."

"Oh yes, Daddy. It's soooo big. I can barely fit my hand around it. Mmmm, you taste delicious," she whispers around the popsicle. "You like the feel of my tongue running along your thick, silky cock?"

"Hell, yes." He lets out a groan. Then, like a flash of lightening Destiny begins giving not only the sloppiest but also the loudest blowjob to the poor popsicle. Completely into her role, Destiny is not only slurping, she's gagging and sucking the fuck out of the thing, bringing "Daddy" to the brink in less than three minutes flat.

"Fuck, yeah, honey. God, take it, yes, take all my seed. Swallow all I give you. Fuck, good girl. That's my good fucking Kitten." With that, the caller clicks off without another word.

"And that's how you get your regulars," she says, waving the leftover stick in front of my face before tossing it into the trash.

"Holy shit. I can't do that!"

"Yes, you can. A few minutes, twenty bucks!" she replies. "Do the math, 69. It's worth it to play along."

Shrugging, I really can't argue with that logic. I mean if she just made twenty bucks in under five minutes, with a cut of half that's ten bucks for a few short minutes of mortification. *She's right, it might actually be worth it.*

"Dude, I legit thought it was your dad at first. I need to get my mind in the gutter," I giggle, shaking my head.

"You really do, Ellie. Watch some porn. Loosen up." She smiles and sticks out a fluorescent pink tongue, moving us back to green to signal again that we're ready. "Like I'd ever let my dad call me here!"

With that, we keel over laughing, and I spend the next hour listening to and watching Destiny—the Phone Sex Superhero—in action.

Chapter 15

Ellie

"HOW ARE YOU feeling about all this, Miss Chanel69?" Destiny asks. "What say you try a call? Our shift is almost done, you've heard me enough, I think. You ready to try it?"

Was I ready? I mean, sure I'd sat here for the last two hours of my three-hour shift listening to Destiny talk to an array of callers, but was I actually ready to try it myself?

"Trust me, its good to try it with me here, that way we can debrief about the call afterwards. Besides, it's kinda a must for me to sign off on you going solo." She shrugs her shoulders, knowing she's got me.

"All right, let's do it. Hook me up." I let out a deep breath.

The system beeps a few minutes later, and I catch my breath.

"See how the comment section is blank?" I look to the screen where Destiny's pointing. "Well, that means the caller hasn't supplied any info about what type of game he's going to want to play. It's a surprise, they can be the most fun sometimes, might even be a little freaky if you're lucky." She winks, and I roll my eyes.

"Yay, lucky me." I raise my arms in a sarcastic cheer. "Shit, okay. I can do this."

"Ready to show me what you got? Or you need a reminder about why you're here...money, Ellie. Money."

"You're right. I'm ready—as I'll *never* be." I give her my best fake smile.

"Oh hush, I'll be right here to coach you if it gets to be too much," she says, grabbing a pen and my Hello Kitty notepad. "I'll write some things here for you as I listen, if I think you're bombing."

"Thank you," I say, as she accepts the call, and the phone begins to ring. She motions for me to pick it up, and as I do, she clicks the speaker on allowing us both to hear.

"Breathless Whispers," I say. Destiny nods and waves her hand in a trail as if she wants me to continue, so I figure she must want me to add the tagline: "Let me leave you *breathless...*" So I say it into the line, which in turn elicits a smile and thumbs up from the happy girl beside me. I guess I was right: *yay, me!*

"I want to hear about your feet," a deep male voice rumbles, and immediately my hands begin to shake. *I'm so not ready.* "Tell me about your feet. I need to picture them in my mind. Are you wearing stockings? God, please tell me they're pretty, that you'd let me touch them. That you'll rub them on my hard cock..." he rushes out, followed by a loud moan.

"Ohhh..." is all that comes out of my suddenly sandpaper-filled mouth.

Well, that escalated quickly! I swear my heart rate rises to about a billion beats per second and I almost drop the phone. The feel of Destiny's hand on my arm reminds me I'm not alone, that I'm fine. I can do this. I look to Destiny who smiles, mouthing: "This is an easy one, just play along. You can do it."

So I begin. "I'd love to tell you about them, and if you're a good boy, I'd love to let you touch them," I say, then look to Destiny for a reaction.

"Perfect," she whispers, "keep going."

"Want me to describe my feet for you?" I ask, in what I hope is a low, sultry voice.

"Shit, yes. I have my cock out, it's so fucking hard, tell me all about them, get me there."

"Well, they're on the smaller side, and they're really smooth. I use lotion on them twice a day. I love rubbing it all over my toes—"

"Fuck. Tell me," he interrupts, "do you rub in between each toe? Oh fuck, do you? Oh shit, do you slip each of your fingers in between, sliding them up and down, feeling the toes hugging your fingers as they move? Oh Jesus, please say yes!" He's breathing heavily now. I look to Destiny to find her dancing around in a circle, fist pumping the air (clearly she thinks her young Jedi is holding her own).

And then it happens. I keep talking, thinking *piece of cake, I got this.* Smiling, I continue to talk feet to my caller, telling him a bit more about how they look. "They're painted a pretty pink colour. I just got a pedicure this morning," I say, which brings out a very strange "ooowwwnnnhhh" from the line. That's when I start to run out of ideas. I'm not sure how to bring a guy like this to the brink. I've said all I can think of, but I persevere. "I do have to get my toes waxe—"

I never finish the sentence. Destiny swats my arm.

I guess saying I get my toes waxed because they're hairy isn't the way to get the "happy ending" we're looking for here. Not that it's true, I just couldn't think of anything else to say.

Thankfully, Mr. Feet gives me an out. "Tell me how they smell, what I'll taste as I suck your, fat, luscious big toe."

I look to Destiny who gives me a "don't you dare" look. I assume she's warning me not to tell him my feet stink.

"Lavender. I wash my feet in warm lavender-scented water. It's divine, and the scent lasts all day. Have you ever smelled lavender? It's perfect for feet, makes them…almost likeable," I cluck out the ending. Another swat from Destiny.

"Oh shit, yes. That's good, so fucking good. I see them. They're perfect. So pretty, fuck, lavender-scented and pink. I'm gonna cum, gonna squirt my cum all over, ahhh, all over your pretty fucking pink toes," he screams, and the line goes dead.

I sit in silence, reflecting on what just happened, and Destiny giggles. "I can't believe you thought hairy toes was sexy talk. Never again, 69. Never again. Now be sure to write that shit down a hundred times in your notebook, and memorize it. *No hairy toes,*" she repeats, shaking her head, before I snort with laughter.

Holy cow, I did it by myself...well, almost.

Chapter 16

Ellie

"HEY, EARLY BIRD, whatcha working on back here, hiding in the corner? Making out with the worm?"

I hear Courtney's voice, and she slides into the booth across from me at the Froth House, a booth that I've been holding captive for at least the last two hours.

"Research," I say, looking at her over my laptop.

"I woke up at seven-thirty for water and found your note on the counter. Class doesn't start 'til eleven today. You know that, right? Which means it was a day to sleep in," she informs me.

"I'm well aware, but I couldn't sleep." I decide to go against the usual BFF Code of Sharing. Courtney doesn't need to hear that a certain black-haired professor with a sexy dimple was the star of my nighttime thoughts, and had me waking early to audition the finger puppets on the Stage of Clitoris. "I tossed and turned all night. Finally, at six-thirty, I decided 'piss it', got ready, and came here to do some research. Figured I'd probably get more work done here than at home, where the TV would convince me to spend time with him and Netflix. I can never say no to that man..." I sigh dramatically, blowing my hair out of my face.

"Wow, Els, you are a dork," Court laughs, shaking her head. "I know you've got a pretty big hard-on for Prof. Ryan, but I don't think you need an 'A' to get his attention, if ya know what I mean. Geez, I'd rather you tell me you couldn't sleep from all the hot sex dreams you were having. Talk about let down, that you're doing school work." She blows a raspberry. "So, truth. Any sexy dreams to share?" Court asks, raising her eyebrows up and down. She knows me too well. There's no way I can tell her she's not entirely wrong, but there's also no way in hell I'm going to admit to her that I just spent hours masturbating to images of Ace, or that I finished the next three assignments for our Sexual Aesthetics class, either. I might be trying to impress Ace, but there's no way Court will let up if she finds out how much of a keener I'm actually being this term.

"Shut up. I'm doing research for work. I have to keep looking up from my screen; I need to make sure the police aren't coming to arrest me. You should see some of the shit I've typed into the Google search bar. My mom would surely be proud," I beam.

"Ohhhh! *Fun* research I can condone. Here I thought you were going for class pet."

"Naw, I'm trying to go for top-rated Phone Sex Superhero. Regulars equal more money," I whisper, leaning in closer across the table.

"Gotcha. Okay, share. Tell me what exciting stuff you've learned, oh dulcet-voiced one. I bet in no time you'll be the Master Yoda of phone sex."

"Master of Phone Sex will I be, yesssss..."

"Not with *that* voice you won't." she laughs. "M'kay, tell me something fun?" Court asks, blowing across her mug.

"Okay. Did you know there are some really fucked-up people out there? I read about one girl who had a 'melon humper'. This guy would call and want her to talk him through how he should fuck a watermelon or a cantaloupe. I guess he would want her to talk him through scooping out the hole and everything."

"That's epic. God, I hope you get that guy." She claps her hands in delight.

"Don't wish that on me!"

"Whatever. It's not like he's asking you to fuck his dog."

"True, but still, it would be so hard not to laugh. And I read that laughing is the worst thing you can do, could even scar a caller, make them feel shamed. They suggest using a pillow to laugh in, if needed." I giggle at the thought.

"We need to get you a bigger box to hold all your props, I think, eh?"

I agree we just might.

"One of the strangest things I read was from a woman who worked a line in Las Vegas. Her name is Lilac. She suggests dressing the part, says to wear sexy lingerie and to let yourself get into it. She says she got off sexually more from being an operator than from her marriage. In the end, she admitted that she had to quit her job because she was starting to picture her callers rather than her hubby when making love. Imagine?"

"That's crazy. I'm sure that's an extreme case. I'm pretty sure we don't have to worry about you not dating because of your job." She gives me a dirty look.

"Shush. You know the last thing I have time for right now is dating. Besides, from the sounds of it, I'm going to be getting more action than you," I joke.

"Shit. Maybe I should apply. Then I can make money, get off, and have extra time to get school work done."

"Or you could actually spend time completing your schoolwork early instead of leaving it to the last minute. I bet that would free up time to date," I say.

"Nah, cramming is the way to go and boys are dumb. Maybe there's something to these phone sex lines. I should give one a try, there's gotta be a man line out there, right? I mean, equal rights and all."

"Oh Jesus. I'd pay to hear that call," I say, packing up my bag and slinging it over my shoulder, having realized we'd better get moving if we're going to be on time for class.

"Please let me be paired with Jax, please let me be paired with Jax..." Court repeats the little prayer over and over as we walk towards our thesis seminar.

Today, Professor Ryan is supposed to be matching us with the Teaching Assistant who will be helping to guide us as we work on our thesis papers. Courtney has made it more than clear who she wants. I, on the other hand, could care less who I'm paired with. Other than Professor Ryan being one of the best mentors to have, I've heard nothing but good things about Jax, Sam, and Joelle too, and that's the same impression I had after listening to them speak at our last meeting. In the end, I'm fine with whomever I get. At least that's what I keep trying to tell myself anyway. Deep down, a part of me hopes to be under Doctor Ryan's tutelage, and not only for educational purposes, either. It's getting harder to deny that I'm not completely attracted to the man, and Court never stops reminding me of that fact, either.

"Please, please, pleeeease. Let me be paired with Jax," Court chants again.

"Why Jax? What's wrong with the others?" I finally need to know.

"Els, have you seen the man? He is delish. And seeing as the professor is already taken, I might as well go for the next best thing. Jax is the second-in-command. And, boy, would I let him command me. Not that I like him or anything."

I both cringe and laugh at her comment. "Sure you don't," I say. "I was wondering why you wanted to sit up front. And here I was, thinking that it was just you trying to show off your big brain. You just wanted a better view of Jax, maybe get him to notice you. Um-hmm," I tease, nudging her.

"No. I sit us up close so that you can keep the apple of your eye front and centre. I know what a smitten kitten you are."

Kitten. "Daddy" and Kitten. Ugh. "Yeah, right," I say, suppressing a shiver. "You wish."

"Aahaha, *you* wish, Els. Just admit it. And admit you want to be in his teaching group, too." she smirks.

I know Court's paying extra attention to the way Professor Ryan and I eye each other. She's been relentless in her teasing about us getting ready to have some kind of torrid love affair. She does all she can to make sure he and I notice each other. Thanks to her, we have permanent seats right in front on Monday mornings. It seems my little sweetie of a bestie is willing to get up extra early to make sure my hot seat is always saved for me. For the past three Mondays, I've woken up to a note telling me that she'll meet me in class. *Isn't she so helpful?*

"Don't start. You know it's not true. He's my teacher. I bet he puts me with Joelle, or maybe even Jax. Stop seeing shit that's not there." I nudge her arm again, only harder. This has been my angle for weeks now. It's all in her head, nothing to see here, move along.

"Oh, it's there. You're just being obtuse," Courtney smirks back.

"I'm not going to sit with you if you keep being a jackass," I huff, picking up my pace towards the seminar room.

"All right, all right. I'll stop. But let's test my theory."

"I bet I don't even want to hear this, do I?"

"Let's say we see if I'm right? That he totally is hot for student? And if I am, I get free rein to tease, bug, attempt to set up, and insinuate that you and that sexy mother of a professor will have a sordid love affair."

"Like losing would stop you." I roll my eyes. "So, what's this test of yours? How on earth are you going to prove this theory?" I ask, becoming annoyed.

For the last three weeks, Courtney's been on me that I should approach Ace and ask him out. She says he totally keeps spying on me.

This I know is true, because he and I have this little staring game going on between us, as if we're both waiting for the other to make the first move. But we both know we can't, either, despite any attraction that might be there. I don't want the man to be fired, after all. And I also don't want to be known as that girl who fucks her way to an easy "A".

"I betcha a bazillion dollars you're in the intriguing man-of-the-hour himself's group. I bet he calls your name third, so as not to draw attention to it, but if we listen closely enough, we'll hear his voice change when he calls out: 'Ellie Hughes'," she mocks, leading us into the already full room.

"You're delusional," I whispercall, moving behind her to our seat, "you need to write and shoot a crazy romance movie to get your inner fantasies out."

"Okay, but only if you and your man are the stars, otherwise I'm out."

"Better yet, let's get you hooked up with your own man so you can leave me alone. I'm going to go find Jax." I turn to walk to the front.

"Don't you dare, Ellie," she snaps.

"Ohhh, what? Can't take the heat? Aww, are you hot for TA?" I start humming the famous porno soundtrack: "*Bow-chicka-wow-wow!*"

"I mean it, Ellie," she says, looking around the room frantically.

"What, you worried he'll find out you wanna 'boink' him?" I laugh out loud, finally taking my seat.

"Point, Hughes," she scowls, slapping my arm, and I smile victoriously.

Chapter 17

Ace

WATCHING ELLIE AND Courtney walk in, I know right away that I should have thought with my brain not my cock.

But, opening my laptop, I still click 'send' on the mass email I'm distributing to each student, including a schedule with times and locations for the preliminary thesis meetings—among other housekeeping items—now that the thesis writing will be in full swing. Beginning next week, my team and I will meet with our student groups and hatch out a plan for the year. I might have switched Ellie around a few times, but in the end I left her in the best hands. *My hands.*

Having recently graded their latest online assignments—the one where I ask the students to tell me about their favourite directors and justify their choices—I knew my decision about Ellie was the right one. As soon as I spotted that she was a Kubrick fan, as well as a Tarantino fan, I knew I needed to work with her. I'm eager to see where her thesis will take her. In the past, I've used this paper to help match the students with the TAs whose tastes in filmmakers are most compatible. I ask my TAs to write the same paper, then divide the students based on the likenesses.

Say, for example, Jax. He's my Francis Ford Coppola guy, so based on student responses, I pair the other F. F. Coppola, Martin Scorsese, Spike Lee and, of course, Sofia Coppola fans with Jax. As for Joelle, she's my Ang Lee buff, so those listing Akira Kurosawa, The

Wachowskis and Zhang Yimou are overseen by her. Sam, he's my wild card, he loves every genre and lists Kathryn Bigelow as his all time fave. I've decided to pair the more eclectic film fans with him, so he'll oversee those listing Noah Baumbach, Mira Nair, and M. Knight Shyamalan. As for me, my all time favourite director is impossible to name (like flavours of ice cream, it's hard to pick just one…), therefore I love working with fans of Hitchcock, Tarantino, Kubrick, Ritchie, Wes Anderson, and other outside-the-box thinkers. I've found my system to be successful, even if it serves as little more than an icebreaker in initial meetings. Having something in common with the person who's to guide you while you write one of the hardest assignments of your life is a good feeling. I've never had a TA/student pairing that didn't work out, so until I do, I'll keep using this method.

Taking my spot in the room's centre, I begin. "Today's class will be our last as a large group until the end of the term. I'll send an email later with our final meeting time. From this point on, you'll be meeting solely with myself, Jax, Sam or Joelle—my outstanding team of TAs—and the other students in your assigned group. I've emailed the schedule for your first meeting time and place and will continue to send info weekly; therefore, it's imperative that you check your inbox often. All meetings will take place on the specified date without exception, please be sure to take note of yours."

Rhyming off the groupings, I avoid looking in Ellie's direction, hoping to God that my naming her third when calling my group out didn't make my intentional placement obvious. After a few beats, feeling it's safe to see if she's looking at me, I chance a look in her direction. My cock instantly nudges against my zipper, when I see Ellie's breathtaking smile. Seeing who she's laughing with, however, makes me see all kinds of red.

Fucking Sam. He's leaning down in front of her table, talking a little too closely for my liking, looking too intently for what's appropriate. But it's him making her laugh that's pissing me off most. The urge to stomp my feet and yell "she's mine!" like a child not getting his way begins to take root in my mind. I hate the way she's giving away her smiles so easily to him; he's probably thinking he stands a chance. Too bad, buddy, she's already on my radar. *I'll* be the one to claim everything she has to give. Smiles, laughs, moans, orgasms. Yeah, the goal is to collect them all.

Mine.

All mine.

Jesus, I need to get a fucking grip, this chick is making me mental. I have to stop thinking this shit. She's a student. My student.

And she's Sam's student, essentially, too. So neither *of us can have her.*

I nod, forcing myself to agree.

Chapter 18

Ellie

WALKING OUT OF the women's change room at the sports medicine gym, I decide that I better start coming more regularly since I was given a free pass. Plus my appointment to try and convince everyone I can still run is coming up in a few weeks. Truth is, between school, work—and the few weeks I wasted trying to find work—my misery over not getting to compete on the Varsity Blues has been the farthest thing from my mind. I'm adjusting my ear buds when I almost walk right into Dr. Robinson.

"Oh jeez, sorry." We both laugh as I right myself. "I wasn't paying attention to where I was going." I raise the iPod clutched in my hand.

"No problem, I saw you. Those things are dangerous. I keep telling my daughter to keep her head up when walking. Maybe you need to follow my advice too," he says.

"Clearly. They need a crash warning, for sure. Maybe airbags."

"They sure do. Anyway, how's the knee doing, Ellie?" Dr. Robinson asks, smiling kindly.

"It's okay. I've been super busy but I've got things sorted, and I'll be here at least four times a week going forward."

"Good, it's all about strength training, keeping the knee joints active. It might not get you back on the track, but it may prolong the need for replacement. Make a few appointments with Doctor Reynolds if you want, tell him I sent you. Anyway, I'll let you get to your workout, no need for you to listen to another one of this old man's lectures. It's good to see you, dear," he says, patting my arm before walking into the change room.

"See ya," I reply, then walk onto the small gym floor, head down, rifling through my iPod to look for a movie I can listen to while I warm up on the treadmill. I know it's weird, but while walking I like to listen to movie dialogue. I only like music when running and working through the circuit. Courtney tells me I'm crazy, I insist it's just a fun visualization game I like to play. I try to see if I can picture the scenes without looking down at the screen. *Hey, whatever, it passes the time.*

Moving through the tiny space, I nod at a few people I've seen from other Varsity Blues teams while making my way to a row of four treadmills. Stepping up, I choose a five kilometre loop, enter my weight, and settle my iPod on the equipment's docking space. I'm about to tap "play" on the screen when a familiar scent kisses my nose. I shake it off as being my imagination, and continue looking for a good film. Scrolling through the list, I hem and haw until I hear it.

It's him.

Professor Ryan. And for fork's sake, he's on the treadmill right beside me. *How the hell didn't I see him?* He's all tight-blue shirt stretching across his solid chest like Superman, five o'clock shadow making him look ruggedly handsome as he jogs, his legs moving in wide strides. The man is like chocolate—sweet and smooth-looking and I want him to go straight to my hips… *Yep, Ace Ryan is chocolate.*

I see his green eyes zero in on me and then dip to my iPod. He's not wearing his glasses, and holy hell do I want those intense eyes to come back and try to focus on me.

"Choose that one," he says. "It's such a great movie. I love Tarantino." He grins slightly, then a devilish smile forms on his handsome face when he glances back up my way. The term "Jell-O legs" is no longer lost on me. Gripping the sidebars of the treadmill, I steady myself.

"Me too. I love him. He really is kick-ass, eh?"

He laughs, "Yes, very 'kick-ass', Ellie."

My name on his lips is also very kick-ass. *Is there a special catch phase for the feeling I'm getting in my girlie bits?*

"I can't believe he remembers my name," I say.

Chuckling, he responds, "Of course I do. I remember a lot about you."

"Oops, I said that out loud…" I groan.

"And that, too, was out loud." He laughs harder.

"I'm sorry. You make me nervous, Doctor Ryan," I cover my mouth with my hand, "and honest, apparently." I smile under my palm, beet red I'm sure.

"It's okay to call me Ace outside of class. Don't be nervous. You're too intelligent not to speak up, and there's no way you can clam up on me now, we need to talk more Tarantino. I have so many questions."

"All right. What do you want to know?"

"A lot, actually." He looks at me, his eyes locking on mine for a second. Then he shakes his head as if talking himself out of something, but with every second I spend near him, I want him to talk himself back into whatever he was thinking "no" to. "First up, tell me: what's your favourite Tarantino scene? Not film. *Scene,*" he asks, sounding pleased with his precise question.

Moving the incline up to six, I contemplate my response as my knee registers a complaint at the increase in grade. "That's a great question. Let me think."

"Right. I should write trivia questions in my spare time. Wait for the ones I have in store," he jokes, and I realize how much fun I'm having working out right now. Or maybe it's Ace I'm having fun with.

I pause for a few beats, running through my favourite scenes. "Got it. 'The Pub' scene in *Inglourious Basterds.* It's kick-ass. He gives us so much with that scene: characters, intensity, conflict, and…*bam!* You're completely sucked in."

"Nice one. I concur, very kick-ass for any fan." He grins and it's beautiful, like seeing the coveted rainbow after the rain, the one you knew would be worth the wait.

I decide to remove my ear buds, hopefully signalling that I want to keep talking, and tell him: "Your turn," wiping my forehead with my towel. The last thing I want is to be a sweaty mess in Ace's presence.

"Now, the right answer, of course, is 'Jack Rabbit Slims' *in Pulp Fiction*, but the honest answer is 'The Bride vs. The Crazy 88' *in Kill Bill, Vol. 1.* That scene is bloody fantastic. 'Kick-ass', even," Ace announces, excitement lacing his tone, and it's contagious.

"Oh my God, yes! That's such an incredible scene. Nice one. It's such a kick-ass female moment in an action movie, pure genius. And are you making fun of my 'kick-asses'?" I tilt my head, taking him in.

"Maybe a little. I like teasing you. You've got a cute blush," he shrugs, like he hasn't just rocked my world. "Seriously, though, the way Beatrix Kiddo spins on the floor wielding that samurai sword like a total badass…it's epic. Honestly, one of the best kick-ass scenes ever."

"So, you thought it was pretty good, then, I guess?" I tease.

"Hey, hey, guys can fanman as much as you ladies get to fangirl. I'm a complete movie buff so, yeah, I get carried away sometimes," Ace says, wiping his face. *A job I'd gladly volunteer to do with my shirt.*

"I love your excitement, no judgment here." I wave my hand. "You get on with your bad self, your secret is safe with me."

"All right, E, what gets *you* passionate, excited?" he asks, and all I can think is *you, and you calling me 'E'.* It's personal, intimate. I want to hear it all the time. If I get to spend even another bit of time with you like this, it's sure to be always be *you*.

"Ellie? You okay?" Ace asks, eyeing my knee brace. "You need to slow down?"

"No, sorry, I was thinking about your question. I zoned out, I guess. Okay, I'd say *The Color Purple*, and movies like *The Notebook, The Godfather.*"

"Adaptations from novels are your thing, eh? I remember from class. But *The Notebook?* That one surprises me, if I can be honest."

"Yeah. I love them. The good ones—the ones where you sit holding your breath because they've managed to capture all the beauty of what the author intended you to see and feel. Gah, sorry, see *my* fangirling? And for the record, Mr. Cool, *The Notebook* was very well done, have to give credit where credit is due, right? Everyone needs some mushy stuff now and then, and that, Professor, is pure mushy goodness."

"I'll take your word for it, but perhaps we can agree to disagree on that one," he says laughing. "Will your thesis be about film adaptations?"

"I can't tell you. I have a week, still, before I have to reveal all," I tease. Not because I'm not ready, because of course I am. But talking about school makes me realize how I'm enjoying being with my professor like this far too much, when the reality is, I shouldn't be.

"My apologies," he says. "You're right. We're both off the clock and I'm ruining our fun."

"And I'm having a kick-ass time, Ace." I give him a cheeky grin.

We both laugh and continue to work out on the treadmills for what feels like hours. I smile inwardly, liking how it feels working out beside him, with his scent, his smile, the easiness of it. By the time we decide to stop working out, we realize we'd been talking on the treadmills for well over an hour, neither of us making it to any other piece of equipment.

My knee even cooperated for the most part, but it will need a good icing.

I fangirled pretty hard over our time spent together that night at home, lying in bed. And I might have fangirled pretty hard over Ace Ryan himself too.

My professor.

Chapter 19

Ellie

"HEY, GRETA," I say, as I walk into Breathless Whispers for my first solo shift. I'm nervous as hell, but seeing her warm, welcoming face settles me a bit.

"Evening, dear. You all set for your shift? Nervous?"

Huffing out a breath, I tell her I'm as set as I can be. "I'm super nervous, I'm not going to lie. I worry that I'm going to be a big flop. I hope I can pull off the sexy talk."

Waving her hand, she dismisses my stress. "Ah, don't worry, Ellie. Everyone is nervous their first time. Erica was a bloody wreck, believe me. She came bawling her eyes out to me after her first call, claiming she couldn't do it." For some reason, hearing that settles me. I mean, Erica is a legend around here from what I've gathered. Greta continues: "By the end of your shift, you'll be a bit schooled, I'm sure, but you'll also be ready to do it again. It really is one of the safest and quickest ways to make good money and fast when you think about it, especially here at Breathless. I'll be here until eleven tonight if you need anything. It's month end, so I'm pulling a bit of overtime."

"That's perfect. I might need a good cry, too," I laugh. "How many others are here tonight?"

"Let me check," she says, rifling through some papers. "Looks like five of you are working the seven-to-eleven. I bet if you go to the kitchen, you'll find them. They always chat a bit before they start, a little gossip and story swappin'."

"Okay, great. Maybe I'll go take a peek and introduce myself. Thanks, Greta."

"Wait. Before you go, I meant to give you this the other day. It's your discount code. The Conrads allow the girls to assign up to three regulars as their VIP's if you want. When you see in the system it's them calling, once you accept the call, type in this six-digit code in the comments section and I'll apply the discount. It's a little thing we do to keep the usual suspects wanting to call us and not the competitors."

"Wow, that's pretty decent. Who would have thought couponing would transcend into the sex-line industry?" I laugh, but Greta looks like she isn't so sure I'm funny.

"Okay dear. You have a great shift," she says, handing me a file with my discount code, a list of a few do's and don't's, and a cheat sheet to help remind me how to work the computer and phone.

Taking the file, I wave goodbye and mouth "wish me luck" as she answers her phone.

Deciding to forego introductions tonight, I head down the hall past the noisy kitchen to find Sweet 22, my assigned room tonight. The butterflies that have been dancing around my stomach all evening before coming here begin to take flight, causing my anxiety level to rise along with them.

"You can do this, Ellie. It's no big deal. It's easy money. A few hours. It's a little sexual simulation. You're the director and star. Tonight's your debut." I mutter this little mantra as I move down the corridor. Noticing how quiet it is helps to settle my nerves a titch. Thank goodness all the rooms are soundproof and private. There's no way I could do this if people in the office could hear me. It will take me some time to find my groove, but as with everything else in my life, I know once I set my mind to it, I'm a natural overachiever. *Can you overachieve at getting someone's rocks off over the phone?*

Opening the white steel door, I move inside, taking the occupied sign off the inside of the door and placing it onto the outside handle before clicking the deadbolt into place behind me. Destiny had said it's important to lock the door, in case you end up getting off with a caller and also for security reasons. Even though I have no intention of that happening, I lock the door regardless. I don't want to worry about anyone coming in and hearing me make a fool of myself.

Despite my denial that I will get myself off during a call, Destiny says what happens between you and your caller is no-one's business and to never feel shame for getting turned on here, that it's part and parcel of the gig. She also explained that the only time management would need to be involved is if a caller crossed the line, if they became threatening to me or disclosed something that was deemed to be of a concerning nature. If that happens, I'm to follow the security protocol in the manual. The protocol basically says to hang up, add notes in the comments section, flag the call in the system and leave it for Mrs. Conrad, as she's the one who deals with those issues. If there's a concern, she'll alert the police and contact me if she needs more information.

Sliding my finger across the trackpad, I quickly bring the computer to life. Typing in my ID number and password, I change my colour from red to green. Then, taking a deep breath, I empty my Phone Sex Superhero kit onto the desk. I laugh, looking over everything as I line it up along the desk. Courtney and I had way too much fun creating this little montage of sex-simulating paraphernalia. I don't think I'll ever look at elastics or my leather belt the same way again.

I'm about to open my laptop and pull up my thesis notes, when there's a beep signalling that it's show time. Reading the description, the caller claims it's a fetish call. *Of course it is.*

Taking a deep breath, I steel my nerves before answering the call using the best breathless voice I have.

"Good evening, Breathless Whispers."

"What colour are your panties?" the caller asks right away, catching me off guard. *Doesn't anyone introduce themselves around here?*

"Um...sorry?"

"I said, what colour are your panties." The panting voice in the line repeats, and I feel my cheeks heat immediately. *Oh God, here we go.*

"Black. They're black," I repeat.

And with that simple divulgence, I'm met with a long "ohhhh" sound, coupled with a guttural: "That's my favourite colour. So fucking perfect. Black is sexy, black makes my cock so fucking hard. I love it when my slut is wearing...*black*." He clucks out "black", while I blanch at his use of the word "slut".

Shaking it off, I try to move on as best I can. I play along, hoping the call ends sooner rather than later. "Oh yeah? That's funny, 'cause it's mine too. I feel so sexy and dirty wearing black. Naughty, even." I roll my eyes at myself.

"Tell me how they feel. Take your hand and run it over the material. Fuck."

I hear him take a deep breath, and some rustling noises.

"They feel soft," I say, the words somehow flowing off my tongue like this is my usual form of dialogue, "like silk. The smoothness tickles my fingers, the silkiness allowing my hand to slide across the material so easily it's hard not to make myself wet."

"Yeah? Are you wet for me, slut? Are those sexy panties exciting you like they are me?"

"Yes, so much. I can't stop my hand from rubbing over my pussy. The combination of silk and slick is gonna make me come so hard. You gonna come with me too?"

"Yeah, doll, stroke those panties. Feel me rubbing your panties over your clit. Fuck it, take them off. I need you to wrap them around my cock. I need you to finish me off. Tell me what you'll do to me."

Fuck. With that I freeze. I blank. I have no idea what to say. It was sort of easy to talk about getting myself off, I could see it. But the vision of me using my underwear on a guy's dick is leaving me speechless.

"I, I, ahem, er…"

"*Well?*" I hear an unhappy voice coming through the line. "I'm paying a fuck of a lot to get off here. I'm waiting. Slip those panties onto my cock, tell me what you see, how you'll finish."

"I'm sorry. I can't think. I guess I'd slide them along your penis."

"My 'penis'? For fuck sakes…now I've lost my motherfucking hard-on. I thought this line was the best of the best?"

"I'm sorry. I froze. It's my first shift," I say, maybe looking for some sympathy? Some understanding?

"Well, you need to practice, sweetheart. You obviously only ever get yourself off. I suggest you ignore my calls in the future. Fucking lame ass bullshit…" With that, he hangs up, and tears immediately sting my eyes. But I will not cry over that asshole. No way. *"Slut". Who* says *that?*

Shit. Am I going to get in trouble for that?

A bit shaken, I move the cursor, changing my colour to yellow. Reaching for my phone, I decide to text Destiny about what happened, asking if being on my first-time solo do they watch or listen to see that I'm actually ready to be on my own? Which, if you were to ask me right now, is a big farkin' "no".

Thankfully, her reply is immediate.

Destiny: *relax no spying. Just in the system when you reject and call times. They might ask why a call is short but no ones listening in. Or video either. It's your show. Relax you got this. Fuck him he was an asshole you're fine Ellie.*

Me: *thank goodness. Okay. A bad call isn't the end of the world. I might need to practice some calls, maybe come sit with you again?*

Destiny: *Yes, anytime come do a shift with me. I got your back. Girl you'll have like ten fuck ups. It's normal. Quit being hard on yourself. You can do this. Think of the $$$*

Me: *thanks.*

I toss my cell back in my bag after turning my status back to green in the system. I'm about to go sit on the chaise and do some deep breathing when the telltale beep signalling a call comes. Slipping on the headset, I adjust it and turn the computer screen so it faces me, click accept, and sit back on the chaise.

"Breathless Whispers. Let me leave you breathless." I decide to add the little tag line.

"Hi," a low voice greets me.

"Hello," I greet back as low, not sure how it really sounds, seeing as I opted to use the voice adapter again tonight.

"I was on Facebook," he says. "I saw your profile picture. So pretty."

I tense at his words. Worrying he knows who I am, my heart pounds. Then it clicks, realizing that's pretty much impossible. Shaking it off, I take a deep breath and play along, realizing this is his angle. He's a creeper caller. Looking at the clock, I decide to try for a ten minute call.

"Oh, you did?"

"Yeah. You're sexy, covered in sand, lying on the beach like that in your cover photo."

"Thank you. I…I love the beach, especially the feeling of sand covering my body. The grittiness of it feels so good. Do you like that feeling? The sensation of having things covering your body?" I ask, pausing.

"I'm going to Aruba," he states, ignoring my questions.

"Ohhhh!" I squeal. "I love Aruba."

"Good. I want to take you with me."

"You do? Oh good. I'd love to go," I reply, not really sure where this call is going. Maybe it's simply a companion call. One where the caller needs someone to talk to.

"Do you wanna come with me, angel?"

"Yes, I'd love to. When would we go?" I enquire.

"Well, you can't come unless you tell me all the clothes you'd pack."

Ding ding ding and cue the freak talk.

"Well, seeing as it's the beach. I'd pack nothing. How's that sound?" I ask, thinking I've nailed it.

"No," he yells. "What will you wear to the beach? Give me details."

"I'll wear my skin. I'll let the sun kiss me while we swim and play," I try again, thinking he wanted more details.

"Fuck. You're not listening. Fine. What about on the plane? What will you wear?

Tucking my hair behind my ears, I think for a minute. "Er, probably jeans and a shirt. Maybe yoga pants?"

"No. That's not acceptable."

"Okay. Well, how about I let you dress me? You pick what I should wear."

"That's perfect. Because I'm actually standing inside the Stag Shop sex store, in the ladies section, and I've got the perfect outfit for you. I love sheer. It all needs to be sheer. I want to see your body through pantyhose. I wanna be able to rip a hole at your pussy entrance and finger fuck you. Whenever I want. I want to feel the sheerness of the material, hear it rip as I take you. Oh God, I'm gonna come thinking about tearing a hole in the material. All you need to wear are panty hose. Fuck, yes. The sound of the tearing, Christ, I love that sound," he pants and I hear a car door slam. "So good. So…fucking…good," I hear him say softly, before the call ends.

"Holy shit," I mutter, taking off my headset. Glancing at the clock, I see that call lasted seven minutes. *Hmm. Not bad.*

Resting my head on the desk, I don't know if I should laugh or cry.

Am I doing okay tonight?

Do I have what it takes to get my superhero cape?

Do I want to come back?

Chapter 20

Ace

ELLIE'S LATE.

I'm sitting behind my desk in my stuffy office, the same office that happens to have a great view, mind you, and I'm agitated. The constant *tap tap tapping* of my pen only annoys me more, but I'm pissed. *Right fucking pissy.* She better have some Oscar-worthy performance once she gets here to go along with her excuse.

It's after six-thirty; the cinema department where my office is located is quiet. Everyone's gone home except me. Again, Ellie is proving that she affects me, hence the bane of my pissed offness. Never have I ever extended my office hours for anyone. I need to get my dick in check here, it's not my liege.

This girl is changing me, and she doesn't fucking know it. And I most certainly do not like it. I need to prioritize, remember my rules where student-teacher relations are concerned. The other day in the gym was the catalyst. I had fun with her, liked hearing her views on topics we discussed, fell a bit hard for her infectious smile and her personality, one I want to get to see all facets of.

In our introduction session, I was clear with my expectations, reiterating that all preliminary meetings were mandatory. That the times were to be respected and upheld, and here I am, breaking my own fucking rules. I knew I shouldn't have let my guard down with her like I did. It's Thursday, my office hours ended at six, and here I sit, pretty much on pins and needles, waiting for the stunning distraction herself to come waltzing in.

The ballsy little thing emailed me last night despite my warning, asking if I could make an exception and change her meeting time. Ellie said that she had something work-related come up. That she couldn't risk losing the job, that she felt she was in a hard spot (*I have a hard spot I'd like to put her on).* She added that she hated to ask, but felt she had no other option. Ellie explained briefly that she'd just started this job, and that she needed the money after losing her sports scholarship due to an injury. Ellie shared how she was embarrassed to ask, apologized profusely, and in the end managed to come up with what I felt was a valid excuse. I can appreciate the struggle to pay your own way, I can relate to the life of the working class, so, of course, I agreed. After creeping her on the university's Varsity Blues website, I know now why she has the athletic department's gym privileges too. I had been planning on asking Mercer, but now I knew why. I replied, agreeing to reschedule, as long as she realized this was the only time I'd be accommodating.

So here I sit.

Waiting.

I hate fucking waiting.

I don't wait for anyone.

Groaning, I take my wallet from my desk drawer, deciding to go grab a cup of coffee before settling in on marking the first assignments from my Sexual Aesthetics class. Might as well stay now and be productive until I meet Mercer and Dylan at the pub in a couple of hours.

Opening my office door, I'm met with a mass of deep-hued auburn hair as it falls into my chest. The scent is an instant dick whisperer—this whole girl is a goddamn dick whisperer—and if I'm not careful, I'm going to be begging her to show me her mad skills up close. I jump back.

"Christ, you smell good," I whisper before I can stop myself, closing my eyes and praying she suddenly has issues with hearing loss.

"Sorry, I know I'm late," she rambles against my chest, before pausing. "Wait. What did you say?" A beautifully confused Ellie Hughes cocks her head, waiting for me to repeat myself.

Fuck that.

"You're late. I'm pissed. I'm going to grab a coffee. Go sit down. I'll be back in five. Be ready to impress me with your thesis topic and research, Ms. Hughes." I don't bother using her first name; she needs to realize I'm not here to be her buddy.

"Okay, yes, sir. I'm sorry. I missed my bus." She shuffles side-to-side on her feet.

"I'm not happy, Ellie," I bite out, before adding for effect, "at all."

With that, I move past her, hopefully leaving her to see that I'm in control here.

Even if I know I'm not.

Chapter 21

Ellie

SHIT. SHIT. I can't believe I missed the bus.

Why didn't I email him? Oh right, because the universe hates me. Nothing like a dead cell phone to piggyback on top of missing the bus, on the day of the most important meeting of the school year. He probably thinks that I think I can take advantage of him now, after we spent some time talking the other night at the gym. This meeting is too important for me to blow, I need to think of a way to turn this around.

Mandatory.

No excuses.

No exceptions.

Except he made an exception for me.

And now I'm late.

"Fuck my life," I mutter to myself as I make a beeline along the corridor of the cinema department searching for Professor Ryan's office. I'm just about to knock, when the door falls away, and my face is introduced to a brick wall—or is it a sexy mother of a chest? That smell, his smell, the earthy vetiver, infiltrates my senses immediately, telling me I'm in exactly the place I want to be.

His office, of course. Found it!

I hear him say something but like a stupid fangirl, my brain goes on lockdown as the eleven-year-old boyband fan in me loses her mind at the thought that he might have just paid me a compliment.

Reluctantly, I pull away, straightening myself with a bit of his help. *God, I want those arms around me.* His green eyes are intense behind his glasses, almost boring into me, his annoyance evident tenfold. His eyes are vibrant, matching the intensity of fresh cut grass in the summer. I could get lost in them, loving the thought of never being found.

"Sorry, I know I'm late. I missed my bus," I start, a bit confused, wondering if I heard him properly. *Did he say I smelled good?*

I try to ask him to repeat himself only to have him dismiss me. "You're late. I'm pissed. I'm going to grab a coffee. Go sit down. I'll be back in five. Be ready to impress me with your thesis topic and research, Ms. Hughes." His rigidness leaves no room for argument. Hearing him telling me to get ready sends a pulse right between my legs, leaving me in no doubt that I'm absolutely already ready.

Stupid mandatory staff meetings. Destiny neglected to tell me that every third Thursday of the month is staff meeting day from four- to six p.m. Her late night text sent me into panic mode. I texted, telling her I couldn't go, gave her shit for dropping the ball and not telling me. She apologized again before calling me to explain that by mandatory it means no show equals no job. With that tidbit of info, I decided to take a chance and email Professor Ryan. There was no way I could risk losing my job, not that I could risk losing a grade either, but I figured it was worth a try. To my surprise, he agreed. A part of me wondered if it was because he had as soft a spot for me as I did for him. I know it's silly, but the way we look at each other, I swear we're heading down a path where our eventual collision will be explosive.

So here I am now, late for my already rescheduled appointment, flailing with how to start an apology after he'd granted me a favour, one I know he didn't grant lightly. And all I can seem to think of is how much my face is missing being buried in this beautifully brilliant man's chest. After a beat, his words finally register with my lagging fangirl brain. I nod and apologize again before he bristles past me, muttering under his breath.

"Again, really sorry I'm late," I whisper as he closes the door behind him.

Moving into his space, I breathe in his familiar scent. I wonder if he realizes just how good he smells or how it affects other people? I would gladly suffer smelling that scent for the rest of my life. Taking in the smallish space, I note the dark-stained desk positioned in front of a pretty big window, a comfy-looking leather chair tucked against it. I also spy a small stack of unpacked boxes, and movie posters of all genres hang on the walls, giving it a relaxed feel. I smile when my eyes land on posters for *Star Wars* and *Casablanca,* and I wonder if Ace likes all the classics I do. I wonder what else we might have in common, and admit that I'd be more than willing to find out. I see a few Tarantino ones and smile, thinking back on our game at the gym.

The more I take in his space, the more my imagination begins to conjure up little fantasies. The fact that I'm alone in his office after hours isn't lost on my imagination or my ladybits for that matter. I'm starting to think my short time at Breathless Whispers is affecting not only the vividness of my imagination but also my needs as a woman. *Maybe I'm not so prudish after all?*

Moving towards the window, I run my fingers along his desk. It's sturdy. Immediately a scene of Ace going down on me while I lay splayed out on top of the dark piece of furniture plays in my mind. Biting my lip, I wave off the thought. There's no way that would ever happen. It cannot happen. Besides, it's such a stereotype: the professor and his student…

"Knock it off, Els. He's your teacher," I chide myself, heading to stand in front of the window. The sun has set, and the skyline has that familiar hue it gets during the transition between early-October evening and night. It's that perfect mix that accompanies the fall weather; a subtle line of pink sky getting lost among the blues and greys of the season. I wish my phone wasn't dead so I could take a photo of it.

The streetlights flicker on, illuminating the small pathways scattered around the campus and highlighting the small nature reserve that we're lucky to have at U of T. A reserve that Ace has a permanent view of when standing in his office like I am now; how he lucked out as a brand new prof is beyond me. I imagine in the daylight he can easily see the lush gardens and the small pond, which are home to some ducks and geese, among other smaller animals. I stare off into the distance, trying to see if I can spot any of them still out. I lean closer against the glass, resting my hand to brace myself, trying to get the best-angled view.

That's when I see his return reflected in the window. He really is a fine specimen of beauty, brains, and brawn, it occurs to me, watching him walking towards where I'm standing. Hitching a breath, I steel my nerves, preparing for him to be angry that I didn't listen, that rather than have my things prepared like he'd asked me, I'm busy gawking out the window like some disobedient troublemaker, like the one he saw back on the first day of class. Swallowing my defence, I watch as he stops directly behind me.

He's silent. Brooding. Is he waiting? Watching? Waiting for me to speak? Whatever he's doing behind me excites me, and my stomach dips at the notion that maybe he's affected by me too. I watch his eyes catch mine in the reflection in the window before he bends his face towards the crook of my neck. He's close to touching me, but not touching me. *Close, but not close enough.*

"It's a stunning view you have, Ace. Sorry, I mean Doctor Ryan," I correct, casting my eyes downward, no longer sure he'd like me to refer to him by his first name.

Feeling the loss of his presence, I look up to see that he's standing tall again. Thankfully, he's still close enough that I can feel his heat, his response to my comment whispered in close proximity to my back. "Yes. It is a stunning view, I couldn't agree more. I think I've lucked out this semester, honestly."

Clearing my throat, I turn around to face him, the move causing him to step back a few inches, making me question if I imagined the whole thing. I digest his words and wonder if he means he's lucked out with the view outside or with me as a student?

Either way, I'm sure of one thing. I'm ready to explore this pull between us. I'd gladly hop on the Ellie-Ace ride to see where it might go. For some reason, the feeling I have is that it might just be the best ride of my life. I don't know this man, but from what I do know and from our brief time together, the words *more, more, more* loop on repeat in my mind.

"Ace." It's barely audible.

Shaking his head, he places one hand on the side of my face, running his thumb along my cheek, and I feel the shift. I know we can't, he knows we can't. "I think we better make it another night, E," he says, setting his coffee on his desk. "It's probably best if you go now. I'll email you a better time."

We're silent for a moment. Ace watches intently while I stand before him, silently relishing all the thoughts of what I just lost. Leaning into his touch, I close my eyes, soaking in the fleeting moment. I'm sad, but I understand. Ace Ryan is my teacher; we cannot do this.

"Sounds like a good idea, Professor." Never ever have I felt the loss of something that I never had to begin with like I feel the loss of Ace Ryan at this moment.

"I'll look forward to your email, sir. Again, I'm sorry," I say, as I move further away and out the door.

Chapter 22

Ace

"HEY, BOYS. LONG time no see. What can I get you to drink?" Liz, our petite waitress, asks Mercer and I as we settle into our usual booth at Riffs Tap House, along with Dylan and his moustache.

After Ellie left, I was more pissed off than before. I'm furious with myself, I fucked up tonight. I let her see that she's having an impact on me, which it turns out is reciprocated, which, hey, makes me one happy son of a bitch. But the reality is, we can't do anything about it. At least, not now. I hated having to brush her off, especially when I know she's that perfect trifecta of brains, beauty and wit. Images of Ellie staring up at me, trying to make out my cryptic words, are doing my head in. Doing that to her was tough, she doesn't deserve mind games, but I needed to reset some boundaries no matter how much it hurt.

Watching her beautiful face fill with hurt and confusion when I flipped the script on her, going from hot to cold, was a hard pill to swallow. I felt like a dick, leaving her embarrassed, seeing her blanch when my demeanour changed abruptly, telling her we needed to reschedule instead of touching her like we both desperately wanted. And what the fuck was I thinking, calling her 'E' again? That's not my place. I can't give her a nickname. I'm her teacher, not her lover or friend, regardless of how friendly we were at the gym or the other times we've bumped into each other. I shouldn't have done any of it. I'm an idiot for putting us in this position. I should have assigned her to Jax, Sam, or Joelle in the first place. I'm such an asshole. *Shit. How are we going to get through the semester?*

"Pitcher of 100th Meridian, please, Liz."

Dylan's order interrupts my inner tirade. I look up, catching him offering Liz one of his perfect smiles.

"You two need to go out. You both spend most of our nights here staring at each other," Mercer says to Dylan once Liz is out of earshot from our booth. "That way, you and that revolting 'flavour saver' thing will never sniff out my sister, so you truly have my blessing."

"Naw, man. Liz isn't really my type," he says, his eyes trailing after her.

"Dyl, she's breathing. What do you mean 'not your type'? You're a regular cocksmith," I add, chuckling. "Isn't that what all your first-year philosophy dudes would say?"

"Whatever, they're all idiots." He shakes his head. "Liz is great, and she's smart as a whip. She'll be done her Ph.D. in a couple of months; she only works here a few nights a week to help her uncle out. But between my work and her school, we'd never see each other. I'm not looking for anything long-term right now, anyway. And she's more of that long-term material."

"See. That right there, how you said that. I agree with Mercer, you got a thing for her, it's obvious." I say.

"Whatever, Nancy Drew. Enough about me, what's up with you and that sweet-looking auburn-haired beauty I saw you ogling earlier in your office when I came to meet you? Tell us about that, why don't you?" Dylan volleys back at me.

"Shut up. She's my student."

"Oh yeah? She pretty?" Mercer, my thickheaded friend, asks.

"She's gorgeous. Short, but gorgeous," Dylan chimes in again.

"Watch it," I interject.

"Whoa, man," he says, raising his hands, "I was just giving my opinion."

"Save it. I don't want to hear what you think of Ellie. Better yet, don't think of her. Ever," I spit out.

"Well, then. How 'bout them Jays?" Mercer asks, trying to break the tension that's taken over. "Wait…Ellie *Hughes*?" he asks.

"Yes."

"Wow, she's a bombshell. Sweet girl. Messed up her knee, used to run for the Varsity Blues. Was fast too. I've helped her with physio a few times. Don't think she'll compete again, though."

"Yeah, see? Told you she was smoking," says Dylan interrupting.

"On the field you mean, right?" I give him an out, but of course he just laughs.

"Sure, if it will help calm you down, then, yeah, that's how I meant it."

I need to get a grip. "Sorry, Dyl. She's doing my head in. I want her. She *is* sweet, on top of looking like a pin-up. And she's smart. I enjoy hearing what she has to say; she's got a quality to her that's rare. It's like I'm a moth drawn to her flame. Seems we have some things in common from what I've seen and heard so far. I'm struggling with my moral code here, hard."

"Didn't realize it was that bad. Ace, you have to be careful. I'm all for taking risks, being the deep thinker in the pack, but this is a big one," Dylan adds.

"Fuck if I don't know it." I smile up at Liz as she places our pitcher down and begins to fill our glasses.

Dylan breaks the silence once Liz is gone, having stared at her the whole time. "Maybe I *should* ask her out. She's a pretty cool chick."

"Great Scott! I think he's getting it." Mercer cuffs him upside the head. "As for you and Ellie, all you'd have to do if you wanted to pursue anything is keep it a secret until the semester's over, or better yet, take two cold showers a day and hold it until the semester's over. It's already late-October. I'm sure you could be just friends for the next six months until she graduates," Mercer supplies, like it's the simplest thing.

"Yeah, but I'm pretty sure as long as she's not your direct student, they can't do anything to you. There's some code or something, listing all the infractions and the fines or whatever," Dylan drops his two cents in, before taking a sip of his beer.

"That true?" I ask, looking to Mercer to confirm it.

"All joking aside, yes. Well, for the athletics department it is. I'd imagine the rules apply across the board. But I think there is a loophole. If you're in a position where there might be a conflict of interest, I'm pretty sure if you write to the chair of your department there are appropriate steps they can take. So, I guess, if you needed to, there might be a way you could pursue things. You could look it up."

"Huh. Good to know," I nod, taking a swig of my beer. The cold bite is exactly what I need. I'm not going to be able to keep resisting her. Christ, I almost kissed her neck when I found her standing by my window, her tight ass displayed in her dark jeans, a black sweater hugging her curves like I wish I could. The whole space smelled like her perfume. Walking back in to find her waiting for me was a feeling I liked a lot. *A hell of a lot.*

The sound of Dyl clapping shakes me from my thoughts.

"I can't believe I'm about to say this, but enough girl talk. It's documentary update time, son. I need to know, how goes the battle? Did you find my perfect girl yet?"

"I might have," I laugh. Dylan is always on the lookout for a girl who can keep up with him in the dirty talk/kinky sex department. Being a philosophy teacher, he's big on sharing every thought, all the time. Sex is an experience in movement and voice and trying out new theories, he claims. Mercer and I just nod and smile most of the time.

"There's this really hot stripper out by the airport. Name's Carly. She's looking for a sugar daddy to take her away. You want her number?" I joke. "She's a real talker, I promise," I chuckle, taking another swig of cold beer.

"Hey, maybe," he replies, laughing. "Think I'd get free lap dances?" He smiles, raising his brows questioningly. "No, for real, man. How's it going?"

"It's good. Really good. I'm about to start the last of my research. I'm going to be investigating phone sex lines for a bit. I'm going to call a few different ones, see what makes one better than the other, hopefully get close with one or two calltakers that might open up, share their stories, their reasons for working. Tell me how it all works; give me some stats to see if calls are on the rise, see if phone sex could pose a threat to places like peep shows and strip clubs. It should be interesting. I'm also hoping I can test how versatile they are, how far they're willing to go to make a buck. Can they roll with the punches, slip into any role, handle any call, see if they ever get tripped up, and so on."

"Hey, I almost forgot," Mercer says, sliding me a piece of paper, "here's the list of names and numbers of lines Chelsea says are top notch. She worked at the one with 'whisper' in the title. She said it's the most private and high-end, and she mentioned it being all about 'Class, Discretion and the Happy Ending', or some shit."

"Fuckers took my motto!" Dylan interjects, gaining another cuff upside the head, from me this time.

"Anyway," Mercer chides, "Chels said the owner is all about discretion, so you might not get too many willing employees to interview. He pays them all very well, making them loyal, keeping them willing to be pretty hush-hush. She said it's a lucrative job, a solid environment with no reason for people to give up any information about it. You might have to become an actual client, build some sort of report. But

Chelsea said to call her if you get stuck, and she'll call a woman she knows who works there."

"Okay, cool. I was planning on being a caller, anyway. I want my research to be authentic. Then, hopefully, I can convince one or two to let me do an interview and get some footage of them in action on the job." Looking at the list of six numbers, I laugh. "The one with the word 'whisper' is good, you say?"

"Yeah, she said it's the best."

"Idiot, three of them have 'whisper' in the title."

He just shrugs. "Guess you'll have to call Chelsea after all."

"It all sounds interesting, man. You nervous about pretending to be a caller?" Dylan asks. "Hey, think you might actually get off? Wait. Fuck, maybe I wanna help with this one. Let me call and you can video me, in all my glory." We all laugh at Dylan.

"You're such a tool."

"Honestly. You don't plan on getting off? Won't it be hard not to?" Dylan asks perplexed.

"Nah, I'm a professional," I say. "I have a job to do and there is no reason I should need to get off while working on this. It's not about me. My goal is research. Besides, how bloody typical would that be? I'll already have critics busting my balls, thinking that's why I chose a sex trade as my topic. The last thing I need is for it to be true. I know it could happen and if it does, it's only me who will ever know, but still, I like to think I can keep control and save myself for real-life action."

"I bet you twenty bucks you get off on the first call." Dylan extends his hand for me to shake.

"Nice support, Dyl."

"Think of it as my contribution to your film. A twenty will buy you, what, at least five minutes, won't it?" he laughs.

"More like three from what I've researched. Thankfully, I got that grant. This shit can be expensive, especially if you need to pull off being a regular caller. I'm hoping I can work my charm. I mean, I did learn from the best after all," I nod my beer towards Dylan before taking a sip.

"Cheers to getting off while getting it on," Dylan says, raising his beer glass. "See what I did there? Get your dick off and your research on."

"Dude, you're a regular Socrates."

"Cheers."

We spend the rest of the night shooting the shit, but I never fully stop my mind from drifting away to thoughts of E.

Chapter 23

Ellie

"HELLO? ER, I mean…*shit*."

"'Shit'?" The man on the other end repeats.

"No, sorry. I meant…'Breathless Whispers'." I try to cover using my best sexy voice.

"Really? This is supposed to get me off?"

"I'm sorry. I'm new. I was caught off guard."

"Who gets caught off guard when the phone rings? Aren't you supposed to be expecting calls? Here's a tip. Quit now. You suck. Fuck, what a waste. I better not get charged for this, bitch."

"Whoa, easy, buddy! I apologized. I'll make sure you're fully refunded."

"You better."

Click.

Well, that went well. Hurray for day two on my own starting off on the right foot.

"Shit," I mumble, reaching for my stress-relief aromatherapy rollerball dispenser from Saje, my favourite essential oil store, the one I discovered soon after my injury. Alternative medicine has been a great way to help me to manage my pain. I uncap the lid and start rubbing it along my temples, and in behind my ears. The soothing blend of lavender, mixed with hints of citrus, vetiver and subtle geranium permeate the air immediately helping to ground me. "I can do this.

Fuck him. I don't suck. I'm still learning," I mutter, placing it back in my bag.

Deciding I need a pep talk, I move the icon beside my name to yellow and make a long overdue call. I call the one person I know who will talk me out of quitting, even when deep down I know I can't really afford to quit at this point anyway, but still it will be good to have my ego and sprits raised. Sliding my iPhone, I move to my contacts, stopping on the name I need.

Erica.

"Hey, stranger. How goes the life?" she greets on the second ring.

"Erica. Oh goodness, I suck. I can't do this, I'm awful already," I confess.

"I've been waiting for your call. Tell Court she owes me twenty bucks."

"Betting on me? Really? You guys suck, you know that? This was your crazy idea, so you better help me!"

"All right, Panic Mode Barbie, what's the issue?"

"I can't pull this act off. It's too hard."

"Oh please, you can so. You're a smart girl and a movie geek, use your drama skills. I did it for over a year, and I'm shy."

"I'm not in acting school, Ric, I'm going to be a screenwriter. This is way too hard."

"Okay, non-actress, it's called *pretending*. I'm sure a serious student of film can handle this easily. Regardless of having acting classes or not, it's all about imagination and letting yourself have fun. We're not going for an Oscar here. It's really not the big deal you're making it. Els, you're crazy fun, sexy, creative, and you of all people can totally pull this off. Put your mind to it and just be confident."

"I don't know, some of these calls are whack," I say, before telling her about my last call and the other crazy ones I've had too.

"Babe, that's nothing. Trust me. You'll get weirder stuff. Listen to me, though. You're making this way too much of a big deal. It's just talking, with a bit of sexy-sexy time."

"That's the trouble. I feel stupid. How the hell did you do it?"

"Honestly, you want the truth?" she asks.

"Erica, of course. I need to get good at this job and fast. I bet they question why I needed to refund that call. I can't let it happen again. I really need any and all help."

"First of all, you need to get out of that head of yours. Use your oil voodoo, play music in the background, dress the part, but you need to work on your mindset first. Remember, no one can hear or see you, so this can actually be a lot of fun. You can channel your inner goddess, hooker, angel and dominatrix all at the same time."

"You sound like Destiny," I quip.

"Second," she ignores my comparison, "get into it. Some of these callers will turn you on. Let it happen. Women are sexiest when turned on. Let the caller's voice wash over you. Allow yourself the freedom to get hot and bothered right along with them. It's natural. We all do it."

"I won't. No way."

"Whatever you say, but know that I know better, Els."

"Not happening," I say again, knowing it's falling on deaf ears.

"Finally, for fuck's sake, Ellie, be creative, adventurous—and like I said earlier—have fun with it. Pretend it's the hottest man you can see. Pretend it's one of your movie project things or whatever. Whatever you do, embrace the phone sex operator job. You won't be successful if you over analyze it. It's money, Els. Lots, if you can pull it off. And I know you can. You've just got to give yourself a real chance."

"You're right. I'm hindering myself. I guess I can do this."

"Damn right you can. Now forget all the calls you've had so far. Become Chanel. Forget Ellie, and pretend you're Chanel."

"Got it."

"Say it: *I am Chanel.* I am a sexy-voiced Phone Sex Superhero with the power to make men shoot cum all over themselves at the sound of my voice and dirty words. I am woman, hear me roar."

"That's disgusting, Ric!"

"What? It's awesome."

"It was way bad."

"Got you to relax, didn't it?" Erica laughs, before we say our good-byes.

Chapter 24

Ellie

AS SOON AS I shift my name back to green, the system beeps. I accept the call and my phone begins to ring. Having decided to always use the adapter to hide my voice, I ensure it's in place before clicking on the headset. I'm hoping from here on out, it might help with boosting my confidence, knowing that no-one is hearing my real voice.

You are Chanel. You've got this. Easy peasy.

"Breathless Whispers. Let me leave you breathless," I say softly into the microphone tip.

"What's your name, lovely?" a rough voice asks, and I feel it in my toes. Maybe Erica was right. I need to let myself be free, put Ellie to the side, allow Chanel to be my alter ego—a costume. Chanel can be a confident, less-inhibited version of myself, a more sexually-versed version who enjoys dirty talk and all things that go along with it. One who has permission to like it, maybe even enjoying the benefits all this sexy talk can bring.

"Chanel. What's yours?"

"It's Jake," the deep voice replies. "I'm hoping you can help me tonight."

"Oh, Jake is one of my favourite names. It was my coach's name in high school. I kinda had a crush on him," I add, giggling for effect, or maybe it's more due to nerves. "I'd love to help you. I'm so very helpful. How can I help you, *Jake?*" I ask stressing his name.

"I need to come, lovely. It's been way too long. I need you to tell me a good bedtime story. One with a happy ending. I'm lying in my bed, ready for to you excite me."

"You're in luck. I love happy endings. Especially ones involving coming." I slap my hand over my forehead. *Nice one, Captain Obvious.* Pausing, I wait for him to call me out, tell me I'm lame. But after a few beats I hear the opposite. He encourages me. He wants more.

"Good. 'Cause I'm really in the mood for a nice sexy story. You gonna give me one, Chanel? Ready to make me come?"

"Hell, yes. I'm more than ready," I say, twirling a lock of my hair between my fingers.

Go for it, Ellie. Show yourself you can do this.

"Can I tell you about my crush, Jake? How I finally got the nerve to tell him how sexy I found him? Wanna hear what a bad girl I was?" I take a deep steadying breath, hoping my brain can write this script as fast as I need it.

"Fuck, yeah, I do."

Giggling again, I start: "I was a cheerleader, you see, and he was the football coach. I spotted him my first day. I was a transfer student. I'd come in the middle of the semester. I'd always been a good dancer so I decided I could cheer. I tried out and made the team. I was hoping maybe the coach would notice me too. After making the team, I got the skimpy uniform. Learned the dances and went on to plan how I'd seduce the coach."

"You sound like a bad girl, Chanel. Are you a naughty girl?"

"Yes. I'm very much a bad girl. So, one day after practice, I waited until everyone was gone. I could hear him on the phone. He was angry. Yelling. I slipped into his office, closed the door softly behind me. I'd left on my uniform. I thought it was sexy. Thought I looked good in it—"

"I bet you looked spectacular in it," Jake says, his voice hitching. "Keep talking, Chanel, it's working. I'm getting so hard."

"I'm so glad. The best parts are yet to come, Jake. Relax and keep focused on my voice, on my words."

"God, I can't wait to hear about your uniform."

Shit, what does a cheerleader uniform even look like?

Smiling to myself, I plan to move into the good bits quickly. For some reason, I'm more determined than ever to make Jake come good and hard. Maybe it's the patience he's showing me, the subtle encouragements. "Now close your eyes and listen while I tell you the story as if it were happening right before your eyes, Jake." I say extending the "k" sound. "Pretending to be all shy, I asked in a low and sultry voice: *'Have you ever fucked a student before, Coach Jake?'* I cocked my head to the side, leaned my back against his office door, hoping to draw attention to the swell of my large breasts. I wanted his eyes to notice the deep 'V' of my shirt, notice it's tightness, and how it hugged my girls just right—"

"Fuck, yeah, I can see your cleavage. Keep going, sweetheart," Jake interrupts, whispering from the other end. I can't deny that I feel myself getting flushed from his getting excited.

"I could tell by the glint in his dark eyes that he was succumbing to my plan. Turning to click the lock in place, I added: *'Or, better yet, ever fuck a cheerleader, Coach?'* just to tease him that extra little bit. Hearing a small growl, I smiled, knowing I had him where I wanted him. Turning back around, I heard him mutter something inaudible over the phone before he hung it up and said my name with a moan, knocking the phone from its cradle in his haste.

"*'I want to suck your huge cock while you sit in your chair pulling my hair, Coach. Would you like that?'* I asked, pushing away from the door. His eyes opened wide in surprise, and a sexy smirk began to form on his lips, lips I'd imagined sucking on my clit a hundred times while I'd gotten myself off in my bed. Standing in front of him, I felt the heaviness of his gaze as it travelled from my white tennis shoes up my tanned, toned legs, pausing at the hem of my barely-there blue plaid skirt. And all the while, I was loving that dark shadow taking over his brown eyes as they roamed over me once, twice more, over my bare legs, stalling a beat on my heavy tits, before finally landing on my face. *'That a yes, big boy?' I said. 'Wanna watch me deep throat your hard cock, see me choke it all down, let it graze the back of my throat?'* Reaching under my skirt, I pulled my panties down, then kicked them off over my shoes as I walked to him where he was sitting in his chair. Tossing the satin thong his way, I let my own smirk play on my lips. Once again, I knew I had him. I mean who can resist the wet panties of an eighteen-year-old cheerleader, right? Ready to make my final approach, I teased him, moving my hips, forcing them to sway until I was standing before him where he was now resting back in his chair, his hand grinding down heavily on his cock—"

"Fuck, yes, Chanel. Tell me more, lovely," Jake says on the line, and I smile again, knowing my words are good, that this is working.

"Coach nodded as I moved to stand between his open knees. I moved my hands over his bearded face; I made quick work of discarding my shirt. My tits sprung free right into his face—"

"Fuck, tell me about your tits. I bet they're spectacular. God, I wanna suck them," Jake blurts out again, causing a pause in the story.

"Yes. I want that too, Jake. I want my hard nipples in your mouth, want your hot wet tongue to kiss, suck and bite each hard tip. I want your hand to roam, and squeeze each heavy double-D. Can you do that for me?" I ask, letting out a soft whimper, because in this moment it's true. My hands move over my chest, stopping at the distended tips under my shirt.

"I'm so fucking hard right now," he growls in my ear.

"That's good, Jake, very good. Now take that big smooth cock of yours out. I want you to touch yourself while I finish my story. Can you do that, handsome?"

"Fuck, yeah, tell me more." I hear his zipper open, a sharp intake of breath, and I assume he's touching his cock. I can't deny, the idea of him touching himself at my words is getting me more excited. Maybe Erica and Destiny are right after all.

"Tell me more, Chanel. I'm so fucking excited right now,"

Letting out a breathy moan, I continue my story.

"After Coach played with my tits, licking, pinching, resting his face in between my heavy cleavage, I leaned in to whisper in his ear: '*Once I finish sucking you dry, I want to try your beard on. I want to sit on your face while you fuck my wet cunt with your mouth, slip your tongue in and out of my sweet heat, slide that beard over and over my pussy. I want to see my wetness dripping off your chin. Can you do that for me, Coach?*' The next thing I know, Coach growled and moved me not-so-gently to sit on his desk. Rumbling and muttering to himself, he pulled my hair back, and tilted my head to face him before he crashed his mouth on top of mine. He kissed me hard while he moved my legs to allow him to get in closer. '*Gonna fuck that sweet cunt of yours first. I can't wait another second. Then I'll lap up every single drop while you ride my beard, sugar.*'

"Knowing I was more than ready to take his hard cock into my soaking wet pussy, I pulled away to position myself with my hands resting behind me, scooting closer to the edge of the desk, opening my legs so he could see my aching, bare cunt was ready for him—"

"Oh fuck, yes. Are you bare right now, sweetheart?" Jake grits out on a heavy breath.

"Yes, completely bare. And Coach loved it. Next, he began stroking my pussy with his thick fingers, with a depth and precision that I'd never known before, bringing me to the brink in no time. Having had enough, I began begging and pleading for his touch, for him to fuck me with his big, heavy cock. I positioned my feet farther up towards my head, giving him the signal that I needed him to fuck me now. That I was ready. Pulling down his athletic shorts, Coach Jake O'Toole gave me exactly what I needed. He slammed his hard cock into my tight, hot cunt. Over and over, deep thrust after deep thrust. He kept fucking me harder than I'd ever been fucked before. My tits were bouncing from his thrusts. My moans filled the air. With each drag and pull, my pussy quivered, my cream began running down my ass, leaving a mess in its wake as I pulsed around his smooth, rock hard cock. I came and came and came. Just when I thought I was done, he slipped out of me and pushed me down onto my knees. Demanding that I suck him dry," I end on a pant, before speaking to Jake. "Do you want me to suck you dry, Jake? Do you want to feel my wet mouth like Coach did?"

"Jesus fucking Christ, yes. Take me, Chanel. God, suck my dick."

Grabbing a lollipop, I channel my inner Destiny and gobble the shit out of that Blow Pop while Jake comes on the other end of the line.

"Motherfucker," is all I hear, followed by a few moments of silence. I'm just about to hang up, thinking I've lost him, when I hear him breathing heavily.

"Fuck, that was good, lovely. I came so fucking hard. I need to talk to you again. Is there a way to get you?"

I explain how it works, giving him my full handle, and telling him how I could give him a discount if he continues to call me. He hangs up with a "thank you", and I can't hide the smile that crosses my lips as I disconnect the call.

I did it.

And I think I just bagged myself a regular to boot!

Chapter 25

Ellie

"NEVER HAVE I ever I had sex in a car," our friend Susan says, taking a sip of her own drink, which causes Courtney to giggle because the poor girl still isn't getting the point.

"Oh Lord, she's never going to get it," Brent whines, taking his sip.

"No, girlie. Your goal is to make *us* drink. To think of things you know we might have done that you haven't. Your goal is to stay sober, to have the lowest number of tallies under your name. The last one standing wins the pot," Courtney says, fanning out the eighty bucks that was resting in a cup in the centre of our oak table.

The four of us decided to play "Never Have I Ever" for Friday Night Game Night. Since I was actually off tonight and my studying was done, I felt a few drinks with friends was a perfect idea. I've been missing out on a whole bunch of friend time with these guys since I started at Breathless Whispers. Susan and Brent seemed as excited to hang out as I was, and Court's always an eager drinker, so it was perfect.

They've both asked me many times where I'm working and why I seem to come and go at strange times, Susan missing me at the gym with her in the mornings. I keep trying to evade telling them the truth. Instead, I've told them I'm working at an old age home and that the shifts vary. They seem to have bought it and haven't questioned me again in weeks. Hearing Courtney's voice trying in vain to once more explain the game to Susan brings me back just in time to hear Court throwing me under the proverbial bus.

"Watch now. I'll get only one of us to drink. Pay attention, the master is going in," she says, rubbing her hands while jutting her chin my way. And I know what's coming before she gets a word out.

"You asshole," I whisper, giving her a sweet smile. Payback is a bitch'n'all.

"Never have I ever been a phone sex operator." Courtney claps her hands, pleased with herself, a huge smile marring her happy little face. Brent and Susan suddenly start moving their faces between us like you would when watching a tennis game. I'm going to kill my *former* best friend. Even though I've been toying with the idea of telling them about my new job—especially since I hate lying, and I know I can trust them not to judge me or tell a soul if I ask them not to—I wasn't planning on telling them like this.

"Ellie, don't you need to take a drink?" Courtney asks, feigning innocence as I feel my eyes bugging out of my face while giving her the evil eye. But I bring the sweet taste of vodka and cranberry juice to my lips nonetheless, while she giggles as if it's no big deal.

"Shut your whoring mouth! What...*Ellie*?" Brent says, bolting up, suddenly excited and intrigued. "You dirty, dirty girl. Please tell me it's true."

Pouring more vodka into my glass, I make quick work of adding a splash of cranberry juice before deciding to acknowledge the elephant that has now arrived in the room.

Deciding *fuck it,* I pick up my recently topped-off drink, lift it to my mouth, and take another huge gulp.

"Breathless Whispers, this is Chanel. Let me leave you breathless," I say, raising my glass in toast.

"Holy shit!" drops from Susan's lips.

"I need all the details, young lady. You little sneak. I never—I mean, never—would have expected this from you." Brent thumbs towards Court. "Her absolutely, but you? I'm shocked and kind of excited for you, sweets, our rebel in disguise. Look at you getting all outside of your square box. I need deets, like, now. And I need to hear about the hottest caller you've had. Things aren't so good with Ed right now, so help give a guy some nighttime ammo. It'll keep me from being a stray until he realizes he misses me." He pours us another round, laughing.

"Aww, I'm sorry, Brent-Brent. You guys will sort it out, you always do." I pat his back.

"Great, now share, woman. I want visuals," Brent deadpans, causing us all to laugh.

"Oh my. Okay, I'll tell you all about it, but first things first. It's my turn. We can talk later. There's eighty bucks with my name on it that I must claim first. You people can suffer with a lack of info for a little while longer. Besides, I'm going to need a few more drinks for that bit of sharing!" I wave my cup in the air.

"Courtney, I can't believe you didn't tell us before, you little ass." Susan lightly punches Court's arm. "It's been how long now that we've been thinking she's been innocently helping the elderly? Lies. Y'all are lucky I love you."

"Sorry, babe. Wasn't my place," Courtney beams, giving me a sly grin.

"Uh, newsflash, bright light. You just told them all now, still wasn't your place." I half-joke, honestly glad it's out and that they took it the way I knew they would. Well, how I knew Brent would.

"I'm all for letting people choose their own paths, but Ellie, I have to ask: why *this?* I mean, you could do any job. Why choose to degrade yourself?" Susan asks, a hint of apprehension lacing her tone. I know her well enough to know she's not judging me, rather she's curious as to why I of all people would take a job in a sex trade.

"No, it's okay, Susan. I know it's a shock. I guess I felt it was the best way to make money fast. There was no way I'd still be at U of T if I didn't get a job that paid enough. Losing my scholarship, I was pretty much up shit creek, and Breathless Whispers was my paddle. It's easy, flexible, and I make good money. Best of all, it doesn't involve any work where my knee will be bothered, it's still healing. Oh, and after literally pounding the pavement for two weeks, it's all I could find," I add, shrugging my shoulders, pasting on a big ol' fake smile.

"I guess that all makes sense. I know it's good money," says Susan. "Believe it or not, my cousin Dale was actually a porn star in college. His roommate's girlfriend's father was some producer. One day he saw Dale and begged him to star in his production of *Red Riding Hood Does the Wolf*. It was some kind of fuzzy fetish film or something and he made like five grand, so he did it—wearing a stuffed wolf head—and no one in our family was any the wiser. And trust me, I feel the pain of the job hunt in this city. Which is surprising, considering its size."

"Wow, that's seriously intense. I didn't realize they made furry films," Courtney barks out a laugh.

"Yeah, it was pretty crazy. He tried to make me watch it, but I threatened to tell his mom if he forced me. I assured him I was proud, but never wanted to see his masterpiece," she giggles, taking a sip of her drink.

I spend the next few minutes assuring them all that it's safe and probably one of the easier jobs I've had. *Once you get past all the crazy fetishes and stuff at least.*

"Are you all done giving Ellie the third-degree? Can we play now? I'm losing my buzz," Brent interrupts, and I'm thankful.

"Again, thanks for the spotlight, Court. I sure hope I can repay the favour soon," I scold. "Now, let's play, so I can drink…a lot."

"Hey, don't be pissy," Courtney says. "That was in the name of learning. It was a great way to teach Susan how to play properly; the poor girl was going to be hammered in no time. I was being a good friend."

"Ha. Good thing we all have you, eh, Court? Well, it's my turn now. Get your drink ready, friend." I hand her the bottle of vodka.

"Oh God. Here we go," Susan says, sliding her drink closer to herself.

"Never have I ever longed to have sex with my thesis advisor. *BAM!*" I shout, feeling smug. Immediately, Court and Brent pick up their drinks and take sips.

"I knew it!" I point at Court. "You want to boink Jax—*hard*."

No surprise that Susan doesn't drink on this one. She's been in a long distance relationship for years with a guy from back home in Thunder Bay. Rory visits, she visits, they're cute and fuzzy.

"And that's how it's done, son!" I mark the scorecard, giving both TA lovers a tally mark under their names. So far, Brent is leading, I might have to dig deep to get this guy. "All right, Brent, you're up."

"Uh-uh, not so fast, Els," Court interrupts, a devilish smile taking over the majority of her face.

"What?" I ask, confused.

"Drink, Ellie."

"What? Why?"

"Pleaaase, don't even try that shit right now. You know you need to take one fuck of a big drink. Does the name Dr. Ace Ryan help to jog your memory at all?"

Fuck.

Double Fuck Squared.

Fuckity fuck fuck.

I didn't think. When I blurted out my masterful question to trip Court into admitting what we both know to be true, I never thought that I'd be implicating myself in the process, as well.

"Damn it."

The upside to "Never Have I Ever" is that you can have a lot of fun getting drunk and learning things about people. The down side is, you can't lie. You're supposed to tell the truth.

"God, this game is fun!" Susan chimes in again. "I'm on total gossip overload," she squeals.

"I hate you." I glare at Court before picking up my glass and finishing it off.

I'm just about to give her shit when my phone beeps beside me, drawing my attention to the email notification.

Opening it up, I almost die when I see it's from Professor Ryan.

To: Ellie Hughes <@EllieH1256@UofT.net>
From: Ace Ryan <@ProfARyan@UofT.net>
Subject: Preliminary meeting
Date: Oct. 16, 2015
Time: 10:40 p.m

Ms. Hughes,

I'll be in my office Monday morning at 8:00 a.m. I'd like to schedule your preliminary meeting for then. Since you'll be here for class at 9 a.m. anyway, I'm assuming this won't be a problem? Please be prepared to choose a follow-up meeting date, as well, as we are now a week behind the original schedule. Please reply to confirm you've received and that you'll be attending.

Best Regards,
Professor A. Ryan
Faculty of Film Studies
The University of Toronto
Work: 416-876-5356

"Jesus, it's like he could hear us…" I hear Brent over my shoulder. "Take it as a sign, Ellie."

"Whatever. Hey, stop reading over my shoulder. Worst habit, it's so rude."

"Well, you can sure as hell expect me to do it even more now that I know how exciting your life is. I'm hoping to catch some taboo call stuff, or better yet a torrid, forbidden love affair involving smutty emails and sexting," he teases.

"Never happening. One, I work in an office, not off my phone, and two, sure, I might have a little crush on my professor, but he's just that—my teacher—so he is very off limits."

"We shall see," Courtney weighs in.

At this point, I'm over them trying to goad me. "Are we playing the game or what? I feel like Miss Susan needs to share some skeletons." I give her a warning look.

After typing out a reply to Ace telling him I'll be there, I spend the rest of the night drinking, playing "Never Have I Ever", and sharing a few of my experiences as a PSO.

Note to self: never ever play "Never Have I Ever" ever again.

Chapter 26

Ellie

IT'S SATURDAY NIGHT. I'm hungover and working a ten p.m. to two a.m. shift at Breathless. I chose to work this terrible block tonight figuring it might be slow enough that I could review my thesis notes for Monday morning's meeting. Ace emailing me without much notice has put me a bit on edge. I want to make sure I'm fully prepared to answer any questions he may ask about my paper. I already have a feeling he might try to dissuade me from my topic.

On top of feeling pressure about Monday's meeting, Brent is driving me crazy, too. Ever since Courtney forced my little revelation last night about my job, Brent has been a needy little bastard wanting all kinds of details. I swear, if I didn't know him better, I'd think he was writing an exposé on my secret life. I'm just about to text to question him about it when the familiar *beep* fills the air. Tossing my phone on top of my iPad, I look at the computer, checking the call log.

"Breathless Whispers, let me leave you breathless," I say to the caller, who's listed role-play as his preference for tonight. These calls are quickly becoming my favourites. I've been working here for almost two months now and I'm discovering a few things about my self-proclaimed vanilla-style preferences. I'm anything but.

It took *this*, taking on Chanel's persona, to discover that I, too, have wild fantasies and desires. Someday, maybe I'll find my own fantasy maker to push and test my limits. The desire to explore role-play to its fullest weighs on my mind with each new call, and I love getting to pretend I'm someone else, pushing my own boundaries and comfort, picturing the words I whisper as they play out for each caller, getting to once again channel my inner movie buff. I pretend I'm an actress starring in the role of a lifetime, in a film written and directed by me; my goal is to chase the Oscar. And I have to admit, I have given some pretty wicked performances.

"I want to listen to you make my wife come. Hard," comes a commanding voice, booming through the line. "I want her to know that feeling. That sensation...I want to hear her breathe and feel her get wet as you touch her."

Well, fuck me. And suddenly I'm completely flailing, my voice lodged in my throat. How can you get someone off if you can't find your voice? It's not that I'm against a little girl on girl action, I'm just the least experienced person on the planet at how the mechanics of it all work. Sure, I've wondered, fantasized a little, if I'm being honest. But these are the thoughts, images, and ideas I keep on lock down in the recesses of my mind.

And now this man wants me to bring them to the stage, to take the lead role in a script I've never seen or experienced. Shaking off my insecurities, I breathlessly agree.

"I'd love to touch your gorgeous wife. I love nothing more than bringing a sexy woman to the edge then slowly giving her the last subtle push she needs to fall."

I cringe, hoping I didn't oversell something I have no clue about.

"Fuck. You're going to be perfect for Rachael. What do you think, sugar?" he asks, and I'm about to reply when I hear a woman's voice come over the line:

"I can't wait, sir. Thank you for this Happy Anniversary, honey."

"Sir"?

"Take off Rachael's clothes...sir," I say. "I want to see her beautiful body on display for us."

"Yes, my wife is breathtaking. After ten years, she's only gotten sexier," he says, and my stomach dips at the obvious feelings he has for his wife.

"That's perfect, our compliments are sure to make Rachael all the more excited for my touch. Are you naked, Rachael? Are you ready for me?

"God. Yes."

"Close your eyes, honey. I'm standing right in front of you, naked, my hard nipples brushing up against yours, my fingers lightly touching every one of your curves. I can see your breathing getting faster. You've got an amazing body, responsive as fuck to me—"

A deep groan resonates through the line, cutting me off; I think "sir" is getting excited.

"Are you with us, sir? Can you stroke your hard cock while I continue to touch your beautiful wife?"

"Shit, yeah, I can. She looks so fucking hot, her body trembling from your voice, excited under my gaze. I'm so goddamned hard."

Holy shit, I'm staring to feel a little rush of excitement myself. To be honest, it doesn't happen a lot, but Destiny was right, it totally happens no matter how much you'd like to think otherwise. With scenes like this, how could it not? *Maybe I should film myself one time? My GoPro App would be perfect.*

"Go lie on the bed now, pet. I want to see your pussy. I need to feel your smooth skin as my fingers dance along your sweet lips, bringing you nothing but pleasure."

"Yes, shit, please do. I'm here. I'm lying down. Please touch me."

"Sir, I'd like your help. Since it's a special night for both of you, let's all play."

"God, I'd fucking like that. You should see her; she's fucking perfect, lying, waiting, goosebumps rising all over her sexy body, her nipples tight with excitement…"

"Perfect. Slowly spread your legs, Rachael. Nice and slow. Tease us. Can you take your fingers and run them along your pretty pink pussy lips?"

"Yes. Yes…"

"Tell me, honey. Are you wet for me?"

"So wet. Fuck, I need more."

"Shhh, no more talking, close your eyes and let my voice guide you. Sir, please act as my hands now. I'll tell you the movements, be my touch."

"Oh shit, Rachael, you're fucking drenched, honey. I'm not going to last."

"Sir, I'd like you to move my hand along Rachael's wet lips, apply the subtle pressure of a lover's kiss after a few days away. Can you feel my fingers caressing you gently?"

"I feel so much. It's so much."

"Mmmm, I can feel you getting wetter with every stroke. Slip my finger inside now, slowly stretch up, now add another and make the 'come hither' movement."

"Jesus Christ, Billy, I'm gonna fucking come…!"

Holy fuck! I shake my head in disbelief that I actually pulled that off. Grabbing my phone, I decide to share my call with Brent. Exposé or not, he will totally appreciate my mad skills on this one.

Chapter 27

Ellie

NOTE TO SELF, the ten-to-two shifts are not the homework-friendly shifts at all. I've only got half an hour left to go, and I notice I've answered twelve calls. Standing from the desk chair intent on moving my tired self to the comfy chaise, the hope of resting my eyes for a moment disappears mid-step at the sound of the beep. Seeing who it is, however, makes me smile. *Jake.*

He called back.

"Hi, Chanel, it's Jake."

"Hi, Jake. I'm excited you called again. I was hoping you would."

"Me too, lovely. Me too. Sorry it took me a few days; work's been a bit crazy. I just started a new job and moved to the city, so things have been nuts."

"I bet. Glad you're calling now, though," I say in a shy voice.

"I was hoping you could help me out tonight. I've got a crazy bet going on with a buddy. He says all women do this, and I disagree. I need to know the answer to a personal question. I figured you could probably help me out."

"I'd like to give you a hand, Jake, anytime," I tell him in a low breathy voice, hoping he gets my drift.

"That's good, 'cause this is sort of a personal question."

"Mm-hmm. That's okay. You can ask me anything, always."

"Okay. Have you ever watched yourself masturbate? Sat front and centre and watched?" he asks, his voice taking on a huskier sound, and it makes my skin tingle to life. I like the sound. A lot.

"No. I mean, of course I masturbate, but never where I can see what I'm doing to myself."

"Jesus. You're making me rock hard hearing that you get yourself off. Would you do it for me? With me?"

"You want me to get myself off for you, Jake? Is that what you want?"

"No, Chanel. I want you to masturbate while watching yourself and I want you to describe it for me while I jerk myself off."

I pause for a minute, wondering if I can do this. I'm feeling adventurous and a little turned on still from the call with Sir and Rachael. Getting up, I push the chaise closer to the wall where a large full-length mirror hangs, ready to give the solo performance of my life. Once again, my sexual naïvety shines through as I suddenly realize the mirror's potential as a perfect visual aid for a situation like this one. *The Conrads must have an amazing sex life.*

"You there? I didn't scare you off, did I?"

"Of course not. I'm just getting ready."

"Thank fuck. I can't wait to hear everything."

"Are you getting ready too? I want you ready to touch yourself. It will make it so much better," I say, grabbing my vibrator from my kit and placing a towel on the chaise just in case I end up needing to use lube for effect. *Wouldn't want to make a mess.*

"I'm beyond ready. Are you naked?"

"Almost. I'm just stepping out of my lacy pink panties." It wasn't quite the truth. I was wearing black yoga pants, not quite ready to give Jake a full-on live performance despite how turned on I might be getting. I was nervous as hell. Thankfully, something about this caller calmed and soothed me and I knew I could do this.

"You've got me all excited, beautiful. I'm happy you're gonna do this for me."

"With you, Jake. We're going to help each other. It's my first time. I might need a little coaching," I say, dropping a subtle reference to the story I told him the first time he called.

"Christ. Tell me you're ready."

"I'm all set." I turn the vibrator on low, so he can hear it's true.

"Where are you?"

"Well, I've got this big chaise. I'm lying on that with my legs spread wide, half sitting up so I can see my reflection in my full-length mirror that's mounted on the wall."

"Tell me what your pussy looks like." I hear a glass clink, assuming he's putting a drink down.

"I'm bare. My skin looks soft, a pretty shade of light pink. Girlie pink, and I feel even better. I feel like velvet. A hint of my excitement is permeating the air now as I think about touching myself for you," I tell him, and hope that it sounds true.

"I bet you smell and look fucking incredible. How do you taste. Give me a little sample."

"I'm running my index and middle finger slowly along my pussy lips, making myself wetter. My fingers are becoming slick from my touch."

"Lick them. Fucking lick yourself off your fingers. Tell me how it tastes," he grits out, and it's sexy as hell. Out of nowhere, an image of Ace standing in his office—voice similar and him sexy-angry—flashes in my mind, and I let out a moan, wishing it has him I was doing this for. Courtney's right, I do have it bad. Those green eyes zeroing in on me in class behind those dark-framed glasses, the way his lip pulls when he gives me that sexy smirk. A second later, I pull off my pants and panties deciding I need this. And I touch myself like I described then do what Jake's asked next.

"Oh God. I'm sweet. I taste like passion fruit with a hint of honey, enough to leave a trail of sweet goodness on my tongue and lips," I tell him slowly licking my fingers. I've never tasted myself before. Sure, I've had a boyfriend kiss me after going downtown but never of my own accord. But after all of tonight's calls, now compounded with images of Ace, there's no way I can't do this for real.

"You're sweet. I fucking knew your tight cunt would taste sweet. Shit." I hear a slow moan escape on his end, which makes me moan as I start to move the vibrator over my clit.

"I'm going to rub myself with the vibrator. I'm so wet. I need the relief. This is making me so hot. It's on my clit, Jake, and it feels so fucking good. I…can't, oh God, it's so good, you should see it."

"Tell me. Fuck, I need to hear. Turn it up higher, lovely, tell me every move you make." It comes out as a command and goosebumps rise on my arms with his tone.

"I'm sliding it along my folds, giving it some of my wetness. Making it easier to slip and slide around my pussy," I tell him, doing exactly what I've described. "Oh God, it looks so sexy sliding in and over and between my lips. The purple tip is glistening, coated with my juices."

"Jesus, that's perfect. Tell me more. Fucking hell. My cock's so hard. I'm circling my head, down along my hard shaft for you. Taking what I wish was your sweet juices and rubbing them with my pre-cum smoothing it all over the head, imagining it's you."

"Oh fuck, Jake. I'm turning it up. I need to run it along my clit, faster, harder," I say, cranking it up.

"Fuck, yeah, do it."

"Shit. It feels too good. I'm spreading my legs wider, I've got my heels digging into the base of my thighs and ass. I'm running the smooth head of it up and along my folds, then up to my clit, alternating the speed and pressure before pausing to let the vibrations tease me. I'm so wet it's hard to keep it in one place, my greedy cunt wants it to slip inside and stay there. Shit, yes. It feels so goddamned amazing."

"Fuck, Chanel, I want to slip inside. I want to feel you clamping around my hard cock. Letting you feel every ridge and vein while I take you fucking hard and fast." Images of what I imagine Ace's hard cock would look like sliding into me pop into my mind. I envision how perfectly his thick, smooth hardness would feel sliding in and out of my wetness as he hovered above, fucking me, so hard and so fast, the fantasy so vivid I'm driving myself crazy.

"Oh my God. Yes, Jake, I want it. Give it to me. Oh, it's slipping inside me. Fuck, Jake, it feels so good. Pulling it in and out, tormenting myself. My pussy's contracting with each push and pull. Fuck, I'm close. Tell me you're close too, Jake. God, I can't hold off. I've slipped it between my lips, the rounded edge now pulsating against my clit, oh shit, ohh fuck!" I scream as I continue to hold the vibrator against my pulsing centre, then letting it glide into my wetness, only prolonging my orgasm as wave after wave of pleasure washes over me.

"Motherfucker, I'm gonna come. I'm gonna fucking cum all over the place," is all I hear as we both go off like explosives. "Jesus fuck, that was incredible. You're amazing."

"Thanks," I whisper, embarrassment over what I've just allowed to happen sinking in. I just finished masturbating over the phone with a complete stranger.

If only I knew how to process how I feel about that.

Should I feel shame or liberation?

Is it okay to feel both?

Thankfully, Jake gives me a rough-voiced, "Talk soon," before simply hanging up.

Deciding to take a cab home later that night, I vow to never allow myself to get carried away like that again.

Damn you, Ace Ryan, for getting in my head and in my panties. I blame you.

Chapter 28

Ace

I SIT IN my office trying to convince myself—or, rather, trying to pretend—that I'm not waiting.

When it's exactly what I'm doing.

Waiting.

Again…envisioning how this meeting will go between us.

Waiting…

For her.

Again.

It's Monday and I'm staring at my computer screen, attempting to respond to the shit ton of emails from the weekend, ones that I told myself were the reason I came in so early, when what I'm really doing is clock watching. I'll make one hell of a timekeeper in my next career. Bet my Ph.D. would give me an edge over the competition. I've been here since seven, sitting. Impatiently *waiting.*

Lucky for her, she's smartened up this time around, and arrives early with almost ten minutes to spare. Rather than make her wait like I could, I invite her in as soon as she knocks, despite not wanting to give the impression that she's my sole purpose for being here.

I stand to greet her. "Good morning, Ms. Hughes. Please, have a seat."

I note how striking she looks, a jacket resting over her arm. She's dressed in a long, deep-purple sweater layered over a pair of those sexy tight jean/legging things that are exactly that—*tight,* showcasing her toned runner's legs. Legs I'd like to feel wrapped around my waist, as the short heels of her ankle boots dig into my ass. I usher her inside, her honeyed voice wishing me a good morning.

"Thank you for seeing me. I'm really excited to speak with you about my thesis."

I'm excited too, but for a completely different reason.

She moves to the small chair where I've gestured for her to sit. I lean against my desk; I've been sitting here for over an hour already.

"Glad we could make this date work for you, Ms. Hughes. Glad you could make it on time, as well." I add the dig, being an ass. I know she felt bad and I shouldn't bring it up again, but I want her to realize I need to be respected regardless of whatever has or is developing between us.

"Again, I apolo—"

I cut her off. "Let's move on. It's in the past. Just know I appreciate your punctuality today." Jesus, I need to tone down the asshole, it's not her fault she fucks me up the way she does.

"I'd like that, to move on," she agrees, her voice low, doe-eyes cast downward, and I hate that I've taken her initial good mood away from her. Hate that I've put tension between us again.

"Damn." I take my glasses off, huff on the lenses, cleaning them, when in reality I'm purely stalling for the words to turn this meeting around. "Honestly, I know you didn't mean to be late. I'm being arrogant. Please accept my apology. It seems you have an effect on me, Ms. Hughes, one I'm not sure how I feel about," I tell her truthfully, putting my glasses back in place.

She mutters something, but it's too faint to make out.

"Pardon?"

"Oh, nothing, I...uh-hmm. I'd never willingly be late to see you, is all. Honestly," she blushes, looking down at her lap.

"Ellie, look at me." Thankfully she listens. "I know, E. I knew it that day, too. I'm the sorry one. Understand?"

"Yes. I think so," she says, gifting me with a faint smile, but a part of me doubts she gets it at all. I'm sorry, most of all, that I can't take her in my arms and show her rather than tell her.

"Please, let's begin. Tell me what the objective of your thesis is and how far along you are at this point," I say, looking into her maple-coloured eyes. I wonder if the colour purple always makes them seem a shade lighter, like they are right now.

"Well, I'm pretty excited about it, albeit a bit nervous..."

I turn her iPad around so I can see the title of her document.

"'*Princess Leia Should Have Wielded a Lightsaber: the Feminist Role Carrie Fisher Never Knew She Was Starring in...Until Now.*' You're kidding. E, tell me you're pulling my leg?"

She's kidding me, right? I'm on a new show called Thesis Jokes and Outtakes, U of T Edition.

"No. I'm not joking. I've been working on this for a while. It's a strong topic."

"Ellie, are you aware that I'm a Star Wars nut?" I point to the shelves where I've recently unpacked a bunch of movie paraphernalia along with having added another batch of framed posters around the room, all Star Wars. "It's my all-time favourite movie franchise. But without sounding unsupportive, I'm completely intrigued and a bit mystified at how this will lead to a forty-plus page paper. I'm sure you've got strong points, Ellie. I'm more concerned with the writing being the required length; you don't want a lot of filler or inconsequential information, with Leia not being the main character. Like, say, if you were to write about a protagonist like Bridget Jones from a feminist perspective, I could see it...but Leia? That might be tough." I cross my right leg over the other at the ankles, bracing both arms on the desktop, wondering if she'll see through my goading her and put me in my place like I expect. Or will she surprise me and back down on this topic?

"It's a favourite of *mine*, as well," she retorts, "all the more reason you should trust my instinct, trust that I wouldn't choose this if I didn't think I could pull it off or do it justice. I know it's a bit risky; I've been doing my research, though. Leia is one kick-ass superhero," she smiles, dropping a reminder of our Tarantino kick-assfest from weeks ago.

"I agree," I say, "she's very kick-ass. Strong and sexy. You'll have to sell this to me, though. Tell me more about your direction. I'm rather concerned that you've wasted precious time on a dead end," I tell her, testing her further. I'm curious to see how she gets when she's passionately defending her ideas, sticking up for something she believes in. And looking up to meet her eyes, I see it immediately—*the challenge*.

"I thought you were supposed to guide me? Support me? You went on in the seminar about all the reasons it's important to trust you guys as advisors, to come to you. And here you are being a jerk. You've not even given me the chance to defend my topic or back it up. I'm not an idiot, Ace…sorry, I mean, Doctor Ryan. Please hear me out before you slam me," she retorts, annoyance more than evident. I'd say pissed is the better term.

"I'm not 'slamming' you, Ellie. Calm down a minute. I think you're bright, so I want what's best for you. Getting published is huge. I'm trying to wrap my head around this. I want to help you to achieve the end goal here. It's my job to push." I put a hand on top of hers, having moved to sit beside her.

"Right. Push. Then pull. Hot, then cold. Nice to not-so-nice. That's what you do best," she says, cutting the air, calling me and my bullshit out without actually calling me out. She slips her hand from under mine. "Now, are you going to listen or do I need to talk to the department chair about how I need a new advisor, seeing as we seem to have an apparent conflict of interest here?" She gestures between us. "One I'm not sure either of us is fully acknowledging, or wants to admit, or knows what to do with, like you said." She crosses her arms across her chest, my eyes following the move.

What the actual fuck? I stand up and lean back on the desk a little, for distance. It's not her threat that confuses me; I know it's empty. The flush on her face confirms she's simply being the passionate Ellie I've come to know and respect in class, the same one who shines when she feels strongly about something. And the idea that this woman just might feel strongly enough about me to have researched what would happen when or if there ever was a conflict of interest between the two of us makes me giddy as fuck. *Hell, I'm an employee, and it took Mercer to tell me the steps I'd need to take if I decided to pursue her.*

We sit staring for a few minutes, seemingly collecting our thoughts, before Ellie makes the next move.

"Now are you ready to listen, Doctor Ryan?" she says, the bite to her voice the hottest sound I've ever heard.

"By all means, E, the floor's yours. Try to convince me your paper is valid." I wave my hands.

"In the words of Master Yoda: 'Do. Or do not. There is no try'. Watch and listen as I '*do*'. Don't '*try*' to underestimate me, Ace," she jabs, her tone now a little snarky for my taste. I get that she's pissed, however, I do admit I've been an ass more or less since she walked in.

"Be thankful I have a soft spot for you, Ellie. Students rarely get away with speaking to me in such a tone."

"Rarely?" she questions, probing for more.

"Well, yes, there are times I can be an ass and deserve a little lip," I share, and her eyes move to my mouth, before making a slow burn down the rest of me where I stand leaning against my desk. It takes a whole lot of restraint not to rush back to her, to show her what I think of her sassy mouth right now.

"And don't call me 'E'. It confuses me. I never know when we're being friends or when you're my professor." A hint of something passes over her face, the sincerity of her voice confirming what I already knew; she's feeling the same thing I am. *Confusion.*

"Friends." I pause. "Drop the 'Doctor' when we're not in class. It's pretentious, and drives me insane falling from your lips. Now, you done with all this bullshit? Ready to convince me, and give me time to figure out how the hell I can help you with this paper of yours, Ms. Hughes?" I ask, raising my brows, unable to hide the smirk pulling at my lips, seeing her flush in response to my words.

"Yeah," she pauses, cocking her head and watching me for a beat, "I can do that. Now that you're over your 'Star Wars is *my* favourite' nonsense and are ready to actually hear me."

Jesus, this girl. My trifecta.

"We good to go?" she says, adjusting her iPad and pulling out her notebook.

I nod.

"I've been doing a lot of research. I'm still working on which aspects of the feminist perspective I'll defend, but I've got heaps of points justifying that Leia's character was actually totally feminist—even if by accident, as some would try to claim," she says, flipping through the pages on her iPad, talking a mile a minute, giving me all kinds of points, a few points I truthfully would never have considered or seen her way until now. "...and she's feisty, fearless, I mean, she took that stormtrooper out in the first scene with her blaster, no hesitation, no fear. And...and, she's the one who leads them to the vent that lands them in the garbage chute, saving them in the end. Right? And this is all pretty much in the beginning. I can do forty pages, Ace. Easy."

"Hmmm, I've never looked at it from this point of view. I have to admit those are pretty good points," I compliment, earning me a sexy proud-of-herself smile before she goes on.

"Leia's wardrobe alone offers the theory that she wasn't seen as a sex object like, say, Wonder Woman with her tiny shorts, caked on make-up and cleavage-baring top." She closes her iPad, satisfied she's explained herself.

"You've not won yet, E. Two words: gold bikini," I smile, knowing I've got her; I've thrown her a wrench. I just hope she doesn't wield it at me. We've been here for about an hour and I'll be honest, Ellie has me convinced. Princess Leia absolutely should not only be given a lightsaber, but be given the right to maim whomever she wants, as the woman certainly earned it. Princess Leia is a completely kick-ass character that I've got a whole new appreciation and respect for. Same goes for the woman sitting in front of me.

Ellie has done an excellent job of explaining as well as defending, all the while justifying how Leia's character is not only a leader and politician, but a fearless fighter. Ellie's done her research, her list goes on and on. I'm sitting here listening, completely smitten with this girl; her tenacity, instincts, and determination. Even though I continue to push her buttons, at this point I'm having too much fun watching her rebut my comments to tell her to go for it, that I'll support her tenfold.

"Please," she says, "have I taught you nothing? Leia might be showing some skin in one out of the many movies in which Fisher plays her, but don't kid yourself, Ace. She kills Jabba the Hutt in that gold little number. Therefore, allowing women worldwide the capacity to graciously accept and not mind fulfilling the stupid fantasies of men around the world as they role-play in replicas of the infamous gold bikini to manchildren oblivious of its irrelevance. The bikini was a ploy to pique the interest of dirty-minded little tweens. And it worked, but in no way does it do anything but add a little tarnish to Leia as a feminist model."

"Well, fuck me," I blurt, causing her to laugh and it's like music to my cock. *Fuck her mind is both sharp and sexy.*

"Convinced now?" she beams, looking to me for the approval she knows she's going to get.

"Beyond." I catch her gaze, holding it. Willing her to see. To know. I'm already convinced, conflicted, and completely interested in the power that is her, that is Ms. Ellie Raine Hughes.

Unfortunately, I'm not sure what to do with her and her Force just yet.

"Now let's hope J.J. Abrams fully keeps up Leia's amazingness in *The Force Awakens.* I'm curious to see how big her role will be and if he'll keep her as a kick-ass heroine," she says, bringing me out of my thoughts.

"Yeah, let's hope. I hear he's done a good job. Respecting the franchise, at least," I add.

"God, he better not fuck shit up. Oops, sorry," she says and covers her face, embarrassed. "Sorry, I get excited. I didn't mean to expose my penchant for potty mouth when I'm passionate about a topic."

"Nothing to worry about, Ellie. I've heard it before, maybe just not from such a passionate young woman." *With such a pretty mouth,* is what I'd like to add, but obviously don't.

"Okay, good," she laughs. "Thankfully, it's out in December, so only a few more weeks before we see," Ellie says, packing up her stuff, an action I hate. I've enjoyed our time together and crave more of listening to and getting to know her.

"By the way, I'm in the middle of setting up an optional meeting time for you and the others in my advisory group. I was able to reserve one of the large study rooms on the second floor of the library. I've booked it for December 13th, from four- to seven p.m. This way, I figure I can assist you with research or anything else you guys may need before the winter break. You might even be able to help each other out, as well. I hope you'll take advantage." *Of me,* I want to add, but, of course, don't.

"That'll be great. I'll see you there. And thanks for finally listening, Ace. I knew I'd convince you." She exits my office with a look of triumph on her face.

"If this shit keeps up, it will be me trying to *convince her*...that she's mine," I mutter, closing the door behind me so I can flag a few feminist film theory articles to help her—and maybe myself—before my next class.

Chapter 29

Ace

I'M SICK.

I need to seek psychiatric advice or help or something.

I bet Mercer will know a good shrink.

I'm sitting on my couch on Monday night, following my meeting with Ellie, watching *Kill Bill* accompanied by a raging hard-on, one that springs to life whenever I think of her. Instead of going out with Mercer and our buddy, Dan, here I am. Just me, Beatrix Kiddo, and my rock-hard cock, along with memories of the wonder that is E.

Ellie Raine Hughes, I blame you.

That punch-to-the-gut beautiful girl who steals a few seconds of my breath each time she walks into the same room as me. Today she impressed the hell out of me. I knew I was challenging her. Of course, Leia is an awesome feminist heroine to explore. What I didn't expect was for Ellie to talk circles around each of my arguments and counter-points, her quick wit and outside-the-box thinking were such a turn on. Never have I wanted to cross the teacher/student line with her as badly as I did today. Ellie's determination alone makes her one of the sexiest women I've ever met. Couple that with her beauty and brains and, fuck me, I'm screwed. I'm not sure how much longer I can control these feelings. I might need to do some serious research on that contacting the chair option. If the little jump my dick just made is any indication of his opinion, I'd say he's on board with the idea.

She's all I can think about whenever anything remotely Tarantino-related comes up. *Shit, who in their right mind sits watching* Kill Bill *with a boner?* I seriously do need to see a shrink.

"Fuck it," I grunt, taking my engorged cock out of my gym shorts, and taking the lube out of the side table. I put a generous amount on my palm before rubbing it all over my cock. Crouching down in the couch, spreading my legs a bit more, I allow my mind to begin playing the reel marked "Ellie".

"Fuck, yes." I stroke my cock to the images, picturing the curve of her ass, the sway in her hips as she walked past me this morning, the way her tits move when she's breathing heavily, how they'll look in my hands. "Oh shit." I move my hand up and down, accelerating the pace. Don't get me started on that delicious scent she gives off, whatever the fuck it is. It might as well be called "Make Me Jizz" in a bottle, because it's a direct hit to my cock every single time I get a whiff of her. *God, how I want to taste every inch of her, see if her whole body smells as good as I imagine. Soon.*

Wrapping my hand around my pulsing cock a little harder, I start moving up and down my shaft, faster and faster while I continue picturing Ellie. I imagine it's her hand in place of my own. Letting out a low growl, I pick up the pace, jerking myself off. "Fuuuck!" I shout, breathing heavily, my cum now covering my hands and stomach.

I'm struggling to do the right thing here. The right thing for both of us. I know there are ways around it, it's a possibility to be together but why risk everything we've each accomplished so far? Why give the school's governing body reasons to doubt either of our credibilities?

But goddammit, it's becoming harder to resist her. That fiery hair when the light hits it just right, her smart mouth, and the way she puts a spin on her answers to all of my questions when in class. Challenging me, knowing full well I love it.

I fucking love it.

But how long can I resist crossing the line?

Chapter 30

Ellie

MY MIND WON'T stop racing.

I keep replaying every encounter I've had with Ace over and over in my mind. Revisiting every stolen glance, harmless touch, and subtle innuendo we've shared. I've come to a realization. I, Ellie Hughes, am indeed irrevocably hot for teacher.

I stretch my knee out a few times to try to loosen some of the tightness I'm feeling after a hard physio session this afternoon. I hate to admit it, but I'm starting to agree with Doctor Robinson's decision not to let me compete. But not even my knee pain can keep my mind from drifting back to Ace. Ace Ryan is handsome, smart, mostly kind, and—best of all—he challenges me. I wanted to punch him in the throat last week at our meeting: who the hell did he think he was, doubting my *Force*? Lucky for him, he converted from the dark side to my way of thinking.

But, seriously, how does one go about telling their professor that they'd like to explore the obvious connection, along with what's under his clothes while we're at it, too? I've looked up U of T's codes of conduct on the topic and it's not like it can't happen, we'd just have to follow the outlined steps. Steps that include writing a letter to the chair and admitting a transgression, which in turn would have them impose third-party involvement where my grades are concerned. It would mean that Ace's judgement would come into question, requiring another person to oversee my grades, and I'd hate to have him put under a microscope like that. *Jesus, slow down, Ellie. Next you'll be standing outside his window in a wedding dress, a love song blaring from the boombox over your head.* It's probably just some schoolgirl crush, a one-sided fantasy I've clearly created, a side-effect from working as a Phone Sex Superhero. Then again, he acts as though he's interested, his words and body language matching my own when we're together. *Ugh. I hate this.*

Beep, beep.

Thank goodness, saved by the beep. I don't bother looking at the screen—I need the distraction.

"Breathless Whispers. Let me leave you breathless," I say sexily into the line.

"It's Ben."

"Hey, Ben. I'm glad you called me, I've been lonely sitting here, I've missed talking to you. Have you been being a good little boy like Mommy asked?" I roll my eyes at how insane I sound, asking him this. Talk about customer service. But this is Ben's thing, so I give him what he wants.

"No. I've been bad, Chanel. So bad, I need you to punish me. I masturbated at work this afternoon while sitting at my desk."

"Oh, Benny, you have been a very bad boy. Mommy's going to have to punish you *hard* for that. You know you're not supposed to touch your cock in public," I tell him in a low, scolding tone. Ben and I have been talking for about a month now, I'd guess he's in his early-twenties and might have a few "mommy" issues. He's into punishment. Nothing gets him hotter than when I virtually spank his bad boy ass. The first time, I had to move the mouthpiece of my headset away so I could giggle. I never expected elastics to have such an impact. Now I play along, being his punishing "Mommy", as he's come to call me. Every call involves him wanting me to consequence him for masturbating in public somewhere: a park, a cab, the TTC, a train, and now at his work.

Grabbing my container of elastics, I give Ben the command I know he's waiting for. "I'm ready to punish you, Ben. You know the drill. Naked, on all fours, ass up, on your bed. Wait for me while I get the best tools to punish your naughty ass. And do not touch yourself. Do not stroke that hard naughty cock of yours." I extend a thick elastic band across my thumb and index finger then position it over the sleek black desktop, ready for the show to begin.

"Are you hard, Ben?"

"Yes."

"Are you Mommy's bad boy?"

"Shit, yes. I'm so bad." *Snap, snap, snap.* "Argh! Fuck. More!"

"I bet you liked that. Your ass is turning a nice shade of pink, Ben. Mommy's just warming up. Would you like more, my naughty boy?"

With a grunty moan, he mutters, "Harder. It feels good."

"It's not supposed to feel good, Ben." *Whack, whack, whack*. I slam a ruler down hard on the desk. "You're a bad boy taking that big juicy cock out at work. Stroking it where anyone could see. Is that what you like, Ben, the rush of getting caught? Men and women watching you touch the smooth skin as you move your hand up and down, slowly at first, then faster and faster?"

Whack, whack, whack!

"Oh shit, yes, yes, ahhhhh…Mommy…thank you…"

I smile. Satisfied, once again having helped my little fucked-up friend, Ben. *Wonder where he'll whip it out next week?* I put my elastics and ruler away.

I'm about to change my status to yellow, when the line beeps.

Noticing it's Jake, I decide that heating up my coffee can wait…

Chapter 31

Ellie

GOOD THING IT'S been quiet thus far tonight.

I decided to work the seven- to eleven p.m. shift because I have a paper due for my Film Noir course. It's probably my favourite class this semester—aside from my classes with Ace—but for different reasons, obviously. We're studying the femme fatale, and I'm seriously killing this assignment. I decided to go with a slightly modern, subtle femme; I'm defending Winona Ryder's role in *Heathers* as being one of the greatest femme fatales of all time, not simply the 80's.

But I've been falling a bit behind lately with my course load. Between working three- to four nights a week, school, plus going to physio and the gym, I find I'm starting to struggle a bit with my thesis for Ace's class. I can't seem to pinpoint the appropriate feminist perspective to apply and defend to help prove my thesis. Thankfully, Ace has been willing to meet with me when I need, and replies to my emails quickly. He really is a great support, not to mention how much I'm enjoying spending time getting to know him, bit by bit. I'm hoping to pick his brain a little more at the upcoming group work session.

Another hour and I'm done for the weekend. I booked off Breathless Whispers Saturday and Sunday this weekend, something I haven't done since I started. I figured one weekend off in three months isn't too greedy.

The familiar beep brings me out of my Ace-induced thoughts. I smile, seeing that it's Jake calling again.

Picking up the line after the second ring, I feel excitement brewing in my belly. I find myself looking forward to Jake's calls more and more.

"Breathless Whispers, how can I leave you breathless tonight, Jake?" I purr sexily, hoping we can get right into it tonight, as thoughts of Ace have me a little more eager than normal. Jake and I have had a few calls that have been more companion than sexy lately, but I'm hoping tonight isn't one of those calls.

"Chanel, you sound sexy, lovely. Have you been waiting for my call?" he demands, voice firm.

"Honestly, yes. I've been sitting here thinking about you. I was hoping you'd call, that we could play."

"I'm happy to hear that. It's actually my birthday. I'm about to go out and celebrate, but I wanted to take the edge off first. I knew you could help me out. I want you to strip for me. I want some birthday sex, beautiful. Think you can do that?"

Smiling, I reach into my camouflage messenger bag, and grab my iPod, the perfect song already in mind.

"Happy Birthday, Jake. Get ready for me to blow your mind, birthday boy…" I tell him, confidently scrolling down to "Birthday Sex" by Jeremih before placing it on the docking station and turning up the volume so that Jake will be able to hear when I hit play. More confident than I think I've ever been, I'm ready to blow his mind. That's what Jake does for me, he gives me the boost I need, never judging. He always seems to support me, like he knows I falter, and when I'm unsure he helps to move our scenes or roles along. It's as if he calls to help me practice, and I want to give him this without hesitation or doubt. Then Ace's face pops into my mind again, giving me the final push I need. I'll do this as if it's for *him.*

"Lay on your bed, Jake. Close your eyes, listen to my moves, my voice, and my excitement at getting to do this for you. I'm so wet and we haven't even begun. It's what you do to me."

"Fuck. I can't wait. Your voice alone gets me so hard. Tell me, is it your real voice or one of those voice changer things?"

"Aaaah, let's not worry about that. Let's focus on giving you a happy birthday."

"All right, I'm ready. I'm laying on my bed."

"Perfect." I put the phone on speaker, hit play on my iPod, and stand in the room's open space, facing the mirror so I can mimic what I'd do if I were actually stripping for a man. Or better yet, one man in particular: *Ace*. As soon as the sexy lyrics can be heard throughout the room, I begin to sway.

"Happy Birthday, Jake. I've just stepped into the bedroom. I'm wearing a black silk robe, and garters attached to sheer stockings peek out beneath the silky material. I'm inching in closer towards the centre of the room, and my hips begin a gentle sway to the music's sexy rhythm. A hint of my cleavage pokes out the top of my robe. Stopping at the foot of your bed, I reach for the clip in my hair and release it, letting my long curls fall, cascading down my chest and back—"

"Fuck, you're beautiful, that sexy as fuck hair. I can't wait to run my hands through it."

"Soon, handsome. I have a show to give you first," I assure him, pulling him back to my show. "Picture me again, Jake, see me as I turn, giving you my back, my hair reaching down, kissing just above my ass. I'm undoing the robe's ties, sliding it off my shoulders now, exposing the soft skin of each. I turn to look at you over my shoulder, our eyes catch, your intense eyes make my breath hitch, and I want nothing more than to please you. I lower the robe completely, tossing it aside, leaving me in nothing more than a black-and white lace teddy with bustier top, my ass cheeks exposed waiting to be spanked, caressed and kissed by the birthday boy. Would you like that, Jake?"

"Hell, yeah, Chanel, shake that ass for me, lovely. God. You really are perfect. I'm so fucking hard. Tell me what's next."

"I've turned around to face you. Climbed up onto the foot of your bed, my legs on either side of yours, you try to touch me, but I swat your hand away. I'm still not done. Reaching behind me, I unclasp the top of the bustier, my heavy breasts needing release. Being under your intense gaze is too much, my body's overheating, ready to combust if you don't put your hands on me."

"Jesus, fuck, I want my hands on you too. God, I want to suck on those sweet tits of yours. I know how tight those nipples will feel on my tongue. Jesus, Chanel. I'm not gonna make it to the end. You've got me wound too tight." His breathing is laboured. I decide to abandon the strip and ride I had planned and opt for a surprise finish.

"I'm slinking myself up your body, Jake. My nipples grazing along your skin excite us both, the feel of you all rough and hard making me crazy with need. Stopping at your hard cock, I pop you in my mouth a few times, coating you with my saliva, prepping you, before moving to push my tits together around your wet cock. Moving forward a touch, I wrap my tits around it in a cocoon, nestling you in there perfectly before I begin moving up and down, your cock gliding in between my deep cleavage, the saliva making it easy for me to fuck you with my tits. You're so fucking hard, Jake, so fucking hard..." I breathe heavily as he moans. "Being too excited, you move our position, making it so that you can touch me. Your big, strong hands move to where I want them most. Thankfully, you know just what I need, honey. You're sliding your fingers inside my heat, do you feel how drenched you make me, how excited doing this to you gets me? Your cock is so hard and sexy between my tits, Jake. God, I might come from the view alone. Oh God, yes, you've given me two fingers, and are now playing with my clit with your thumb, which is making me move faster and faster over your cock, squeezed right up tight between my tits."

"For fuck sakes, I knew those tits would feel incredible. Fuck, Fuck. Yes, fuck, I'm gonna fucking come so hard right now..."

Chapter 32

Ace

WATCHING DYLAN AND Liz makes me nauseated, yet I'm happy for my friend.

Mercer and I are sitting in our regular booth at Riffs, and I'm dying to rib Dylan. The guy's been scarce for the last month and it's because of the fine young waitress that is Liz, the same one both Mercer and I knew would be a good match for our little Dyl.

"Okay, babe. Have a good shift, I'll be here until your shift is done then I'll drive you home." Dylan kisses Liz on the nose, and Mercer and I both chime in a little "aww" at the same time.

"Shut it, assholes," Dylan says, and Liz laughs.

"Sorry guys. How are you? It's been longer than usual," a smiling Liz asks.

"We're good, thanks. You?" I ask her back.

She beams, "I'm excellent." She glances at Dylan and he grins back at her. It's fucking adorable. I never would have thought that Dylan would be this guy, but it looks good on him. Reiterating that I want this. With *her*—Ellie.

"Okay, welllll, I better get back to work. Have fun, good to see you guys. I'll see if I can pop by in a bit," she says, waving bye after kissing Dylan one last time.

"What a difference a month makes, eh, Dylan?" Mercer jabs as Dyl finally sits down.

"Cheers." We all raise our beer glasses.

"To Dylan, finally taking the plunge," I add.

"Piss off, you both knew I'd ask her out sooner or later."

"Yeah, I'm still shocked she agreed, though. I mean, she could have had all this," Mercer points, circling his face. "I've been told that I'm one hell of a tall drink of chocolate milk. Just as sweet, too."

"Fuck me. I'm surrounded by idiots," I chuckle into my beer.

"Whatever, man, I know I'm hot," Mercer laughs, and I roll my eyes.

"Speaking of love lives, how're things with the forbidden student?" Dylan asks.

"Ellie. Her name's Ellie."

"Right, sorry. How are things with her?" Dylan probes.

"Complicated. I'm all over the place where she's concerned. I'm getting to my breaking point. I think it's time I sit us down and speak honestly about how we're both feeling. I know I'd like to take her out, spend some off-campus time together, get to know each other better, but we need to be careful about it. Maybe it's better to wait until she graduates in April? It's already December, I'm sure we could hold off, if we decide to give it a go. Besides, the documentary is taking up all my spare time right now, anyway," I share, before taking a long pull of my beer.

"Blah, blah. All right, you like each other. Who cares about waiting? Just be discreet. Touch behind closed doors," Dyl quips.

Who says shit like this?

"I can't believe they let you teach higher education," Mercer says, shaking his head.

"Whatever, I'm a philosopher. I see things differently," Dylan retorts.

"Understatement," I cough.

"Piss off. Now let's cut to the chase," Dylan says, leaning in.

"How're the phone sex line calls going? You're a shit text-er. Leave your best friend hanging without any deets for weeks. I mean, who the fuck does that?"

"Me, I guess, eh? Like I've got the time to text you back enough details to satisfy that enquiring mind of yours."

"True. But Liz is into a bit of role-play, so share, man," he whispers, and Mercer cuffs him upside the head.

"You'll probably have to block his number. I can only imagine his texts," Mercer says, then adds, "Our very own Barbara Walters." He bursts out into a deep chuckle.

"Whatever, man. I only care that things are going well. It's a big deal, it's TIFF!" says Dylan.

"Right. It's not that you want the smutty details for your own sex life, like you just said," Mercer points out.

"No, no, I do. But I want to make sure it's going smoothly, too. I mean, if not, I know a few—"

I cut Dyl off. "Nope. Thanks, but I'm good. Actually really good, now if you'll shut up, I'll tell you about it."

"It's about bloody time," Dylan says, handing out the round of beers the server just dropped off.

I spend the next while telling them about the four places I've called, share a few of the experiences and how awkward it was the first few times, and how I opted to use the Voice Changer app I'd found in the App Store, a precaution to ensure I'd never have to worry about having my voice recognized. I know it's pretty out there to think someone I know would be a phone sex operator, but since Chelsea was, I didn't want to take a chance. *You never really know, right?*

"Have you gotten off, though, is what I really want to hear. Don't get me wrong, I'm glad you're getting good stuff but come on, I need more than that."

"All right, only because you've been so patient and a good listener,

I'll share a few secrets with you."

"Thank fuck," Mercer sighs, "otherwise, we'll never hear the end of his whining." This time, it's Mercer who gets the cuff upside the head.

"There's this one chick. I've gotten off with her once." I don't bother telling them that she reminds me of Ellie, that she's got a quick wit about her and the times we've just talked she seems like an intelligent girl, like Ellie. I'm dying to ask her her story, but I worry she'd freak out if I got too personal. I don't bother telling them that I picture Ellie every time we role-play, either. Some things need to remain secret.

"I knew it. I knew you'd get off while doing this movie. How could you not, it's all sex, all the time," Dylan says and I need to clarify this right now.

"Calm your voice, Dyl. You can't tell anyone that I got off. It's not exactly my proudest moment. The last thing I want is for that to get blown up out of context. It was one time and I won't let it happen again."

"Of course, man. We'd never say anything. You know that."

"It's not like I expected to, but this one girl, she's gotten under my skin. I called in one night, and we got to talking, she got down to it quick and the next thing I knew I was jerking off to her voice" *(picturing Ellie)* "and the crazy story she was telling me. Now almost every time I call, my dick ends up hard as fuck, but I ignore it, knowing I have a job to finish and my getting off isn't a part of it. It's crazy, though." I also leave out that we've spent time just talking too, spending ten or fifteen minutes sharing random thoughts and questions about life and so on. That with her, I feel like I've developed a friendship, which is all kinds of fucked up I realize, but it's true.

"That's awesome, man. Your job is the best. Maybe I should have gone into film," Dylan jokes.

"Question. Don't you film and record all of your calls and interviews? So are you telling us that you've made your own brand of Ace Ryan porn?" Mercer asks before he and Dylan break out in laughter.

"Yeah, I had been. But I've since deleted those particular ones and I've stopped recording when I feel the call will escalate, so sorry, guys, no Ryan originals for you."

"Thank God," Dylan adds, lifting his beer. "Honestly, are they really that good, though?"

"Yeah, some really are. It's crazy how versatile and completely professional they are. I've thrown some crazy scenarios at a few of them and they take it all in stride, determined to see me to the end of my fantasies. It's insane how they can slip in and out of different roles. I've been impressed. The biggest downside for me still is trying to convince Dee, that underage girl I told you about, to meet me so I can get her some help. I'm still trying to convince her. I was thinking of talking to Chelsea to see if she might be free to help me figure out a way to make it happen. I have another girl I'd really like to interview, too, but I'm not sure she'll believe that I'm not just the regular caller I convinced her I was over the last few months."

"I'll update Chels and see what she says. Maybe she can talk to Dee, maybe if you call and have Chels talk to her it would help? And I'm sure I could probably get my buddy Diego to get her a job at his diner; the tips would be crazy seeing as it's over in the finance district. It might help to entice her to talk, knowing she'd have a safer job lined up," Mercer offers.

"Hey. That might actually work. From what she's told me, she isn't making as much as the other places. But she's in deep, so she can't walk away unscathed. I guess the boss has been roughing a few of them up, a means to send a message."

"Fuck, Ace. We need to get her out of there," Dylan huffs.

"I know. I'm working on it. I've been in constant contact with Detectives Hernandez and Muller. They work in Vice and Drugs, here in the city. The more I spoke with Dee and her friend, I realized I needed to involve the police; it was getting too big for me to try and save them alone. Besides, I have all the recordings, which might really help down the line if it ends up going to court."

"Jesus. That's impressive, Ace. Those girls are lucky you care enough to help."

"Yeah, in the long run, I hope. Maybe once the dust settles and they see they can have a better life. I have a feeling they're going to be pissed for a long time once they process everything that sleazeball of a boss has done to them."

"You're doing the right thing. I know it's tough, but you're a good guy, Ace. The girls will see that in the end," says Dylan.

"I agree," says Mercer, before adding, "we're here for you if you need our help in any way, eh? You know that?"

"I do, and I appreciate that."

"Fuck. I really did pick the wrong job," Dylan remarks. "You're like a detective filmmaking-savant superhero for the sex trades. Your film is not only going to cause waves, bringing awareness about real issues, it might actually stop a few assholes from exploiting kids. I'm fucking impressed, man," Dylan says, saluting his glass my way before taking a sip.

"Thanks, guys." I raise my glass. "Now, let's hope all the pieces fall into place to make everything happen the way I'd like it to."

Chapter 33

Ellie

"I CAN'T BELIEVE you're going on a date with Jax, and that you're dragging me into this mess. I doubt Professor Ryan would condone you banging your thesis advisor," I say cheekily, slipping a gold hoop into my earlobe in the small hallway mirror.

How I wish Ace would condone banging me, though! This tension and back and forth between us has been killing me. Being with him in his office again last week nearly did me in. The need to kiss him, to feel him, to finally be with him, was extremely hard to ignore. Needless to say, I left his office a needy pile of wanton frustration.

"I'm not going on a date with him. *We* are," she says grinning, applying a coat of pink Devine lipgloss by Mac right beside me.

"No, I'm your tagalong to make it look like it's not a date when we both know it is."

"Whatever, chaperone."

"And you say I make googly eyes at Ace? Hello, pot, have you met my friend? We call her kettle." I step back, the quick movement making my knee twinge, as I assess my appearance.

"It's still not a date. It's a bunch of friends going to see the most anticipated movie of all time. You of all people should be happier than a pig in shit right now that I managed to swing these tickets." She gives me a stern look.

"Oh, trust me, I'm flipping out. I'm so excited I could die. But I'm not blind to your tactics, my friend."

"Hey, it's not my fault Jax happened to be the one who invited us. And insisted that you come. But honestly, Els, it's Star-fucking-Wars! You never turn that shit down."

"You're right. I would have had to cut a bitch if you'd told him I didn't want a ticket," I laugh.

"See? Not a date. We're all friends," she harrumphs.

Rolling my eyes, I still call bullshit. I know damn well this is a date disguised as a group outing. Apparently Jax's little sister, Jade, works at the Varsity and VIP Theatre over on Bloor Street. From what I understand, Jade won some employee contest they held last month; the prize, an exclusive pre-screening of the *Star Wars: The Force Awakens* for up to one hundred guests. So she was super sweet and gave Jax a bunch of tickets for the screening to invite whomever he wanted. Court happened to be top of his list, as she described how this "non-date" came about.

"Do I look okay?" she asks, smoothing down her mid-length sweater dress, which is paired with a black cinched belt and knee-high boots, fitting her like a glove, accentuating her subtle curves.

"You look stunning for our date. Can we go now, please?" I ask, putting on my black faux fur-lined hooded winter coat from Rudsak. Unlike Court, I opted for casual tonight, pairing a dark green v-neck sweater with my favourite pair of jeans and tan Ugg boots. I'm not trying to impress anyone; therefore, I'm comfy, although the sweater dips enough in the front that I'll still look sufficiently sexy should we decide to go out somewhere afterward.

"YOU HAVE GOT to be shitting me. Courtney Liza Pierce, tell me you didn't know he'd be here," I demand, squeezing Court's arm as we make our way to where Jax is standing inside the expansive theatre lobby surrounded by a group of people. A group that includes Ace-flipping-Ryan!

He hasn't spotted me yet. He's too busy laughing with two guys, one who looks likes Dr. Mercer Reynolds, but the hat is making it hard to be certain from this distance.

"Can't do that, bestie. Sorry. It was top secret. I knew you'd deny yourself this once-in-a-lifetime opportunity if you knew he'd be here."

"Easy, Drama. It's a preview screening, not an invitation to write the screen adaptation for *She's Come Undone* by Wally Lamb. *That* would be a once-in-a-lifetime opportunity. I could have waited like the rest of the world to see this." I try to steer her to the side so we can make our way to Jax unnoticed.

"Yeah, that's a lie. We both know this is right up at the top of your geek list, to see *The Force Awakens* before the masses. I know you, Els."

"Okay, okay, you're right. It's totally once-in-a-lifetime. But you should have told me he was going to be here."

"Boo-hoo. You'll get over it. Besides, you two are close. We both know it. I'm hoping this will help push you two to even more closer-ness. That would be epic."

"He's my professor, Court. It's a conflict, as is whatever's going on with you and Jax," I remind her.

"Well, sometimes you've gotta take a risk to see if it's worth it. You'll never know if you hide behind the whole 'he's my teacher' crap. We're adults, and on top of that we're graduating in less than three months. Soon it won't make a lick of difference."

"Huh. I hadn't thought of it like that."

"That's why you pay me the big bucks." She winks at me. "Want to wait here, and I'll shoot over to Jax and let him know we're here, then we can grab our popcorn? That way you can avoid Ace for a few more minutes."

"Okay. I'll meet you right here," I agree, standing off to the side.

"You're such a chickenshit," she mutters, walking off towards Jax.

After what feels like forever, I decide I'm tired of waiting in the corner like a loser. Court's obviously in a Jax trance and needs a reminder that I'm here. Moving through the crowd, my eyes find my targets. I'm too focused to realize I'm heading into the eye of a hurricane, one I was set on avoiding for as long as I could. I'm a constant voice of "excuse me's" and "sorry's", and I'm almost to them when I smell it.

Him. His now familiar scent that has created an imprint on my senses even when he isn't around. I'll know his smell for the rest of my life. The earthy smell that is purely his and his alone.

A gentle grasp on my arm to steady me confirms I've walked right into him. His hard chest acts as a cushion for my face, another clue, as I slam right into the storm that is Ace Ryan.

"Shit, I'm sorry. I wasn't paying attention," I say, meeting his surprised eyes.

"E, are you okay?" He slides his hand down to my wrist to take my hand, but quickly releases it, realizing what he's done. I feel the loss, and think I hear him murmur something about soft skin. I want to ask him if he'd like to feel more, maybe, say, my whole body? But I bite my tongue instead. *Who knows if I even heard him correctly?* Clearly, Courtney is getting inside my head.

"Yeah. I'm good. I'm so sorry. I was keeping an eye on Courtney, trying to make my way to her. It's so busy in here, I was worried I'd lose her."

"No. It was my fault, Ellie. I was focused on something too." I'm trying really hard to pretend he didn't mean his focus was on me, because that wouldn't be good. *Right?*

Meeting his gaze, I see him smirking as a throat clears beside us and I step back. Ace puts his hands in his pockets. I nod to Mercer.

"Hi, sorry, let's try this again. Good evening, Doctor Ryan, Doctor

Reynolds." I try to regain some composure and offer them both what I hope is my least awkward smile. *Oh God, do they realize their last names combined make…?* I tilt my head, assessing them as they stand before me. They must know, but I can't not ask. "Hey, do you guys kno—"

Laughing, predicting the epiphany I've just come upon, Ace finishes my thought. "Yes we are aware that together we are Ryan Reynolds. It's been years of jokes, trust me." He rolls his eyes.

"Yeah, in university they called us 'The Ryan Reynolds'," Mercer adds, shaking his head. "We are that lame."

I nod, unable to hide my laughter. "That's so bad. I can only imagine. Ha! Ryan Reynolds." I motion between the two. "Well, it was good to see you both. I'd better go find Courtney, she has my ticket." I wave. I'm about to move around Ace and Mercer when Ace moves in close to my ear.

"See you around, E," he says, and rubs the inside of my wrist as I pass.

My voice is non-existent, I can't seem to find any words. Instead, I'm too focused on how much more I'd like to feel him touch me.

"Hey. Els, where ya been?" Court asks, as I rock up beside her.

"Are you kidding? You were supposed to come back to me. What, being around Jax makes you that forgetful? Are we that smitten, my little kitten?" I say, using her words against her.

"Whatever. He's hot. My brain goes mush. I'm a bad friend, blah, blah." We both laugh.

"You really are. Luckily, I understand. Now let's go find our seats. And then you can buy me popcorn." I nudge her.

"About that," she pauses. "Don't kill me."

"You know when you start a sentence like this I know it's bad, right? What's going on, Court?" I ask, hoping I'm not going to have to kill my friend in public.

"I've got bad news, babe," she says. "Seeing as there are so many of us, we have assigned seats. Just like with *Fifty Shades*, it's too busy. This is their way to control it. So we're not sitting together." She drops the tiny bomb. I sigh, then she leans in to whisper: "I'm beside Jax, though. You okay if I don't ask him to trade you, like the good friend I usually am would?"

"You really are the worst friend. You know this, right?"

"The worst." She jumps up and down.

"Fine. Ditch me. Give me my ticket and let's go so you can get me my popcorn before you go suck face on your date, you ass," I smile, looping my arm in hers as we walk to the concession stands.

"Thank you. You're the best, Els. Layered butter for you tonight."

Chapter 34

Ellie

YOU'VE GOT TO be kidding me.

Now I know what Courtney was referring to when I overheard her telling Jax that she thinks they pulled it off. And cue the "it" she was talking about…

"Ellie." Ace's husky voice appeals to every inch of my body as I slip into my seat. The one right next to his, of course.

"Ace, hi. No Mercer?" I swear my voice squeaks, as I look past him, clearly my name *should* be Captain Obvious.

"No, we got separated, too." He looks past me, referencing my missing friend. "Looks like it's you and me." His voice drops, and I swear it takes all my might not to admit how good the words "you and me" sound used in the same sentence when he says it.

"Yeah, looks that way." I jam popcorn into my mouth, causing him to laugh out loud, the deep sound making my body hum with awareness. *I'm so screwed.*

"You're cute, Ellie." He leans in close, something he seems to like to do, and I wonder if he realizes how much I like it. "I'm excited to watch this with you." He runs his thumb under my bottom lip, and I almost jolt off the seat with the force of his touch.

"Butter. There was a bit of butter there. Sorry," he says, moving his thumb to his mouth and licking the butter off.

"No. Don't be sorry. I liked it," I whisper, so low I'm not sure he catches it, but he does. *Oh. My. God! Did I just say that in my outside voice?*

"Jesus. You're killing me," I hear him mutter.

"Mmm," I stuff more popcorn into my mouth, mortified, as he chuckles beside me, his shoulder brushing mine as he shakes.

"Fuck, you're sweet."

"Mmm hmm." I stuff more popcorn in my mouth, still speechless, but saved by the dimming of the lights. Knowing we're both huge Star Wars fans, I know I'm safe from further words.

He chuckles, gripping my knee. "Let's sit back and watch your girl."

I nod, appreciating his Leia reference.

After a few beats, swallowing, I find my voice and lean into him this time, "My *woman*, you mean. And I bet she's totally kick-ass."

My comment causes him to bark out a deep laugh before looking me in the eyes and telling me: "I think *you're* pretty kick-ass, Ms. Hughes."

"Ssssh!" someone hisses behind us.

With that little revelation, I spend the rest of Courtney's "non-date" enjoying one of the best dates I've had. And if I had big green ears, they would most definitely be twitching. *Like him I do, yes.*

Chapter 35

Ellie

"BREATHLESS WHISPERS—"

"Chanel, lovely. How are you?"

"Hey Jake," I reply excitedly. "I've been hoping you'd call again soon. It feels like it's been a while."

Seeing his name across the screen did make me happy. It's been weird not talking to him for a few days. Strange as it may sound, I feel an attraction to this stranger. Talking to him excites me, and not only sexually, either. I'm curious about him, what he looks like, how he acts, what he does in his day-to-day life. Over the last few weeks, he's disclosed little things about himself: he's in his early-thirties, his favourite band is The Tragically Hip, he recently moved here, he's a movie buff, and Star Wars is his life, apparently. I might have fallen a little bit with that last revelation.

Truth be told, I'm intrigued. Jake sounds like my type. I know it's insane but I want to meet him in person. I think we'd make great friends, maybe even more. I know I can't (it's a serious no-no at Breathless Whispers; the Conrads would have my head on a plate) and that it's a silly *Pretty Woman* fantasy, but I do think about it. Maybe it's because I can't have Ace. Maybe on some level my brain is trying to manipulate my heart, when in reality both notions involving both men are beyond fucked up? One's my teacher, the other's a stranger. I definitely need a reality check. I'm sure even Destiny would tell me to put down whatever I'm smokin'. Lost in my wavering thoughts, Jake's voice soothes my uncertainty, his words bringing me back to him, or, rather, to my job.

"I missed talking to you too, lovely. Work's been crazy. My stu— pid job has been busy." He's quick to correct himself and I can't help wondering what he was going to say. "With the holidays coming, I've been on a deadline at work, trying to get things wrapped up before the break. Then I'll be taking some time off and working on a big side project."

"Well, I'm sorry to hear that. I'm glad you're calling now, though. And please tell me that this side project is something fun and sexy," I tease.

"I'm glad I called too. It's a fun project, there are some elements that are sexy, but I don't want to think about that right now. I need this tonight. I won't be calling again until after the holidays, beautiful."

"Boo." I offer my best pout. Over the past few weeks when Jake calls, it's not always to get off. Sometimes he simply likes to talk. He'll ask me things about my life—well, Chanel's, anyway—we talk about movies, books, dating and relationships. A few times I've even shared a few crazy caller stories with him. He tells me those ones are his favourites to listen to me talk about. Says he wishes he could see me telling him my adventures, wants to see if he's imagined my facial expressions and mannerisms the way I actually look when sharing my stories. Sometimes I feel as if I'm Scheherazade in *One Thousand and One Nights,* telling Shahryar different stories night after night. If you were to ask me honestly, I'd say Jake and I are sort of friends. Maybe even friends with phone sex benefits, if that makes any sense. Except that he pays for it, of course, and I do have a job to do. I clear my throat.

"I need you too. Are we gonna play tonight, Jake? You going to get me off as hard as I plan to get you off?"

"Fuck, yeah. I'm wound so tight from work and this gir—other shit going on."

"I'm sure I can help you relax. I happen to have a little present for you. I know how much you like Star Wars, and with Christmas coming this week, I ended up finding the perfect present when I was out shopping. I was grabbing a few new sets of panties and matching bras when I spotted it. Right away, I knew it was perfect, that I needed to grab it so I could send you off into the holiday season with a special treat if you called on time, and lucky for me, you did," I say in my sultriest voice.

"Oh yeah? This sounds promising." His deep voice sounding rich with excitement spurs me on.

"There I was in this lingerie store called *Avec Plaisir,* when I come across a table featuring Star Wars merchandise. With the new movie coming out, it seems *Star Wars* stuff is everywhere."

"Oh fuck. Chanel. Tell me it's a bikini."

Smirking, knowing this is going perfectly, I continue on. "Spying a sexy gold bikini, a perfect replica matching Princess Leia's, I thought of you right away," I pause, letting that sink in.

"You thought of me, beautiful?"

No, I thought of Ace, but I'll keep that bit to myself. Instead, I keep going.

"Yes I did. I thought of how I could buy it and wear it just for you. Give you me as your Leia for Christmas. Then let you tell me all the things you'd like to do to me for a change."

"Fuck, you might be perfect if not for this no-seeing, no-touching conundrum we have going on. You make me so fucking hard." His breathing increases, and, of course, so does mine. "Tell me about how you tried it on, Chanel. Describe how it didn't fully cover those amazing tits."

"That's exactly what happened. How did you know?" I giggle teasingly.

"'Cause I imagine your tits to be perfect. Beautifully formed, with pink-tipped nipples that beg for my touch. Fuck it, let's take turns telling this one tonight. Sound fun?"

"Yes," I reply, sounding out of breath.

"Let's pretend I'm your boyfriend and I knew you were trying it on, and I came into the change room. I got so turned on knowing what you were doing that I had to come in."

"God, that would be so hot. Let's do it."

"Okay, ready, lovely? I think we're both going to come so hard tonight."

"God, me too. Please, Jake. Let's continue," I say, needing to see how this all plays out. Once again, the idea of this very thing happening with Ace fuels my desire.

Jake's husky voice brings me back from my Ace-induced thoughts. "You've just finished trying it on and I'm so fucking turned on knowing what you're doing behind the curtain. I charge into the small change space. Tell me what happens next."

"I gasp. Then I say 'Jake, you can't be in here.' I try to scold, when really I want nothing more than for you to see me like this, my tits spilling out of the bikini's front, the small gold panties barely covering my aching pussy."

"Shit, that's perfect. I step in closer to you and tell you how fucking beautiful you are. I reach for the tie at your neck and pull."

"Yes, it falls, releasing my huge tits, my nipples instantly hardening with the cool air's kiss."

"I take them between my finger and thumb, rolling each tip and pulling, convincing them to get even harder for me."

"I moan, and beg for you to suck on them, aching to feel your tender bites and the swirl of your tongue as you drop your mouth to each one…"

"Hell, yeah, I love when you beg. Sucking on your nipples, I drop my hand down the front of your gold panties and rub your clit. Feeling how wet you are makes me growl."

"You push me back against the mirror, taking my mouth hard with your own. Then, next thing I know, you've turned me, my hands now bracing myself against the mirrored wall."

"Shit. I look you up and down all ready for me, sexy as fuck. I drop my jeans, grabbing my hard-as-stone cock needing to slip it inside you. Wanting nothing more than to feel your tight cunt hugging my cock while I thrust so fucking deep inside of you. Our eyes never break contact in the mirror."

Jesus, I'm soaked. This scenario is killing me. I'm lying on the chaise and it's taking everything in me not to slip my hand down the front of my jeans and get myself off. Despite being turned on by this man more times than I care to admit, I've only ever touched myself that one time. But right now, I'm wondering what the hell I found so wrong about giving into this type pleasure?

"You feel so goddamned good, Chanel. Seeing my cock slipping in and out, the sheen of your juices coating my cock, is going to make me come hard."

"Yes, keep fucking me, Jake. I move my hand to my tits, pulling each nipple while you watch in the mirror. God, I'm so close. I can feel my pussy quivering, it's intense, my legs are shaking, the drag and pull of your cock feels so good. Oh fuck, it's all blurring, I see flashes of lightsabers. Oh, oh, oh, fuuck, the stars…I see the staaaarrs!"

"Oh fuck. I'm coming…I'm gonna fucking come."

"Have a Merry Christmas, Jake," I whisper over his moans.

"God, you too, Chanel. Thank you."

Chapter 36

Ace

"GREAT SESSION, DOCTOR Ryan."

Melody Richards pats her pink mitten-covered hand against my chest while batting her blue eyes my way, thanking me as she walks through the library's exit door that I'm holding open. She's thanked me now at least ten times. I get it, but of course I simply tell her that she's welcome and that it was indeed a productive three hours.

Three hours of absolute torture for me, however. Tonight's study session went very well, and all of my students showed up, including Ellie—the torture factor. Ever since the movie, I've wanted to talk to her, to discuss whatever this is between us, but to my dismay, I haven't had a real chance to get her alone. Other than the couple of short office meetings since she began to really delve into her thesis (every time she stops by, it seems I'm booked, only having a couple of minutes to talk), we've emailed a bunch of times, but it's not like I can ask her how she feels about me over campus servers, now can I?

Now it's the last time I'll see her for three weeks and I hate it. I hate not knowing where things stand. Sure, we flirt, there are rare touches and glances, but I need verbal confirmation. And I want to stamp her body with my body, claiming her. I want her to be mine.

Fuck, I'm completely screwed. I tried to pretend that the only reason I set this up is because I'm a good professor and wanted to make sure everyone was on target with his or her thesis timeline. I'd be lying, though. I also set it up so I could make sure I saw her once more before the holiday break to make sure *she* was on track with her thesis, seeing as I know it's a difficult one. *Or so I try to tell myself, anyway.*

"I hope you all feel good heading into the break, but remember, the goal to keep up your pace is to work on plotting your first argument, and try to get ten pages or so done from that," I share, as I hold the door for the rest of the students.

The December air is cold. A few flurries flutter around us as we stand outside in the brisk night air, the breath of our words turning that familiar hue of greyish-white that accompanies winter, as we all give our final goodbyes and good wishes for the holiday. Most of the group is heading home for the almost three-week break. I myself will be staying in Toronto for most of the break this year. With the TIFF submission deadline around the corner, my goal is to be done sooner than later. Submissions timelines run from February to the beginning of July, but I want mine in with lots of time to spare. I have too much to work on if I want to submit it by mid-April. My plan, however, is to make the almost two-hour drive home to Kingston for a few days over Christmas, then come back and lose myself in the film. My grandparents would disown me if I tried to skip coming home altogether.

"Shit, I think I left my cell phone back on the table…" Ellie's distressed voice as she rifles through her purse breaks my train of thought. "You guys go ahead, I'm fine to walk from here. I'm just off campus, over there." She points across the expansive campus to where I can barely make out a set of traffic lights, then turns and heads back up the stairs.

"We can wait, Els," Dom calls out.

"Nah," she stops. "Honestly, I'm fine. I was planning on going to The Froth House to do some work anyway, so I'll actually be heading the opposite way. You guys go on, I'll see you next year," she laughs, while encouraging them to go. They all agree, waving goodbye.

The fuck I will.

The sound of the door opening draws my attention. Seeing Ellie walking down the library's steps, I make my way over to the bottom of the stairs where I've been shifting from one foot to the other for the last five minutes to keep warm.

"Jesus, Ace. You scared me," she says, finally looking up from her phone, her hand flying to her heart.

"You should be paying more attention to your surroundings, E," I chide, not happy that it's dark and she had no clue I was standing there until she practically collided with me. She would have no clue who or what could have been waiting for her.

"Oh please. It's the safest campus in Canada. Besides, I knew you were there," she lies.

"Bullshit. You need to pay attention, Ellie. I don't care what you say. Eyes wide at night, always."

"Yeah, yeah, okay, Professor. Now tell me, what are you doing here, anyway?" She cocks her head before making a show of looking around, to see if anyone else hung back.

"You're such a pest. You know that?"

"What? I was just making sure we were safe is all."

I want to kiss the shit out of that sassy mouth of hers.

"No, seriously, Ace. What are you doing?"

"Waiting for you. There wasn't a chance I was letting you walk home alone, and I felt like a coffee. Heard you were going." I step in closer to her, my nose immediately pleased to be reunited with its favourite scent. *Her.*

"And you assumed I wanted your company?"

"I know you do. As much as I want yours." I run my gloved finger along my bottom lip.

"Ace." She looks all around us again.

"*Ellie,*" I imitate her. "We need to talk, E. Seriously, I think we need to discuss us. This." I gesture between us.

"Us?" she questions. "Whatever do you mean, Professor?"

"Yeah, E. *Us*. I mean, I think we both feel the same way." I step closer, then take a quick look around us before leaning down to meet her ear. "Well, at least I hope you feel this too."

Thankfully, exhaling, she agrees. "I feel it. So much. Sometimes I worry it's unhealthy how much I feel it. I'm freezing. Let's go talk," she nods, giving me a heart-pounding grin.

Now to make her agree with my proposition.

Chapter 37

Ellie

"I'LL GET RIGHT to the point," Ace says, placing both of our lattes on the table I'd found for us while Ace insisted he buy our drinks. Suddenly, I find my hands sweaty and my heart making its way up my throat.

Did we really both admit to feeling this pull between us? Or is the December cold freezing my brain cells?

"Ellie, are you listening to me?"

"What? Sorry?"

He smirks. "I said I'll get right to the point."

"Yes. Right. By all means." I pick up the wonderfully hot mug, appreciating its warmth as it thaws my frozen hands.

"Look, I like you. For some reason, you affect me. I like being around you and I want more time with you. I'd like to get to know you, see where this could go. There. No more hot and cold," he says matter-of-factly.

"Wow, you have such a way with words. Could that have been anymore robotic, Wall-E? For a film guy, that sounded pretty lacklustre." I place a hand over my heart, having set the mug down for the full effect.

"Sorry. But I've wanted to say that for a while now. The thought of being interrupted made me rush it." He holds my gaze, the sincerity I see making me feel bad for teasing him. "In my head, it was much more eloquent. Honest." His nervous smile and that bloody dimple on his right cheek help to convince me.

God, this man could be my undoing.

"Take two?" I say, glancing around us. Thankfully, it's just he and I sitting in the back right now.

He nods.

"And...*action*," I call, leaning in closer to the table.

"Ellie. I like you. Aside from being the hottest woman I think I've ever had the pleasure of laying my eyes on, your intelligence is mesmerizing, and your brain is sexy as hell. The way you look when you're passionate about something makes my body yearn to be closer to you, to be on the receiving end of that force—that look. You surprise me with your brilliance and make my cock hard with your quick wit, especially when you demand that I hear you out. And please note, I do hear you, but it seems I have a one-track mind where you're involved. I'm sorry but I do. My brain can only focus on all the ways to make you mine. You are the trifecta: beauty, brains and wit, all in one hell of a package."

I sit back, my mouth surely agape. I think I blink a few times—maybe even close my eyes for a minute—before opening them, checking to be sure he's actually sitting across from me. No-one has ever said anything remotely close to that about me before. Lucky for me, each time I reopen my eyes he's still right across from me, camel-coloured button-up shirt enhancing those already piercing green eyes, waiting for my response. *Would mounting him in The Froth House send the right message?*

"Better?" he says a bit cockily, knowing it was pretty damned epic.

"Was all right," I shrug, despite a huge grin escaping.

"I did make some great points, did I not?"

"Indeed." I pause, shake my head. "Okay, first things first, I need to get this off my chest before we talk about 'us'. I need to pre-book my advisor meetings with you moving forward. I've been avoiding you and me in confined spaces. And this typing up everything I have to ask you in an email is killing me." I rub my wrists, feigning carpal tunnel syndrome. "We will have to make sure we stay focused," I add for clarity.

"*We,* eh? Who's to say I wasn't always focused on the tasks at hand? It's all becoming clear now, though. I was wondering why our communication had turned to strictly emails. You *do* like me, Ms. Hughes." He gives me a devious grin.

"Ace." I give him a dirty look, which only makes his smile bigger.

"What? It's perfect. I'd like to make steady appointments with you too," he says, and I roll my eyes.

"Not like that. Wellll, not yet, anyway..." I add, gaining a full-on smile.

"Soon, I hope. I've thought about you and me in my office. A lot," he tells me in a low, gravelly tone, one which sends tingles down my spine.

"Whatever," I say, rolling my eyes.

"Now tell me the rest of your thoughts," he says, leaning in even closer.

"Okay, well, I agree that I am pretty brilliant," I say, to break the lust-induced spell he's putting me under.

"E," he huffs, "what about the other stuff? The me and you bit."

"Give me a minute. I'm thinking here. That was a lot to take in. It's not everyday that a girl gets a gorgeous man giving her a speech like that. Allow process time." I rub my hand along my chin.

"You think I'm gorgeous?" Ace smirks. The bastard knows full well I do.

"Definitely." My eyes move over each of his facial features, noting how handsome Ace Ryan truly is, before moving back to his lips. Lips I can't wait to get my own on. Feeling brave, I ask, "Would I get to kiss you, if we did this?" I gesture between us. "I've got to be honest. You've got the sexiest lips. I've imagined how'd they feel moving into mine probably a million times, wondered if the friction would be as all-consuming and hot as I imagined."

"Christ. If we're going to start this, we're going to need ground rules. I can't be walking around campus with a hard-on all day. People will think I'm weird," he says, his hands disappearing under the table, and I burst out laughing. "First rule—" he begins, but I interrupt him.

"The first rule of *Fight Club* is…" I laugh, imitating his deep serious voice, "You're so serious-sounding. You make it seem like what we're talking about doing here is completely illegal or something, Ace."

"Well, it isn't like I can sing about liking and wanting to date you from the bleachers like I'm Heath Ledger now, can I? Not if I want to keep my job."

"You want to date me? Like date, date?"

"Of course I do. I thought I was clear about that. Do I need to find a bleacher to perform on tomorrow, Ellie?"

"Gah…no. That would be so cool, but I imagine it might not go over very well with the other students or the chair, though, eh? But, God, that would be so hot. I'd definitely need to kiss you after that."

"Right there, that is precisely why we need rules so we don't get caught, at least not until after you graduate."

"I agree. We do need a few rules and maybe some clarity."

"Clarity. What aren't you sure about, E?"

Looking around again, I'm suddenly feeling a bit embarrassed to ask what I need clarification about. I want to know if we're going to be exclusive. I mean, look at the man, there's no way he'll limit himself to only getting to know me. *Right?*

"Ellie, what is it, sweetheart?"

"Uh, er…" I pause for a beat before blurting out. "Will you be dating other people while we do this? I mean, I get that you might, but

I want to be clear so I know if I should date too. Or not." I feel my cheeks heat at the question.

"Not a chance. I'm not sharing you, I'll barely get to see you enough as it is. Why, are you seeing someone else? Shit. I never thou—"

I stop him. "No, Ace. I only want you. I mean, to get to know you." I offer an impish smile; again, no doubt my cheeks are like cherry tomatoes.

"Okay, now that we've settled that, I think we're going to need to address some of those ground rules I was talking about. Because right about now, seeing that flush on your cheeks, all I can think about is coming over there. I'm curious to see where else I can make you flush. We'd better get back to rule-making."

"I can't wait to kiss you!" I blurt, but it's true, and he's being completely adorable right now.

"Number one. You cannot say shit like that about kissing me on campus. It's going to be the death of me knowing I can't."

I try to stifle a giggle at the pained look on his face. "Right, sorry. I don't want to kiss you."

"Jesus, you're going to kill me, aren't you? I think you like driving me crazy, Ms. Hughes."

"Whatever. I'll be good. I promise. All right, what should our next rule be?" I ask, drumming my fingers on the sleek tabletop.

"As hard as it will be for you to resist me, there should be no touching each other while on campus, either," he offers, that damn dimple leading the way.

"You're right. That one's going to kill me," I laugh. "In all seriousness, that is an important one. I agree, we need to be careful. I'm close to graduating and you're still new here. There's no sense bringing on any unwanted issues for either of us. But I think our no touching rule is a bit unrealistic. Maybe we could have a no sex rule until we know we can safely be together? But we can still kiss and maybe have a little over-the-clothing foreplay? I mean, we're going to want to fool around a bit while we get to know each other, right? In private, of course," I add, and Ace nods, a satisfied look on his face.

"Good, that was easy," he nods, pleased with my compromise. "Knowing I'll get to touch you on our dates will hold me off, I hope."

"'Dates'?"

He all-out laughs at this point. "Yeah, E. I do plan on taking you out from time to time; the point here is to get to know each other. We'll have to be creative, and find some safe places for us to be with each other. Thankfully, Toronto is huge; it shouldn't be a problem."

"Glad you've thought of everything."

"I've been thinking about this for a while now, E. I needed to have it figured out. There was no way I could let you tell me no." He reaches across the table and squeezes my hand.

Smiling, I bring up the one thing that still weighs on my mind about this arrangement. "No favouritism. You can't show me any kind. I don't expect an A grade, unless I deserve it. This is a non-negotiable." I meet his eyes, hoping he sees how serious I am.

"Trust me, E. I don't give out easy A's. I'll probably be harder on you, anyway. I have high expectations for that paper of yours."

"No pressure, of course." I shake my head, "As long as you're fair, I think I'll meet your expectations. The last thing I want is an A because I rode your casting couch."

"Casting couch, that's new." His shoulders shake with laughter.

"I need your Red Pen of Sorrow to give me detailed notes about my hits and misses on all my work."

"'Red Pen of Sorrow', eh? I like it. I'm that tough of a grader? Does my red pen offend?" he asks in jest.

"You do realize we all hand in our work on white paper, yes? Have you noticed that once you're finished marking them, they tend to take on a pinkish hue?"

"Can't say I've ever paid attention."

"Court's papers from Jax never come back looking that way. Maybe I should have him as my TA?" My shoulders shake at the mock look of hurt on his face.

"Not a chance. You're stuck with me," he jokes, taking a sip of his coffee.

After a few moments of silence, Ace looks at me with sincerity and asks if I think I need a new advisor now. All joking aside, he said he could ask Sam to take me on, since Sam was the one with the least amount of people in his group. The fact that Ace offered made me fall that much more.

Of course, being the teasing shit I am, I pushed his buttons with my reply: "Why don't we wait and see how things go between us, then decide? We might not even like each other that much."

"Oh no, Ellie. Make no mistake: we definitely like each other." His eyes trail down to my chest where my nipples had been vying for his attention since we sat down. "If anything, I bet we only like one another more as time goes on."

"Hmm. What do you do in your spare time, Doctor Ryan?" I ask, trying to ignore the heat in his eyes.

"I'm actually in the middle of wrapping up a documentary I'm entering in TIFF this year. It's why I don't have a lot of free time in my personal life at the moment and the main reason why I won't always be free. You'll have to be patient with me for a few more months."

Unable to contain myself, I more or less freak out with excitement like a fangirl. "Holy crap! That's huge, TIFF! Ace. Congrats. It's amazing! Tell me all about it. Can I help?" I clap my hands excitedly. "Are you getting grad students to assist? You need to let me help! What's it about? Please tell me everything." I move my chair closer to the table, showing him that he has my full attention (not that he's ever lost it, really).

I freeze as the words "sex trade" and "phone sex lines" fall from his lips.

I begin to panic, my bad knee aching from the pressure of my feet digging into the floor. *Does he know what I do? Holy shit, this has to be simply some insane coincidence. He can't know, he'd say something, I'm sure. Wouldn't he? Nah, there's no way he could know.* With that, I begin to relax, but remain guarded as he talks.

"It's been an amazing adventure, to say the least. I'm happy with where it's going." Ace's voice helps to bring me back from panic mode.

"That's incredible, I can't wait to see it," I say honestly, because it does sound like it will be one of those documentaries that is going to have a definite impact.

We spend the next few hours discussing Ace's project, how he's investigating the intrusion of the digital age into the sex industry. I was completely fascinated and literally smitten listening to him exude passion for his film. At one point, however, I have to admit I felt a little guilty for not telling him that I would be a perfect subject for his documentary. But, seeing as I'd never agree to be filmed and the fact that he sounds like he's almost finished, I decided to let the guilt go and to keep my secret, especially since I'll be quitting soon. Besides, it's not like we're a couple or anything, really—not yet, anyway. I'm hoping we will be soon, but in the meantime, I can still keep a few secrets, right?

Lying in bed later, I can't keep the smile from returning to my lips when I think about how Ace took the elevator up with me and walked me to my apartment door. I knew he wanted to kiss me, and Holy Mother Hubbard in Her Cupboard did I want him to. Instead, he walked away, leaving me disappointed. Well, until I'd put the key in the lock and then felt him at my back. A quiet "fuck it" made me turn to find Ace in front of me, an "I'll take my chances" falling from his lips before they brushed against mine. A touch so soft I barely had time to register it before he whispered a sweet "see you 'round, E," as he gave my hands a squeeze and walked away.

"Rules schmules," I mutter, brimming with happiness and reaching to shut off my bedside light.

Chapter 38

Ellie

"BREATHLESS WHISPERS, THIS is Chanel."

"Hey, babe. How's it going tonight?" a deep voice greets.

"I'm good, really good." I reply softly. "You've got a very sexy voice, sugar. It makes me tingly in all the right places. What's your name?" I ask, while expertly matching five candies in a row, which has now created a colour bomb, heck, yes! This is sure to earn me a high score for this level in Candy Crush.

"Oh yeah? You're sounding pretty sexy yourself. Name's Hale. What are you up to tonight?" Pausing my game of Candy Crush, I take a deep breath, trying to think of a good scenario to share with Hale. I hate to say it but sometimes this job is boring. As much as the calls differentiate, in the end they're all pretty much the same. Trying to think of original stories and fantasies is trying sometimes, more so because if I recycled the same material I'd surely go batshit crazy from boredom. For me, the challenge of thinking up new material keeps the job fun and me on my toes. Looking back on the last few months, it's funny how comfortable I've become. Greta and Destiny were right; it's definitely easy money. I can pretty much get a caller off in under four minutes if I want, but of course I always go until I guarantee the customer their "happy ending". Who'd have thought I would have lasted this long, or that I'd come to like my job? Not me, that's for sure.

"What are you doing tonight, Chanel?"

"You want to know the truth? Do you think you can handle hearing how bad a girl I am?" I ask him, deciding on the perfect story for Hale.

"Yeah. Tell me. You know a real man can handle—and only ever wants—the truth. Right? And we all love a dirty girl," he drawls.

Oh please! "You can't haaandle *the truth";* Jack Nicholson's voice as Colonel Jessup from *A Few Good Men* pops into my mind. Imagine if I could tell some of these callers what I really thought of their fetishes or insane penchants, or better yet, how I think they really need to go out and get a life, to stop paying for my made-up stories? But, then again, I wouldn't have a job now, would I? *And we all know I need this job.*

"Okay, don't judge me. It really is kind of naughty. I've been a bit of a dirty girl, I'm afraid."

"Yeah? Tell me. I'd never judge, sweetheart."

Giggling, I gear up to give Hale my tall tale, one I hope leaves him satisfied and allows me to get back to my game within five minutes. Having built up my call list, I'm not as worried about trying to keep callers on the line for a long time, now I'm more worried about getting to all of the calls in my queue. It turns out that I, Chanel69, have developed quite the knack for this job.

"As long as you promise, I guess I can share this with you, big boy."

"I can't fucking wait, sweetheart."

"I've been lying here, in nothing but my baby blue boy shorts and tank top. My nipples are so hard because I've been sitting here getting myself incredibly horny."

"I'm getting pretty fucking excited too, doll. Just your sexy voice hitching like that is making me hard. What's got you all excited?"

"I'm reminiscing about the amazing threesome I had last night. It was sexy as hell. Who knew fucking your best friend and her boyfriend could be so crazy hot? You ever have a threesome, Hale?" I ask, my voice laced with seduction.

"No, can't say I've had the pleasure, but I'd love to hear about it. Love to hear you tell me everything," he says, his voice cracking, and I know I've piqued his interest.

"Okay, but remember, you promised you wouldn't judge me, or tell anyone. It's got to be our little secret, Hale."

"My lips are sealed, doll. Go on."

"Well, my friend Lettie and I had been drinking this super-strong concoction called Mermaid Juice all afternoon, and after the fifth or sixth drink, we started playing 'Truth or Dare'. Have you ever played that game, Hale?"

"Yeah, it can be fun." I hear a sharp intake of breath.

"It sure can. Maybe we can play sometime, if you call me back. I'd like to give it a go with you."

"I think that'd be a good plan. Shit, doll, you've got me on the edge of my seat to hear what happens next."

Hook.

Line.

Sinker.

Hale is right where I want him; putty in my hands.

"Anyway, after a few rounds, I chose 'dare'. Lettie giggled and dared me to go surprise her boyfriend, Nigel, by sneaking in and giving him head while he slept. I've never done something like that before, but I can't lie, Hale, the thought excited me a lot. I could feel the dampness of my panties as I sat contemplating what the right thing to do was. I mean, after all, Nigel is Lettie's boyfriend." I pause, waiting for a reaction.

"Did you do it? Say you did. Say you were a needy little whore."

See, it's okay for me to refer to myself as "whore" or "slut" because I'm role-playing, but I blanch each time a caller uses degrading terms.

Chanel is my costume and I've learned to don her with pride, but I'll never enjoy being called names. It's something I guess I'll never accept because I am no such thing in my real life.

Ignoring the "whore" comment, I continue.

"Of course I did it. Nigel's hot. And Lettie and I had been doing a little bit of kissing and touching with each other during our game, so I was feeling a bit needy, truth be told."

"How'd you do it? Tell me everything." I hear the telltale clink of a belt buckle coming undone and a zipper being lowered.

"I snuck inside the bedroom, leaving the door open for Lettie in case she chose to come watch. I was pretty sure she would, I mean, we're close, you know what I'm saying? Lucky for me, Nigel was sleeping on his back, a black satin sheet barely covering his huge cock. Padding quietly across the room, I peeled off my yellow sundress, tossing it aside, leaving me in just a tiny white thong. My breasts began to sway as I made my way to the foot of the bed. My nipples were insanely hard, aching to be touched. I ran my hands along the distended tips, pulling them, trying to relieve some pressure."

"Shit, that's hot. I love when a woman plays with her titties. It makes my cock so damn hard," Hale lets out with a deep breath. "Sorry, go on."

"Sliding onto the bottom of the bed, I removed the sheet, exposing Nigel's full girth to my now salivating mouth. I wanted him in my mouth so bad I could taste it, Hale."

"Fuck, this is so fucking hot, doll. God, I wanna pull on those titties of yours. Mmmm," he says, and I wait to make sure he's listening.

"Making sure he wasn't awake, I looked up, relieved to find him passed out. Positioning myself to hover above him, my tits almost touching his legs, I slipped Nigel into my mouth. Immediately coating him in my saliva, I began moaning and swirling my tongue around his growing hardness. My pussy was so wet and excited I could feel drops starting to run down my thighs."

"Shit, that's hot. What did he do when he woke up? Did he freak when he saw it was you?"

"No, quite the opposite. When he opened his eyes, all he said was 'Fuck, yeah, Chanel, keep fucking my cock with that hot mouth of yours.'"

"Jesus. What did Lettie do?"

"Well. Just thinking about what happened next makes me so wet. I might have to touch myself while I tell you. Is that okay, Hale?" I ask, knowing he'll love the idea.

"Fuck, yes. I'm thinking the same. You've got me so hard."

"That's good. I love a hard cock. Now, let me tell you about Lettie. So there I am, deep-throating Nigel when I feel the bed dip behind me. Suddenly, Lettie's hand is moving along my back, lowering her hands to my ass where she pulls on my thong, pulling the material, teasing me with the fabric as it rubs my sensitive pussy. Moaning at the feel of her touch, I spread my legs in invitation, silently begging for more."

"That's hot. Jesus, you're gonna make me come, you keep talking like that."

"What's even hotter is when she started to trail her tongue along the small scrap of material, teasing and taunting me, making me a needy mess. Finally, she gave in, pulled off my panties and put her wet mouth on my greedy pussy."

"Fuck, I bet that looked so hot. Her eating your ass out from behind."

"Oh yeah. She was so good that I stopped sucking off Nigel so I could lie down on the bed to give Lettie a better angle."

"What did Nigel do?"

"He got up and started fucking Lettie from behind while she sucked the fuck out of my clit," I fake giggle. "It was incredible. Then I rode Nigel while Lettie rode his face. It was fantastic. Best bonding experience ever."

"Fuck, I need two wild girls. God, I'm so fucking hard."

"Are you stroking that hard cock of yours, Hale?"

"Yeah. It's so hard from listening to you. I wish you could jerk me off, I wish I could stick my cock in your tight cunt. I'd love to feel your heat wrapped around my cock while I fill you up with my cum."

"That sounds so hot, I'd like that too. Let's get each other off, Hale, let's finish together. I'm so wet, I need to come."

"Hell, yeah. I'm fucking close, doll."

"Are you touching yourself like I want?"

"Oh fuck, yeah, Chanel. I am."

"Good. I'm touching myself too. I'm running my fingers along my wet pussy. I'm dripping wet from imagining you touching me right now," I say, reaching for my pocket pussy, the one I've just added a bit of lube to, to mimic how wet I want Hale to hear I am as I move my fingers in and out of it.

"Fuck, you are wet. I can hear your greedy little cunt."

"Uh huh. My pussy's hungry again tonight. Your fingers feel so good, fuck, yeah, you know the right place. Yes, yes, right there, there! Oh shit, yeah…"

"Ahh, fuck, yes! Fuck, yeah…" Hale shouts, the sound of sweet relief lacing his voice before he hangs up.

I resume my game of Candy Crush, and wait for the next call.

Chapter 39

Ace

DATING ELLIE HAS been both agonizing and wonderful, the perfect pleasure/pain combination.

Pleasurable in the sense that getting to know her is making me fall head-over-heels for this woman. She's amazing, and the more time we spend together, the harder it's getting not to lay claim to her publicly. I'm rethinking the whole not-pulling-off-a-Heath-Ledger-move like in *10 Things I Hate About You,* because, honestly, if I saw Sam or any other man try to make a move on Ellie, I might have to make for the bleachers and claim her as mine right then and there. Ellie is mine and I eagerly await the day when everyone will know it. The best part? She feels exactly the same.

I thought she was going to lose her mind last week when Lucy Westman was leaving my office and offered me her cell phone number. For "educational purposes only, of course" she said, once she saw Ellie sitting in the waiting area outside the door. Seeing Ellie all huffy and pissy when she came into my office, flustered and trying to deny that she was riled seeing Lucy flirting with me, was a sight to behold. I laughed and told her I was glad we were on the same page. My little cavewoman is adorable when she gets possessive.

Along with being pleasurable, things have been rather painful, as well. The blue balls I've been sporting for the last few months are going to be what takes me out in the end, I swear. This whole "waiting until she graduates to touch each other" thing is literally killing me. It's been months of jerking off and, trust me, it's not the same. All I want to do is sink myself deep inside Ellie and never return. It's taking everything I've got to stick to the stupid rules we laid out that night at the coffee shop. I want to take a Mulligan on that, have a do-over. I want the freedom to touch, kiss, and explore her all I want.

Speaking of blue balls, I must admit that one of the characteristics I admire most about Ellie is her *balls*. Despite being paranoid about getting caught together, she's willing to take risks when she feels it's necessary. Just last week, my spitfire showed up at my apartment unannounced, once again showing me what an incredible woman she is...

Placing my laptop on the table, I get up to answer the door, assuming it's Mercer checking to see that I'm still alive after I cancelled on both our weekly coffee and our bar meeting.

Looking out the peephole, I'm surprised to see Ellie, a pizza box and a six-pack of Alexander Keith's in hand. Seeing her reminds me how pissed I was earlier when I had to cancel our date tonight, but when Detective Hernandez called saying he needed my help with Dee's case, I knew she'd understand. And she did.

"Hey, you," I greet, opening the door.

"Surprise. I come bearing brainfood in the form of the best pizza Toronto has to offer, and the best beer to accompany said pizza," she says in a singsong voice. But I see the flash of uncertainty crossing her face about showing up unannounced.

"You might be the most perfect specimen in the world. I'm famished. Come in," I say, taking the pizza box from her hand.

"Oh no. It's okay. I don't want to distract you," she waves her free hand, "I just wanted to drop off some dinner. I was assuming you hadn't eaten yet," Ellie says, looking past me to the mess of papers, files, and my

laptop covering the coffee table. "I see you're busy. I totally get it. I just wanted to make sure you ate," she beams, her beautiful eyes shining.

"I'd love to have you as a brief distraction. Come in. Eat. Talk. I deserve a little Ellie-time. I've been working on sorting the footage and recordings for hours." I let her pass.

"Okay, I guess you do deserve a break. Besides, I miss you too." She kisses my cheek as she walks by. I slap her bottom with my free hand as she passes, nearly making her drop the six-pack and eliciting a laugh from Ellie.

"And you're wearing tights. I cannot pass up the opportunity to spend time with those. You know we're practically best friends, right?" I tease, following her into the kitchen.

"Well, then. I must allow you two to continue to bond," she replies, playfully taking two bottles of Keith's out and setting them on the grey countertop. "How's it going?" Ellie asks, placing slices of steaming pepperoni-and-mushroom pizza on our plates.

"It's good. I'm almost done. I didn't realize how much Dee had divulged to me. Thank God I record everything. I have two tapes left to go through, then I'll have everything in a file I can send to the police for their case. I'll just have to pop in to give a statement sometime this week, then I'll wait to hear when the court date is."

"That's incredible, Ace. Your research and hard work is really going to help those girls. You're giving them a voice. A way out. I'm so proud of you. And I'm proud of Dee for agreeing to talk to you, too. Who knows? Maybe she was waiting for you to come along," she says sincerely, taking a sip from her beer.

"Yeah, it feels good. I never expected this film to be the springboard for a police investigation, but I'm glad it is. Chelsea was great at talking to Dee with me. Having another woman who could relate to Dee's situation, to tell her she shouldn't have to deal with being degraded, threatened, and severely underpaid, really helped. I still can't believe Dee's going to be the

key witness against her former boss. I'm proud of that girl," I add, moving to sit in the living room. I make quick work of piling a few folders and other papers to make enough room for our plates.

"It's incredible. Good thinking using Chelsea to help. Are Dee's parents around?" Ellie asks, concerned.

"Unfortunately, no. Dee fits the stereotype to a 'T'; runaway, sixteen, trying to survive on her own. I put her in touch with Covenant House to help her get set up with some transitional housing."

"Wow, that's a lot for a young girl," Ellie sighs, resting her plate on her lap. "Anything I can do to help her, please let me know. Even if she needs clothes or someone to talk to, help finding a job. Anything."

"Thanks, baby, that means a lot. Mercer's helped her find a job, so she's getting a fresh start. Now, enough shop talk. How about I clean this up, and you let me cuddle those tights for a bit before I get back at it?" I offer, raising my brows up and down, trying to lighten the mood and because I want nothing more than to feel this incredible woman as close to me as possible.

It was a perfect date, one of my favourites, despite my need to continue working. We spent more than an hour snuggling on my couch, talking about everything and anything. It was the perfect distraction…until she began teasing me, making me hard as nails for her.

"I love these lips. They're so soft," Ellie said, running her finger along my bottom lip. "I can't wait to feel them on mine," she adds softly, from where we're lying stretched out together on my couch.

"Funny, I have similar feelings about that ass of yours," I say, palming her behind. "I can't wait to see it up close and personal. Not that I'd ever give up my friendship with these tights we both love, but we could always just pull them down a little so they wouldn't feel neglected." I laugh, kissing her forehead. "Anyway, moving on. I'm glad you came over tonight. I'm sorry I had to cancel our date. It was the last thing I wanted to do."

"I know. Don't be silly, your work is important, Ace. Never apologize

for doing what you do. I'd be mad if you didn't make this your priority. It's a big deal. I'll be here when you're done. I plan on being around you for a while, Doctor Ryan," Ellie says, a satisfied grin on her face.

"You know it drives me crazy when you call me 'Doctor', E."

"I know. That's why it's sooooo much fun to do. I swear your eyebrows almost get knotted in your hair, you raise them so high," she snorts, her body shaking. I take the opening to give her a tickle attack as punishment.

"Oh my! No, no, don't, Ace. Okay, okay. Truce. Truce. I give!" Ellie shrieks, thrashing beside me at my onslaught of tickles.

"So, no more 'Doctor Ryan', then?" I question, pausing to let her answer.

"Okay, fine. No more," she laughs, and offers her hand to shake on it.

Ellie left shortly after that, again offering to help Dee in any way. It was hard to let her leave, but I knew I'd never get my work done if Ellie and her tights had stayed much longer.

Chapter 40

Ace

ELLIE HUGHES IS everything I knew she was going to be, and a whole lot more. Our weekly dates have been incredible, despite the "no sex" rule we continue to follow with difficulty.

We've seen a dozen or so documentary films over at the Bloor Hot Docs Cinema. It turns out Ellie is almost as big a documentary fan as I am. It also doesn't hurt that they have a fantastic selection of local craft beers, either. Another thing we have in common: the love of all things local, including awesome beer. Touring the Mill Street Brewery was another date where I fell a little harder for Ellie. She's easy to impress and never hides who she is from anyone. She's becoming my favourite person.

I smile at the thought of her walking through St. Lawrence Market last Sunday—when she suddenly freaked out, convinced she saw my teaching assistant, Joelle, with her boyfriend, Daryl. It took me about twenty-five minutes to get Ellie to come out of the alley she'd hidden in, although I did get to spend those minutes staring at my beautiful girl, while trying not to laugh at how she looked freaking out about the possibility of being caught and all the risks we were taking. After letting her get it all out, I may have manoeuvered my way in for a comforting hug, one where I pulled her in tight and managed to nestle my face into her neck to offer words of comfort, all the while battling my own urges, as I stood inhaling her incredible scent and enjoying her soft curves.

Reminiscing in my desk chair, my cock twitches at the memory. But just as I lean back to adjust myself, my office door flies open, revealing a tear-streaked Ellie. Rounding my desk to meet her, I immediately tuck her into my chest.

"Ellie. What happened?" I ask, placing my hands on her back.

"I can't do this. I need to drop out," she sobs, her shoulders shaking.

"Do what? Drop what, E?"

"This." She lifts one arm up and waves it in a circle. I know I shouldn't laugh, but she's adorable even when she's clearly upset.

"Are you laughing at me?" She pulls away and looks up at me, her face scrunched with irritation.

"Er, no, but that was kind of cute. That whole arm thing…like that would explain anything to me." I move my hand, making the same gesture.

"Ace," she cries, "I'm serious. I can't do this. I have to drop the class." Ellie's tears fall again, and I start taking her seriously.

"Stop. Ellie, look at me," I say, placing my hands on either side of her cheeks. Catching her tears with my thumbs, I tilt her head a bit, forcing her to look at me, needing her to listen. Her beautiful hazel eyes glisten, turning almost green under the tears, which continue to fall down her face. Running my thumbs along their wetness, I back her up to sit on my desk and move myself closer in between her legs.

"Calm down, beautiful. Tell me what's going on in that brilliant head of yours." I kiss her forehead.

"I can't…you were right. My thesis is a joke. The topic's too hard to get enough decent arguments to fill forty pages. I never should have convinced you I could pull it off. I can't. I'll never get it done," she whispers, her shoulders shaking from how upset she is, and it rips me apart. I never want to see her like this. Guilt pierces my gut for having given her a hard time in the first place. It's truthfully an impressive topic, one I have no doubt she'll pull off.

"Ellie. Listen to me. You're an intelligent, capable woman. Your paper is impressive."

"It's not. I'm stuck. I still have a final argument to think of. It's already March. I'll never get it done, Ace. Between work, the gym, and all the dead ends I'm running into with my research, I might as well drop the course and save face."

"Ellie. Look at me. Hear me. There will be no quitting. This is what we're going to do…" She cuts me off.

"And I'm sexually frustrated. The "no sex" rule is stupid. I need…I'm too stressed," she blurts, her hands immediately moving to cover her mouth. "Oh God, I can't believe I said that out loud." She covers her face with her hands and I place mine overtop to peel hers away, unable to hide my smile at her admission.

"Me too. I swear I'm going to pass out, my balls are so blue." I kiss her nose before moving to her ear, an idea forming, a way to help relieve a little tension. Either way, I know it will snap her out of her current mood. "I have an idea," I whisper.

"Does it involve me visiting the registrar's office to try and convince them it's not too late to drop the class?"

"No. Even better. It involves no rule breaking, well, maybe just a slight bend, because I will be kissing you and touching you a little, but nothing under your clothes. All you have to do it sit back, relax, and trust me. Let me share my non-touching talents with you. I dare you to let my words torture you until the day when I can truly touch you like I plan. I promise, this will be the best hands-off experience of your life."

"Oh yeah?" she looks up, meeting my eyes.

"Definitely. You'll feel so relaxed when I'm finished with you."

"I like the sounds of this."

"Me too. I love the idea. Especially getting to watch how you react, E."

"Yeah? You think I'll react to whatever 'non-touching' plan you have?" she whispers.

"Yeah." I run my nose along the side of her face. "I'm going to kiss you now," I tell her, letting my lips ghost over hers. "Would you let me kiss you, E? Let me kiss you all better?" I ask, before I connect our lips softly, resting mine like a whisper over hers, waiting for her reply.

"I think that might help, a bit anyway..." she shrugs, and I go for the kiss I crave, moving my hand behind her head, holding her gently in place while I take her bottom lip, tugging it enough to elicit a sexy moan. Running my tongue along her bottom lip she opens her mouth, her tongue meeting mine. We battle instantly, both of us struggling for control, our tongues swirling and chasing one another's. She tastes incredible, and my cock wants to come out and play something fierce. So badly, in fact, I swear it's going to *Escape from Alcatraz* right through the zipper of my jeans.

"I'm going to make you feel good," I whisper into her hair, the sharp intake of breath confirming that my plan is working, her mood is changing. "First, I'm going to give you the stress release you need, then we are going to look over what you have so far for your final argument. Next we're going to work on beefing up your points and then I'm going to kiss you a bit more. Finally, I'll walk you home."

"That might really help. Might even be what the *doctor* ordered." She gives me a cheeky grin.

"We will repeat this process every day if you need it, Ellie, but there will be no quitting. Not an option. Understood?" I tip my forehead to hers.

"Yes, Ace. Completely."

"Do you like that plan, E? Feel it needs any amendments or additions?"

"It's the best plan I've ever heard," she says with a wicked grin, "but one suggestion. Can we do the work first, then reap the rewards? I think I might have an idea."

"Sure, whatever you want, Ellie, you keener. Work first, play later." I shake my head as she bounces off the desk, forcing me to step back as she rounds it to stand in front of my computer.

"I just remembered that article you saved for me, the one with the Carrie Fisher interview. I think that will help me big time," Ellie smiles, while opening the folder marked "Leia" on my desktop. I have a folder for each of my thesis students, one where I add things I come across that I think might help them. A bit sexually frustrated, I nonetheless take a seat in my chair and watch her hover over my computer. After fifteen minutes of staring at her ass, I can't take it anymore; I need my hands on her, but I remember how much fun it is to torture each other. This waiting for sex is proving to be the best foreplay I've ever had.

"Have I told you how sexy these jogging pants are?" I say, lifting up her t-shirt with the edge of the pen I'd been twirling (flirting with the boundaries of our "no touching on campus" rule). I let the pen's tip expose her sexy ass even more as she stands in front of me, looking at the monitor way too intently for what I had in mind. But I'm happy that the Carrie Fisher article will help her with her paper. Seeing the relieved look cross her face as she rereads it confirms its worth and makes me happy for her. I'm glad she'll be able to pull this off, just like I knew she would all along.

"Tights, Ace. They're actually a few steps up from jogging pants," she laughs.

"Whatever. I fucking like them."

"Caveman."

When she came barging into my office in tears, I didn't take notice of the loose shirt and tight pants, formerly known as *jogging*. I was too busy trying to calm her down, to get to and to help solve the issues. But now I can't stop noticing. *How is it possible that a grubby shirt and tights can have the adverse effect and make her look hot as hell?*

"Eep, Ace, this is going to be perfect!"

"You're damn straight it is."

She peers over her shoulder. "This article, Ace. Not my ass."

"Your opinion," I deadpan, before standing.

"Jeez, you're a pain."

"Get used to it. You're mine, Ellie. It's your new lot in life. Here, take my chair, you look like you might be at this for a while." I give her my best shit-eating grin as I rake my eyes blatantly down her back to her ass again, before taking my chair. Once she's sitting, I move in, placing both of my forearms on the armrests. Leaning in, I move my mouth to her neck, savouring her scent. "Fuck, you always smell so good, E. Maybe we need a quick study break." I run my tongue along her neck, causing my already needy cock to strain against my zipper.

"Ace, please. We can't. It's too risky. The door's not even locked. Someone might come."

"I know who's going to come, Ellie. You."

"Ace," she pleads. "You need to stop, you know my neck is my weakness."

"I know. But you're fucking killing me. These things are my weakness." I move my hands down the outsides of her legs, teasing her by avoiding where I know she'd like me to rub.

"In tights? I look like a grub."

"Sexy. You're curvy in all the right spots, with long, toned legs and a perfect, tight ass," I growl.

"Ace." It's an appeal, but know it's an idle attempt. She wants this, too.

"Let me tell you what I wish I could do to you, Ellie," I say, leaning in close to her ear. "Please, E…listen while I talk. Let me tell you how much I want to touch you," I say, while shifting to sit near her on my desk.

"Tell me. How would you touch me right now?" she relents, squeezing her legs together. I can't hide my smile, knowing she's giving in. She has no idea what's coming.

"First, I'd rub my hand in a circular motion over the material covering your hot pussy, applying just enough pressure so I know you'll feel it in that perfect spot—the one I can't wait to rub my hard cock against," I say. Immediately, she leans back in the chair, gripping the arms to support herself. My lips crave the taste of her skin, but instead I stay seated, just lean in a little closer and whisper all the dirty things I want to do to her in her ear: "I'd slip one of my fingers inside your warmth, loving the way your greedy pussy hugs around it, wanting desperately for it to move, to explore, and stretch you in the most exquisite way. I'd add a second finger, while my thumb started making deliberate circles over your smooth clit."

"Oh shit, keep talking." Ellie slips her hand inside the front of her pants, spreading her legs to accommodate herself. The sight has me gripping the edge of the desk to the point of pain.

"Have you any idea how badly I want to slide inside you? How often I think of the day I get to experience you, Ellie? I want to feel your warmth, your pussy squeezing my cock."

"Jesus, Ace," she moans, squeezing her legs together, trying to relieve the pressure building from my words.

"You look fucking sexy, baby." The urge to rip her pants off is on the tip of my brain, but I know we can't. I'm pushing the boundaries as it is. I shouldn't be doing this, especially not here in my office. But I don't stop. I keep going. "I bet you'll feel so good wrapped around my cock. And be ready, E, I'll be going in rebel-style—nothing between us, because we're both clean. My cock, your cunt, and the sweet drag and pull as I fuck you bare. The only thing we'll be feeling is each other. The only things we'll hear are each other's names as we scream them out when we come."

"Oh fuuuck," she moans, "I want that. God, I do, your words…you've got me so hot. We need to stop this, I'm too close. Ace, you need to stop or I'm going to come."

"Slip your other hand under your shirt and pull those hard nipples for me, Ellie, while you grind down on your hand. Finish for me, that's it, beautiful. Let me watch you. Circle your clit like I want to, give it the tiny circles that are sure to push you over. Do it, Ellie. Show me."

And she does.

"Aaaaace, oh God…" she says, having picked up the pace.

"A little more, let me hear how wet you are. Fuck, you smell so sweet. I can smell how excited you are, Ellie. Pretend it's my hand. I wish it was. I'm dying here, E."

"It feels so good, Ace. I'm going to come, ahh, fuck…" she says, increasing the pace even more as she gets herself off in my office chair.

"I want to touch you with nothing between us. It's killing me how badly I want to slip my hand down the front of those tights. I love those tights, by the way. Love how easily I can see what you're doing to your pussy—*my pussy.*"

"You're gonna make me come again, ohhh," Ellie says, breathlessly.

"That's it. Stroke the pad of your thumb over your clit, now move faster, now a bit faster. Jesus, listen to how wet you are. I can't wait to see how wet you'll be for me, how tight you'll feel wrapped around my cock while you milk every drop from me."

"Ace, oh God, I'm gonna…I'm gonna come so soon!" she whisper-calls out, while she increases both her speed and dexterity. And I'm like a teenage boy who's about to come all over the inside of his pants at the vision of Ellie falling apart at the sound of my words. "Oh…we need to stop, Ace. This is your *office.*"

"Fuck the rules. Let go, Ellie," I stand now, moving my mouth closer to her ear, whispering: "I can't wait to feel those sweet pussy lips around my cock." Then I pull her hand from her pants and lick off her slippery fingers, the act propelling her to spiral into bliss, and she goes off again like a rocket. I cover her mouth with my other hand, masking her howls as her orgasm rocks through her body.

"Jesus, that was the hottest thing I have ever seen." I step back, assessing her appreciatively from head to toe. This woman is incredible. I watch, unable to hide my satisfied smile, as her breathing evens out, and she floats back down to me.

"Ace, that was incredible. But maybe next time you should just email me all the article links and files. Clearly, we have issues following rules," she chuckles.

"I think we need to add a rule," I say, sitting back down on the desk and adjusting my still rock-hard cock.

"Oh yeah? What's that?"

Ellie looks perfectly disheveled, and I will my brain to commit her to memory in this very moment. *Beautiful and perfect.*

"Going forward, we can only meet in public. 'Cause next time, I'll be contacting the chair. There is definitely a conflict going on here." I gesture from my hard cock to my brain. "I let my dick take the lead on that one. I'm not really sorry; I know I should be. But did it work? Are you relaxed?"

"Yes, completely, but it was risky, Doctor..." she smiles, rolling the "r", knowing I hate it when she calls me that, "...but so worth it," she beams, softening the blow.

More and more, I'm convinced that *she's* worth it...*all.*

Chapter 41

Ellie

"HEY, 69, HOW'S it hanging?" Destiny calls from her spot at the table, where she's sitting with Cherry, Mercy, and Diamond. I rarely come into the staff lounge, but as soon as Destiny mentioned that I was the resident recluse, I decided to put in more of an effort. Over the last several weeks, I've made it my mission to interact with and get to know the other girls a bit more.

It turns out we're all in the same boat: working here for the money. The differences? Our reasons. For Mercy, Destiny, and myself, it's school. Destiny's taking cosmetology classes at the Canadian Beauty College and Mercy's a student at Sheridan who'd rather work here than end up with a ton of loans to pay off after school, which I can appreciate and relate to. As for Diamond, she's a single mom trying to make more than ends meet; with a one-year-old at home, things have been tough for her. Turns out the baby's father, along with her parents, wanted nothing to do with her once she decided to keep the baby despite their protests. Having flexible hours, Breathless Whispers keeps her and her daughter living above the poverty line. With babysitting help from her aunt, Diamond is able to work straight nights while Charlotte sleeps.

"Hey, ladies. It's hanging. Just getting ready to pull the midnight-to four a.m. shift. I'm hoping it'll be quiet, I've got a paper to finish."

Not all of the girls here are friendly like these ones. There are a few who are here because they have a habit to feed and they could care less; they'll try to steal your callers, take the prime shifts, and, if you're not careful, will try to get you in trouble if you don't bend to giving them what they want. These are the girls to steer clear of, Destiny warned me. According to her, these women are in way too deep with gambling, addiction, or other sketchy things, so they need this job to support that side of their lives. Despite the Conrad's best efforts to keep the girls clean, according to Destiny, they can't control everyone, so a few girls have managed to keep their jobs despite breaking the rules. She's convinced it will only be a matter of time before they are caught, but warned me nonetheless to avoid them, which, thankfully, I've managed to do thus far.

"Oh, honey, I did that shift last night and I was swamped. Had the most fucked-up caller too. For the first time, I thought I was gonna have to drop the call. Guy wanted me to role-play I was his dog!" Cherry shares. I inwardly cringe, hoping to God she doesn't say she did it.

Noticing my silence, Mercy jumps in. "Relax, Chanel. She didn't go along with it. She pulled a Houdini and flipped the script."

"Yeah, turns out he just needed to be dominated instead. So I made him my bitch," she shrugs, and we all laugh.

Cherry is the resident comedian. From what she's shared with me, she works here simply because she loves it. Apparently, her husband and teenage son both support her career choice. She told me the other day how she was writing an erotic novel and was using her Breathless experiences as material. Cherry also asked me to share any of my exciting calls with her, as well. Needless to say, I was very excited to hear that she was writing a book, and immediately offered to turn it into a screenplay when she was done. One quick handshake, a round of girlie squeals, and our deal was solidified.

Grabbing my Diet Pepsi from the fridge, I join them at the table.

"Shit. Hopefully he doesn't call back tonight and get my line. I'm finding I've not yet been able to pull off the Houdini; the other night I had to pretend I was a dude! I swear, we're going to turn this experience into one hell of a movie in the future, eh, Cherry?" I nod, taking a sip.

"Tell me about it. I've got half the book dedicated to the weirdos who call. Seems we get them the most, ladies." We all agree that it seemed that way lately.

"I gave a golden shower last month. And it was so good, the guy's called back six times for a replay," Mercy pipes up. "It's a good thing the Conrads pay me enough to deal with this shit," she adds, and we all agree again.

After a few more minutes of chatting we go our separate ways: Destiny and I to our suites, the others heading home. It looks like it's just a few of us on tonight from the names I saw listed on the shift board as I passed by.

Once inside, I pull my props and thesis binder out of my bag. I'm really hoping my shift isn't too crazy, I've got my final meeting with Ace in a few days before we all meet next week to defend our theses in front of the thesis committee. I have a bit more to edit and rewrite, but I think I'm actually going to pull it off. I'm grateful Ace didn't let me give up like I wanted to last month. *God, that man is amazing. I'm falling for him more and more each time we're together.*

Our last movie date was incredible…

"Wow, you look stunning," he says, when we meet in our row at Bloor Hot Docs for our weekly movie date.

"It's dark. How can you tell?" I ask him.

"I just know," he replies with finality.

"You really are good with words, Ace," I laugh. The next thing I know, I'm being pulled over to his lap.

"I know because when I picture you in my mind, you're always beautiful, but then when I finally get see you in person again you manage to take my breath away. Every. Single. Time."

He grins, looking a little smug, knowing he's just turned me into a pile of girlie-goo. Of course, that damned dimple joins in the fun.

"Okay, maybe you do have the words." I move my hand to cup his jaw, the day-old stubble—along with those dark-framed glasses—making him look more rugged than usual. "I love when you wear your glasses." I kiss tug on his bottom lip. His hand moves to my ass pulling me in closer.

"I love this tight ass. I can't wait to get up close and personal with it. These rules are bullshit, E. I'm going to combust soon," he groans, pushing my centre against his hardness. Looking around, I see that the theatre is still empty, the opening credits haven't yet begun, and I decide it's time to bend a rule. "It's my turn for a little payback, Doctor Ryan," I say, leaning in close. "I need you to close your eyes and listen to what I'd like to do to you here one day in the future. Think you can do that for me, Ace? Can you be a good listener?"

"Oh, hell, yeah, I can," he says.

"Perfect. Imagine it's our usual date, but suddenly I move off your lap from where we've been having some pre-show cuddles. Instead of moving to my seat for the previews, I position myself down onto my knees. Right between yours."

"Sounds good so far, keep going."

"You're not quite sure what I'm doing, because—me being such an innocent girl—we've never done anything like this before. Little do you realize, however, I've thought about it every single week that we've come here. Pictured doing just this," I whisper, blowing into his ear.

"What are you doing, Ellie? Don't stop, tell me more," Ace says a bit breathlessly, and in the amber glow of the theatre lights, I feel the slight twinge of his hardening cock under his jeans as I continue.

"I'm being a rebel. Rules are made to be broken, right?" I ask. "Lean-

ing up, I place my hands on your belt, waiting for you to give me the go-ahead."

"Like I'd ever tell you 'no', you know I love a rebel streak every now and then," he shares.

"Now, because you're such a cooperative man, you lift yourself enough that I can lower your pants, making it easier for me to get at that big, hard, beautiful cock of yours," I smile at his intake of breath and the grip he has on the armrest, knowing I'm affecting him.

"'I can't wait to have you in my mouth. I've been thinking about it for a long time, Doctor Ryan,' I tell you, as I spring your thick cock, the same one I can tell will fit me like it was meant solely for pounding into my waiting pussy."

"Jesus, fuck, Ellie. That mouth," Ace mutters, and I try not to giggle. I love that my plan is working.

"Keep talking like that and you won't need to touch me. Blue balls, remember?" he quips, and I laugh.

"Once I've got you out, I reach for my drink. Opening the lid, I take a sip and slip a few ice cubes into my mouth. You eye me suspiciously, not sure what I'm up to, but your cock jumps with excitement."

"Know that everything you say and do will be repeated. I'm hard as stone right now, Ellie. Goddamn it," he says, shifting underneath me.

"Quiet. Let me finish this part, it's so good. Taking your cock in my hands, I look up into your eyes. 'How about we cool down that fireman's hat with a little cold water,' I say around the ice, placing my hands around your hard length."

"'Fireman's hat?' And I'm the one with word issues?" he chuckles.

"'Shhh,' I say, moving my mouth closer and blowing the cool air over your cock, waiting for you to relax and let me continue."

"Call it what you want, as long as you suck it. Fuck, please tell me you put it in your mouth next. I need you to tell me how you'll suck it, Ellie," he hisses.

"With the ice in my mouth, I wrap my lips around the head of your dick. The ice begins to melt from your heat, and I start swirling my tongue around the sensitive head, coating you with my saliva, branding you as mine, making you all wet and ready for my mouth's assault. Using my tongue, I tease the tip, applying the perfect blend of pressure and suction. You're so turned on, you move your hands to my hair, and start kneading my head, holding it in place, and I fucking love it," I say, pausing, taking a moment to let it all sink in and to see how he's reacting. It doesn't take long to see I'm doing a good job, even as the lights go down for the previews.

"Shit, that feels so good, E. Fuuck," he whispers, his eyes closed as if he is picturing everything I was describing.

"As my mouth makes its way down your smooth shaft, I nibble a little bit, running my teeth gently along. I drag my lips and tongue over each ridge and vein before moving my hand up to play with your balls."

"Jesus Christ. I'm going to come, if you keep that up. Fuck, yeah, I can't wait to watch you take it all…" he says, as his hips start moving and I move my lips within millimetres of his ear and tell him that I can't wait either, and then the opening credits start to roll and…

Beep.

And I'm taken from my happy place by that familiar sound.

Chapter 42

Ellie

FUMBLING FOR MY headset, I click "accept" and speak into the line without looking at the caller specs: "Breathless Whisp—"

"Your only job right now is to listen. You understand? I'm in control here. I call the shots. Your only job is to say 'yes' and come on command. Understand?" the male caller bites out, cutting me off before I've even begun.

"Yes, I understand," I reply in my lowest voice, assuming this caller is going to be an aggressive one who might be best dealt with using my soft tone. Sometimes you get these types of callers, ones where they need an outlet, a place where they can prove they are capable of being in control of any and all situations. A caller desperate to let their dominant side shine, because most likely they aren't the ones wearing the pants in their reality.

Destiny warned me about these types of callers. She said to play along initially, then work to take back the control. She says that by the time you've taken control back, they're so far gone they rarely notice they're on the bottom again.

"Good. Now take your clothes off, pinch your nipples, get them ready for me. Tell me how it feels."

"Exciting. The pulling is sending a little tickle to my…"

"Shit, I can't wait to eat that cunt of yours. I'm gonna eat that pussy like a fucking cannibal."

His words are harsher than I'm used to, but I shake it off and play along.

"Oh good. I can't wait. I bet your mouth will feel so good on my pussy. It's been too long, I need…"

"Fucking right it'll be good. Once I get to you. But first I wanna watch you suck the fuck out of my cock. Get on your fucking knees. Now. I wanna listen to you gag and choke around my dick while I fuck your mouth and throat with my huge cock."

"Yes, I'd like that," I say, rolling my eyes, moving to grab a popsicle from the bar fridge's freezer.

There's a strange laugh that comes across the line, immediately causing dread to pool in my stomach. The hairs on my neck stand on end. I pause in the unwrapping of the icy pop.

"I don't want you to 'like' it. You'll fucking hate it, and I'll love the fact that you hate it. That's what sluts like you are good for, cocksucking. If I were there with you right now…in fact, I might just come down and find you, for being such a mouthy fucking whore. Oh yeah, darlin', I know where you work. I could easily come and get you. Anytime I want."

My hands begin to tremble with that admission. Whether it's true or not, it's never crossed my mind that it could be a possibility. I mean, I'm sure the Conrads have disgruntled past employees and other weirdo callers. I bet this is why they need that secured entrance. *Oh God. It's just me and Destiny and maybe two others here.* I'm trembling by the time his words begin to register again.

"Are you listening to me? Tell me you're ready, whore."

Shaking it off, I answer: "I'm here. I'm on my knees. Ready." I whisper. Hoping I can appease him and move this along. "I've got your cock in my hands," I try, hoping it's the right thing to say.

"No. Fuck you. This is my show. Now I want you to sit and listen to me. I'm pissed you've ruined this for me. I should come find you, bitch. Wait for you in the shadows when you leave the building."

My heart begins to thump wildly in my chest. *Ellie, he's bluffing, it's all just part of his fantasy, right? Just tune him out, do what he says.*

"I'll grab you. Wrap my hands around your stupid fucking neck, rob you of your breath. I'll take you when you aren't expecting it. Once you've walked far enough away, thinking you're safe. I'll grab you and push up against a brick wall, 'cause worthless sluts like you deserve it rough."

I gasp audibly, and it only spurs him on. I can't seem to stop listening, my body is frozen. I can't convince my hands to click the off button.

"You like that, bitch? The idea of me taking you? Knew you were a whoring cunt. Next, I'll fuck you in that nasty-as-fuck hole of yours. Stretching those butt cheeks, while I switch from ass to dirty cunt! Your asshole taking me over and over, in and out. When I'm good and fucking ready, I'll pull out, only to slip it back into your filthy mouth. You'll swallow my cum, taking my seed down that stupid whoring mouth of yours while I fuck your throat. Then, I'll grab my blade an—"

"Noooooo!" I yell, finally breaking free from my frozen state and disconnecting the call. I'm shaking. Tears stream down my face and I can't catch my breath. I'm a mess. A complete wreck, not just from his words but more because, deep down in my gut, I know that he's some creep who actually gets off on that violence shit. I'm mad at myself for not ending the call sooner, for freezing up—that, and allowing him to make me feel this way. For letting him degrade me like that. I'm suddenly angry at my fucking knee, at Dr. Robinson, at school. I'm angry for having to work in this kind of environment because of my need for money. *Fuck the money.*

Without thinking, I leave everything as is and exit the room in search of Destiny. I need to debrief and compose myself. I text her and she said to walk into Sweet 16, her door would be unlocked. But as I make my way along the hall, I find myself face-to-face with Greta.

"Oh goodness, Ellie, dear! What's the matter?" she says, walking me to the couch near her desk where she sits us both down.

"A bad call," I hiccup. "I didn't know y—you were here," I barely get out.

"Yes, I'm here. I decided to work the night shift. I need a day off next week so I figured I'd come in tonight and get stuff done. Is this your first bad one?" she asks, and I nod, taking the Kleenex she's offering.

"He was so mad, said he'd come and get me. Said he wanted to *hurt* me," I say, wiping away the tears that refuse to stop falling. "I can't believe I let him talk to me like that, let him say all these terrible things. I'm a *person*, Greta. I don't need to let anyone talk to me like that," I huff angrily.

"You're right. You don't. No call is worth you getting upset about like this. You hang up. Know it's the right thing. You hang up and flag it for Mrs. Conrad, and she'll look into him."

"No-one should have to deal with that. I'll make sure I go back and flag him."

"Good. And you're right, Ellie. When the job starts taking more from you then you're getting from it, its time to reevaluate what's important. You have to remember to keep Chanel separate from Ellie, though, too. That caller was using your character, not the real you. He's probably some lonely man with a distorted sense of reality, one who's hopeless and is counting on having made you feel scared. Let Chanel take that on and laugh at it, and allow Ellie to simply let it go when you log off. Walk out of here knowing Ellie is safe."

"I try. I do, but it's getting too hard. I don't think I can keep doing this job. I'm keeping secrets from people, my mom, my boyfr—. Never mind, I'm good. I just needed a minute away. Sorry, I'm having a bad night."

"We all have them. They all have them." Greta gestures to the hall. "I've sat here with almost every one of you girls, listening to the same thing. You're going to be all right, Ellie."

"Thanks, Greta. I know. Like I said, I'm mad at myself for letting him get to me. Never again, next time I'm hanging up right away. Regardless. I won't ever let a caller make me feel like that again. They can fire me…well, if I don't quit first." I nod, agreeing with my own words.

"We love you here, Ellie. Trust your gut, always, and know they won't fire you for not finishing a call like that. They care about you girls; they know they need to keep you all happy and safe. This isn't like those other places," she waves and I think about the two young women Ace had told me about. *God, I can't imagine what they must deal with.*

I wish I could talk to Ace right now; I wish I could tell him everything. I will, one day. I'm just not ready to see the look of disappointment that's sure to cross his face at my disclosure. I told him I worked at call a centre; I just left out the phone sex part. *I hope he understands.*

Then it hits me: *what if we've talked on the phone before?* I use a voice adapter. Who's to say he hasn't? I know he told me he's called a few lines for research. *Holy shit. Imagine? Oh my God, what if he was that guy tonight?*

"You going to be okay, dear? You suddenly went all pale…" Greta asks, bringing me out of what-if land.

"Yeah, I will be. Thanks, Greta. But I think I'm going to clock out early tonight."

"I think that's a great idea." She smiles warmly, patting my leg.

I take a taxi home.

Chapter 43

Ace

SITTING IN THE cafeteria, I can't keep a smile from crossing my lips when I stare at my phone, reading this morning's text exchange between Ellie and me. Reading it over a few more times, I'm extremely confident that I'm about to do the right thing.

Ellie: *what are you doing?*

Me: *the usual.*

Ellie: *oh yeah? What's that involve?*

Me: *thinking about you*
Wanting you
Wishing we were together
You know, the usual…

Ellie: *sweet talker ♥*

Me: *I speak the truth*

Ellie: *I'm gonna kiss you so hard.*

Me: *can't wait.*

Ellie: *see you soon, Doctor*

Me: *E!!!!!!!*

Ellie: *LOL, it's just so fun!*

Me: *har, har. See you soon.*

Ellie: *can't wait xo*

"Sam. Thanks for meeting me," I say, as my teaching assistant takes the seat across from me.

"No problem, Ace. I've got class in the next building in half an hour, so it's no trouble."

"How are you? How are your classes going?" I ask the man I'm hoping will be willing to assist me this late in the term.

"Good, pretty light right now. I ended up not needing to take The Origins of Animation, so I've got a lighter course load than I'd expected."

"That's a nice surprise, I'm sure."

"Yup. I was able to get tuition fees back, too, so that was a huge bonus."

"Listen, Sam. I won't keep you too long. I asked you here because I need a favour."

"Sure, what can I do for you? I mean, I probably owe you a few."

"I need help with a student. Do you know Ellie Hughes?"

"Yeah, I do. I'd help her with anything, if you know what I mean. She's hotter than hell," he says, winking smarmily, and the urge to lay this shithead out instantly consumes me. But I'm a professional scholar, not an MMA star.

"Not appropriate, Sam."

"Right, sorry, sir. Sure. I can help out, no problem. Tell me what you need," he says honestly.

"Well..." I pause. "I need you to mark her thesis and go over her other papers. I need you to see if you agree with my grade assessments."

"I can do that. Why, though? I mean you're the profess—oh shit. I get it. You've got the hots for her!" He claps his hands together. "You dirty dog. Well done, man. I'd let her have all A's." At this point, I realize this was a fatal mistake.

"Sam. You shut your mouth. You have no idea what you're talking about. There is nothing going on between Ms. Hughes and I. I've had some things come up and was trying to lighten my load."

"I bet you have," he interjects. I shake my head, trying to pretend that I misheard even though I know he said it. *Idiot.*

"You know what, punk? Consider this your final warning. You're off my team. Enjoy an even lighter load," I grit out.

Leaving Sam, I make my way to talk to the last person I wanted to, but the first person I should have.

Chapter 44

Ellie

READING THE EMAIL from Ace—saying that students who had previously been working with Sam as their thesis advisor needed to attend a mandatory meeting with Ace on Wednesday in the library's second floor conference room—has my curiosity piqued.

I hope everything's okay with Sam, he seems like a great guy. But by now, I'm getting a bit frustrated with Ace. I've texted him three times to check in and make sure that everything is all right and to offer my help if he needed it, but have yet to hear back from him.

Assuming he's dealing with something, I decide to take my irritation to the gym for a late night work out. My knee has been locking up on me a lot more often since I've been slacking at the gym. I'm coming to terms with the fact that I might not run competitively again. My new immediate goal is to learn to live with the pain, using the pain management routine Doctor Robinson and his team created for me.

Since I've not been competing this year, I actually feel somewhat better; I sleep better, my body isn't always sore, I can eat whatever I want and I love having all the extra time for myself. I didn't realize how much running took up my life. I'm happy to say that jogging for leisure now sounds like a pretty good goal to aim for down the road.

Entering the gym, I wasn't too surprised to hear a couple of machines going as I made my way to the change room. There are usually a few people here at this time, although normally by eleven I have the place to myself.

Whom I didn't expect to see when I walked out of the change room were Ace and Mercer, running on treadmills. My steps almost faltered when I walked out, catching Ace's eye and an accompanying lurking grin trained on me. I could almost feel his eyes blatantly *boinking* me from my toes up to my nose. Wanting to ward off the awkward feeling I was having with both men staring and smiling at me, I offer a small wave then bee-line it to the back of the gym and out of sight. Where exactly I was going, I had no clue. But if Mercer's subtle, knowing grin told me anything, it's that he knows something's up between me and his friend.

Finding a rowing machine in the back corner, I hop on, relieved when I can't see them anymore, giving me a bit a reprieve before I have to loop back into the main area to work on the strength-training machines. *Back to Ace's heady stare.*

Sooner than I'd like, I'm finished rowing, so I slink back into the main gym, feigning nonchalance. You know in tennis where you're moving your head left-to-right—then right-to-left, over and over again—to make sure you don't miss anything? Well, right about now, I feel as if I'm watching a three-way tennis match. One where Ace watches me, then I watch him before quickly diverting my gaze to Mercer, whom I catch watching Ace, then me, the whole time trying to hide a Cheshire Cat smile. *He totally knows!*

It's almost midnight now, and I have yet to utter more than simple "hey" to Ace or Mercer, despite the game of tennis we've been playing since I rounded back to the weight and cardio part of the gym, where I hopped on the elliptical while they did the training circuit. And the only reason they got that "hey" from me was because of Ace calling out my name, saying "Hey, Ellie," when I reappeared.

Finally, after nearly twenty minutes of working out on the elliptical I hear Mercer's voice. "Be sure to hit the lights before you lock up, eh?"

The double scrutiny was killing me, and I'm thankful he's leaving.

"You got it, boss. We won't be too much longer," Ace says, looking for my agreement.

"Yeah, I'm almost done too," I acknowledge.

"Right. 'Night, guys." He waves, a curious expression on his face as he looks between us one last time.

"'Night, Doctor Reynolds."

"Mercer, Ellie. Call me Mercer, please."

"I can do that." I smile. "Good night, Mercer. Thanks for letting me finish up."

"Not a problem. You're in good hands with Ace here." He clears his throat and closes the door behind him.

I'm mid-stride on the elliptical when I hear Ace's commanding tone.

"Come here, Ellie."

Immediately, my head jolts up to find him. My heart rate might have jolted a bit at the tone of his voice. And I might have gotten that Jell-O-leg feeling, too. Just maybe.

"Come here, Ellie," he repeats.

Looking up, my eyes find him easily where he's sitting at the chest press. As if guided by a force beyond my control, within a nanosecond I find myself standing in front of his muscular knees.

"How's the workout, E? Your knee?" He cages me with his thick thighs, his touch on my waist causing my nipples to harden under my sports bra. The result doesn't go unnoticed by Ace.

My tongue is taffy-stuck as he begins trailing his hands along my exposed sides, the deep green pools of his eyes never leaving mine.

"I'm all sweaty." I try to squirm from his grip.

"I bet you're sweet and salty—my favourite combination," he says, running his stubble across my exposed skin. "I want to snack on you, Ellie. It's killing me not to touch you. I can't stop thinking of what's under those tights," he whispers, dipping his head low onto my stomach, his lips brushing softly over my skin as he references that time in his office, the time he made me come without really touching me.

"It's killing me too," I say, and find I can't hold myself back. I cup his strong jaw, tilting his head to meet my eyes. Reaching up, he pulls the hair tie out of my hair, and simultaneously I pull off his glasses. Suddenly our faces are sheltered by my messy tendrils; our eyes lock again. His trail down to my mouth, and in turn I bite my lip, stifling the moan that tries to escape at being so turned on. He hesitates a few beats before meeting my stare again. Taking his glasses from my hand, he drops them beside us.

"I wanna bite that lip of yours, E. You look like sin right now." Leaning up, Ace positions himself to take my bottom lip between his teeth. He sucks gently on my bottom lip before running his tongue along to soothe the bite.

My hands immediately fall into his hair, the need to anchor myself to him while we continue to kiss is all consuming. I never want to let him go. Our tongues battle for dominance, he tastes like nothing I've experienced before: passion, sweetness, *mine*. All too soon, he's pulling away, trailing his tongue down in a slow path towards my stomach. "See? You're the ideal tasty blend—sweet, salty, and sexy. You going to let me eat you now, E.? Let me run my tongue over the sweetness between your legs? Let me nibble on that aching clit?" he asks, walking his fingers up my thighs, teasing me lightly where I want him the most.

"I want that, but someone might see. Might walk in," I whimper, tugging a lock of his dark hair, trying to make him pause in his endeavours.

"I could give a shit right now. All I care about is taking what's mine. You are mine, Ellie. And I know you want to give it to me, baby. I can smell how excited you're getting," he says, looking up at me while pushing my shorts and panties to one side and skimming one of his stealthy fingers along the lips of my soaked pussy for the first time.

Chapter 45

Ace

"GOD, ACE, YOU feel so good," Ellie whispers, as I continue to gently move two fingers over the outside of her wet pussy.

When she walked into the gym earlier, I almost came in my pants. I'll need to have a little chat about appropriate gym attire if she ever expects us to work out together. There's no way I could operate heavy equipment with her around in those tiny shorts without getting my swollen dick caught in the machinery.

"This feel good, E?" I ask, inserting two fingers inside her.

"So good," she says breathlessly, clenching her pussy walls around my digits. It wasn't my plan to touch her here, or like this, tonight, but when Mercer—the knowing bastard—left, I couldn't stop thinking about finally getting a feel of what I've been dreaming about for months.

Withdrawing my fingers, I stand, quickly switching our positions. I sit Ellie down, making quick work of pulling her runners—and both her shorts and panties—from her body before positioning myself on my knees in front of her on the chest press's small bench seat.

"Open up, E. It's time to let me taste your goodness. You've made me a starved man and I'm done fucking waiting." Reaching behind her waist, I pull her ass to the edge of the seat before spreading her legs to exactly where I want them. "Beautiful. You are a cinematographer's dream spread out like this. Look at that glistening pussy. You ready,

Ellie? You ready to come all over my face?"

"Oh Jesus. Yes. Oh God, Ace. Do it. I'm ready," she says, and I laugh at the hitch in her voice and the tremble that wracks her body. We both have so much pent up sexual frustration that I know it won't take me long to get Ellie off.

"I can't wait to break the last rule. A few more weeks, and I'll be inside you, finally feeling all of you."

"Ace..."

"Nothing between us, Ellie. I warned you," I remind her. Gripping her ass with both of my hands, I pull her slightly further towards the bench's edge to meet my mouth in perfect alignment.

Christ, she tastes perfect. I swirl my tongue over her clit before sucking on it rhythmically, giving her the perfect balance of pleasure and pain before lifting her legs and tossing them over each of my shoulders. Ellie's now leaning back low on the equipment, her pussy and ass hanging where they belong—over my face. I lap up her juices as I slide my flattened tongue along her slit and run my stubbled chin softly down over her lips, clit and inner thighs in a pattern that I know will drive her crazy. Her legs start jerking on my shoulders and her thighs are trying to clench my head in closer.

"Such a greedy girl with a greedy pussy to match. I fucking love it," I chuckle adding my finger into the rotation. I'm hard as stone, but I could care less—this is all for her.

"Yes, yes. Oh shit, don't stop, Ace. Please don't stop," she says, leaning up and trying to tangle her hand in my hair.

Picking up my pace, I rock the pattern a few more times before she detonates on my tongue. I pull her off the seat and we fall onto the floor with her laying on top of me, my hands running down her back soothingly as she comes back down to Earth.

After a few minutes of silence, Ellie looks up at me, eyes still hooded. "We shouldn't have done this. We're breaking all of our rules, Ace.

And we're on campus," she says, when her breathing finally evens out.

"It's fine, E. I took care of it," I say, rolling us over. I kiss her nose before shifting to stand up. Grabbing her shorts and panties, I pull her up, and then help her dress. Once I've got her shorts back on, I pull her into my chest, nuzzling her neck, taking in her sweet scent. And letting what I've said sink in.

"What do you mean?" She pulls back, her face confused, her eyes seemingly worried.

"Exactly what I said."

"Stop being evasive. What's going on? Does this have anything to do with Sam? I saw your email and you didn't text me back." She reaches up to cup my cheeks to make me look at her.

"Everything is good. We don't need to talk about it now."

"Tell me. Right now, please."

Taking her by the hand, I lead her to the mats where it's more comfortable. I sit, then pull her down to straddle me. Her arms wrap around my neck instinctively, and I revel in her closeness.

"I talked to Sam earlier. It didn't go very well. I needed to make sure we would be safe in case he decided to make trouble, so I went and talked to the chair of my department about us today," I shrug, pretending like it was no big deal, when in fact it was a huge deal, and says a lot that we haven't yet said to each other out loud.

"Holy shit." Tears start to surface in the corner of her eyes. "So that's it, just like that? So now what? Am I expelled? Do I lose the right to graduate? Are you fired? Was all this just a helluva goodbye present?" She gestures to the chest press. "Oh my God, Ace, what will we do?" Ellie huffs out all at once, a few tears starting to fall.

"Shh, E. We're both fine. Everything is more than good, actually."

"How can that be? You told them about us, and you're my professor?" she says, bewildered.

So, for the next forty minutes I sit with Ellie on my lap and tell her everything. How Doctor Mehta (my department chair) was understanding about our situation when I unloaded it all on her following my meeting with Sam. She also agreed that I did the right thing in dismissing him.

"She understood that these things happen, and believed that we had yet to cross any major lines, so that no-one in any of my classes had reason to think that we've had a conflict of interest. She was somewhat disappointed that I hadn't come to her sooner, but was willing to let that go since I've been such an outstanding employee. She made a few calls on her end, and it's been decided that Jax will re-mark all of your assignments this term, acting as a third-party to ensure that there wasn't any favouritism on my part. Jax will also grade your thesis paper—with Joelle's input, and mine—after you defend it next week. And that's pretty much it."

"Wow. I can't believe you risked getting in trouble for me..."

"For us, E. I did it for us. I hate feeling like we're doing something wrong when deep down I know it's nothing but right. They will keep everything a private matter as long as we continue to be respectful and don't start flaunting our relationship, so it's best to keep things quiet for a few more weeks until you graduate," I say, catching another escaped tear.

"So, no bleacher song-and-dance just yet, then, eh?" Ellie teases, giving me a sexy smirk.

"Way to ruin your graduation present."

"I think, after tonight, I just might have fallen pretty hard for you, *Doctor* Ryan," she winks, before hugging me close.

"You better have," I whisper in her ear.

Because I've already fallen.

This girl is definitely my trifecta.

Just one final phone call to make everything right in my world.

Or so I think, anyway...

Chapter 46

Ellie

"YOU'LL BE GREAT. I have no doubt that you'll impress them as much as you have me."

Ace kisses my forehead outside the small seminar room where the thesis defences are being held. It's been a long road, and the journey has led me on a path I never expected to find myself walking, but it's one I'm happy I took. I feel a confidence I never thought I exhibited before, even when running track, and I know that whatever questions Jax, Joelle, and Dr. Mehta ask me today, I'm ready. Unfortunately, Ace isn't permitted to sit in on my presentation with circumstances being what they are, but he's here to wait and offer support, and has been helping me prepare all week.

"Thank you for everything, Ace. I mean it. I don't think I could have done this without you," I say, taking a deep breath.

"I'll be right here when you're done." He squeezes my hand as I turn to enter the room.

"Oh, and E," he beams, "remember to *use the Force.*"

I let out a nervous chuckle before walking in to face the Galactic Senate waiting in the seminar room.

"Ms. Hughes, welcome. I must say, I thoroughly enjoyed your dissertation," Dr. Mehta states, "Please, sit. We have a few questions for you."

I nod and give all three a warm smile before sitting down.

"Question one: Do you think Princess Leia could have freed herself from the Death Star without the help of..."

Almost two hours later, I left that seminar room grinning from ear to ear.

Chapter 47

Ellie

"E*VER WONDER IF we'd get along in person? Do you ever imagine what I look like? I try to picture you...*"

"*What was your childhood like?*"

"*What is your biggest fear?*"

"*...and sometimes I feel like I know you. Do you ever get that feeling?*"

Snippets of conversation after conversation between me and Jake run through my mind like a highlight reel tonight, as I take in what he's just asked me.

He wants to meet. In person, face-to-face.

Over the last few months, Jake has become not only a regular caller, he's become more. I think it would be safe to say that we've become sort of friends. Partially because he reminds me of Ace in some ways, especially when he calls just to talk. It hasn't always been about sex with Jake, and tonight, it makes sense why. I can't put my finger on it, but there have definitely been times where I feel the same easiness when speaking with Jake that I do with Ace. I know deep down that Jake and I could have some semblance of friendship in the outside world, but am I willing to test my theory by meeting him in person? *A caller. What would the Conrads say?*

Granted, we know things about each other; or at least I feel like I know things about the real Jake. For example, like Ace, he grew up without his parents in a smaller town; I know that his first kiss was with a girl named Sabrina; his job is taking up all of his time right now; he loves *Star Wars,* and also knows the every single word of the *Rocky Horror Picture Show* (a piece of info that I might have been a bit overexcited about, seeing as I can recite every single word verbatim, too. *But who's to say it's not all part of a role, the game? Just because Jake's told me this, doesn't mean it's necessarily true.*

It's because of this that I'm struggling with what I should do.

"Do you think we'd be friends if we met?"

"Have you ever thought of me when we aren't talking?"

It's weird, because I do.

I have thought of Jake. Not often, but I have.

Now don't get me wrong, I don't feel the same pull for Jake that I do for Ace. Not even close. And I'd never compromise what I have with Ace, either. That's why, when Jake proposed to meet me tonight, in the end I told him no.

With that decision also came the decision that it's time to take the costume off and pack Chanel69 away for good.

Thinking of Ace causes a wave of guilt to crash in my stomach. I need to tell him about Breathless Whispers. Especially after what he did for us, the risk he took by coming clean to the chair, in case Sam took his anger too far.

I owe Ace the truth. I have to be honest and tell him about Chanel, this job, even if it is my last shift. He deserves to know.

And maybe he'll want my input for his documentary? *Yeah, if he still even wants to be with you after he hears what you've been doing for the last eight months...time will tell, I guess.*

I can't believe I've been working here for eight months; I'm going to be a graduate next week! Giving my notice felt incredible. Ever since *that* call, I've barely picked up any shifts anyway. Greta's words rang true: *"When the job starts taking more from you than you're getting from it, it's time to reevaluate what's important."*

I decided I didn't need to put myself through the stress anymore, that I no longer felt safe, and that it just wasn't worth it anymore. It's not like I needed more money; school would be done soon enough. I've managed to save a fairly large nest egg, one that can sustain me for a few months while I pound the pavement with my bad knee again in search of a job. Only this time, I'll be looking for a full-time job in the film industry!

I've already sent out a ton of resumes. Having pulled off an A on my thesis will be an extra boost to make me stand out. According to Ace, Dr. Mehta told him that I'm one of three finalists competing to have highlights of my thesis featured in *The Canadian Journal of Film Studies*. *How amazing would* that *be?*

And with all the changes and excitement in my life, I'm happy to say my mom is coming to watch me graduate. I have yet to decide if I'm going to tell her about Chanel. I'd like to think that one day I might, but now probably isn't the best time. As for the sperm donor, unfortunately, my mom's lawyers weren't able to find that loophole to get the money back that he'd stolen. It's okay, though. I told her that sometimes it's better to leave the past in the past, and move on. Surprisingly, she agreed. Tom might have something to do with that, too. He proposed to her, and I haven't heard my mom this happy in forever. I'm excited for them to meet Ace. And as soon as that diploma hits my hand, I will proudly introduce him as my boyfriend. I can hardly wait until we can go public with our relationship.

"Chanel? You still there? I didn't scare you away, did I? I'm sorry. I shouldn't have asked to meet you." Jake's apologetic voice brings me back to the here and now.

"A journalist? Wow, I wasn't expecting *that.* I'm sorry, Jake. I'm just processing everything."

"How much would it cost to meet you?" he had asked minutes ago, barely above a whisper. Despite knowing there's a huge possibility that

he's some pasty, basement-dwelling creeper who sits in front of his computer masturbating to anything deemed erotic while smoking cigarettes and pounding back two-litre bottles of Pepsi, I considered it.

Because it's Jake.

My friend.

My regular.

My safety net at this job. The one caller who's been consistently kind, almost caring, one who sees me as a person, when I'm otherwise surrounded in a sea of piranhas.

And I have this gut feeling that he's the complete opposite of Pepsi Guy. I believe him when he says he's doing an article about the reasons women turn to phone sex lines as a way to make money.

Similar to Ace's work in his documentary.

It's research I've helped Jake with to a point, albeit unknowingly. Knowing that he was role-playing as much as I was makes my liking him seem somewhat less crazy, in my mind. Jake has been the only caller that I felt any connection with. So, I'm tempted, but unfortunately for Jake, I can't help him with his story. Not when my own boyfriend hasn't a clue about my job and could probably use my experiences to fill any gaps in his own project. The project he's finishing up as we speak, working to make as perfect as it can be so he can submit it to TIFF for judging next month.

Ace is amazing, and I have no doubt that his film will receive all the accolades and attention it deserves. It's probably the most informative and thought-provoking theme for a documentary I've heard of in a long time, from the snippets I've seen here and there while he's been working on it.

I just hope I'm still around to celebrate his achievements with him. I owe Ace the opportunity to hear the truth.

And, most importantly, meeting clients is not safe. *I know exactly what the Conrads would say.* I'd never risk my safety, even if I "think"

Jake's a nice guy. There are just too many crazies out there, and I have no way to know for certain that he's not one of them.

"I'm sorry, Jake, but I can't meet you in person. I'll gladly answer any questions you have, but I'm not willing to meet you for a live interview. I hope you understand."

"I understand. Of course I do. I can't say I'm not disappointed, because you're the perfect candidate for my piece, but I get it. No hard feelings, I hope? Anything I can do to make up for lying to you?" he asks.

"No, I'm okay. Thank you for understanding, and for helping me out along the way, too. I wasn't sure I could do this job at first, but your calls always helped to build my confidence, so thank you for that."

"You're welcome. It was my pleasure. Wow, it looks like this will be my last call. Thank you for the help you've given. You're excellent at your job, Chanel. I wish you all the best," he says. And then I get an idea.

"Hey, Jake? Before you go, I have a request. Will you do me a favour?" I ask, excited at the prospect of putting the shoe on the other foot, as the saying goes.

Laughing, he agrees. "Sure. What can I do for you?"

Chapter 48

Jake

I HAVE TO admit, I'm disappointed she won't agree to meet me. Maybe I should have told her the truth? Maybe she'd be more inclined to come in for an interview if I had?

But I honestly can't blame her. It's not like she knows me. Other than the few superficial things we've talked about, I could be some serial killer for all she knows. Funny, though, I always told her the truth when we talked. There was an easiness that came over me whenever we spoke. As if I knew her, as if we were already friends. Part of me is proud and relieved that she said no. It showed me she's aware of her boundaries and that safety is important to her.

Luckily for me, I managed to get interviews with two other phone sex operators I had spoken to a few times, although they weren't as talented as *her*.

Crazy how after seven months of talking, I see her as a friend, one whom I would like to see move on to bigger and better things. If things were different, if I weren't already serious about someone else, I might have even offered to help her if she needed it. But I would never jeopardize what I have with my girl, especially for someone I've never actually met. Don't get me wrong, she's absolutely been the best phone sex operator that I've talked to and I would have loved to have her showcased in my project, to know her motivation for working the line, her life plans, her perspective on the job itself since she's so articulate about it. But it is what it is.

Thankfully, she's at least agreed to let me include some of our recorded conversations, since I won't be identifying her. Out of all the contacts I had, I spoke to her the most, a part of that instant connection. My calls may have been a bit unorthodox, but she was flexible and adapted to my moods, scenarios, and managed to get me to easily become a regular, continuing to call long after I'd needed to.

"...how about you tell me a story for a change tonight? Let me be the caller?" she asks, and I agree. "You could add your own perspective into your story, what the job feels like, the thought process, how quickly it all moves, and whether or not it's easy to pull off?"

Looking at it like that, I think that might be a great addition. I could speak a bit more honestly about what it feels like to be the one trying to maintain a caller's interest, adding another layer, and share how I performed in that role. As this was our last call, I figured I could do that. I'm not going to be getting myself off, and this is a great opportunity. One I'm sure my girl might find amusing, me being on the other side, seeing what it's like. *Hey, maybe she'll let me practice my newfound skills on her sometime soon?* I can't wait for her to sit down with me to watch the whole documentary from start to finish, to get her take on my hard work. It's always been about her for me, anyway, when I was talking to Chanel, and the other places I called, too. I can never get her off my mind.

Only once did I allow myself to jerk off while conducting my research, and it was while I was talking to Chanel, before my girl and I were serious. I had called in and tried to trip her up, testing her to see if I could get her flustered with my scenario and questions, but instead she guided me through how she masturbated.

But all I could picture was Ellie. I was done. That girl had me wound up so tight that I couldn't breathe. So completely fucked right up that I couldn't help picturing Ellie during Chanel's descriptions while I got myself off. All the other times, I simply sat back and listened to my personal Scheherazade tell me stories that all featured Ellie in my mind.

"What should I talk to you about? Any last requests?" I put out there, not having a clue what she might want to hear.

"You're supposed to be the professional, Jake," she teases.

"Okay, then help me. Give me some idea of what you might like," I ask, honestly drawing a blank. This shit is hard to think of under pressure.

"What's your biggest fantasy?" Chanel asks, and it's easy. Instantly, I picture my girl and I in my office, me finally taking her on my desk.

"I'd say having sex in my office would be a big one."

"Oh yeah. That'd be hot for sure."

"Yeah, it would." My dick twitches at the image of Ellie spread-eagled for me.

"I think we should play it out, Jake. For old time's sake. And, truth be told, tomorrow's my last shift. I quit. I can't do this job anymore," she shares, and I'm happy to hear that she's quitting. I don't ask for the whys, because it's not like I can't imagine why someone would quit in her line of work. I want more for Chanel, and it makes me feel good knowing that she won't be subjected any further to the shit I now know goes on at these places. "This would be a perfect good bye, and a thanks for the secret help," she says, and I hear her smile at the other end of the line.

"That's awesome news. I'm excited for you," I tell her honestly.

"Thanks. Me too. Glad to finally be done school, and not needing to worry about tuition payments anymore."

"Aha! the reason for the job comes out," I tease.

"Blah, blah, yeah, yeah. Anyway…are you going to share this fantasy with me or what? I'm an excellent listener. It will let you experience how this crazy job really is, writer-man," Chanel teases me back, and I feel a flash of guilt for bending the truth, for saying I'm a journalist, but I was worried she would freak out if I told her I was actually a filmmaker and that this was all for a documentary, one I'm hoping will be featured at one of the largest film festivals in North America. For some reason, people clam up when there's a chance they feel they might be exposed on camera instead of just in the written word. Especially when they hear the word "documentary". It's like it's some sort of exposé out to ruin them, even though I would, of course, disguise each person and their voice upon request.

"All right. Let's do this. You ready to hear what I hope to accomplish one day soon? My biggest fantasy?"

"Hell, yes. I've even busted out some popcorn. I'm way too excited to get to listen for a change."

"Well, Happy Graduation. Sit back and enjoy."

"And *action,*" she says, and, right away, Ellie saying the exact same thing to me in the coffee shop pops into my mind.

There's no way. I mean, her voice doesn't sound the same, but that's such an Ellie thing to say…

Chapter 49

Ellie

"AND *ACTION,*" I say, wondering what Jake would say if he knew his fantasy was also one of mine.

One I plan on fulfilling with Ace, when I surprise him in his office next week. In my fantasy, I finally let him take me on his desk. *Hard.* Not being his student anymore definitely has some perks. With the fear of consequences gone, I feel it's time to give Ace and I something we've both been waiting for.

Maybe I'll get inspired by listening to how Jake's fantasy plays out.

"I'm actually a professor, you see. And I've had the hots for one of my students. We'd been skirting around our attraction for months. But one night, she shows up to my office and all bets are off," he says huskily. My heart suddenly accelerates its pace at the irony unfolding as I listen.

No way. It can't be.

"Sounds promising. Please continue," I whisper, barely audible.

"At the sound of her soft knock, my cock twitches, knowing she's on the other side of the door, here to see me. Waiting for me to let her in. I'd been waiting impatiently for what felt like hours. She was late. I was pissed and planned on letting her know it. Planned on showing her how frustrated I was."

Holy shit. It can't be!

"Okay so far?" Jake asks, stopping midway.

"Perfect. Keep going, don't stop. I'm intrigued. Tell me more."

"Okay," he sniggers.

Little does he know, I'm freaking out big time.

"Opening the door, she stumbles into my office, or rather, into my chest. She was about to knock again, but instead fell face-first into me. Looking up at me, her hazel eyes seem to take on a darker shade alongside the flush of her apologetic face, and my anger dissipates. Suddenly, it's replaced by feelings of hunger, of longing. A hunger to kiss her, to ravage her right there in that moment. Wanting to touch, to hold, to finally feel the silkiness of her skin, her hair, every part of her sexy, lithe body as it moves beneath my own." He pauses, allowing me to take in all in.

"Jesus," I whimper—wetness pooling in my panties—knowing I'm right.

"'You're late,' I tell her. 'I'm not happy. I don't wait for anyone,' I say, once she's inside and I've closed and locked the door. 'You need to realize that my time is valuable,' I say, walking forward while she inches back. I keep seething, walking forward until her back is against my desk. She's cornered, with nowhere else to move. Taking one more step, I cause her to lean back over the edge of the desk. It's then that I pounce, like a hunter stalking his prey. I lift her legs simultaneously, wrapping them around my waist and I deposit her on the desk, nudging my way in to stand between her legs, hard against her."

"God, that's hot," I utter unintentionally, slapping my hand across my mouth, because this is going sideways fast.

"'You're in my head. I can't stop thinking of you,' I say, cupping her face with my palms. Inching in closer, I inhale her scent. 'You always smell so fucking good, baby. Tell me, E, do you taste as good?' I ask, laying her down, my intentions clear—"

Oh fuck!

"E"?

I knew *it!*

"Oh God...*Ace*?" I blurt, cutting him off.

"*What the fuck?* ...Ellie, is that...is that...*you?*"

I can't answer him. All I can do is hang up. And I do.

I'm shaking, my body in shock.

All this time? How...how can it be? It makes sense. I get the "why", but how...how didn't I know?

I need to get out of here. Moving the cursor to red, I log Chanel out—permanently.

Looking around Sweet 44, taking in the chaise, the mirror, the desk, and finally the bar fridge in the corner, I nod, and give a small smile before closing the door on this scene of my life.

I just hope my decisions haven't ended my story before I get my happily ever after.

Chapter 50

Ellie

DEFLATED, I STEP into the elevator, pushing the button for the seventh floor. I lean my head against the back wall, wishing Courtney were home. She and Jax went away for the weekend to celebrate her graduation; they turned into quite the couple after their "non-date" at the movies months ago. They've been pretty inseparable ever since. *Man, could I ever use her advice right now, along with a few shots—or better still—bottles of tequila.*

So, Jake is Ace.

And Ace is Jake.

Life is one long movie reel of fucked-up coincidences, and Faith and Karma are a tag team of bitches that no-one can deny.

Jake is Ace.

Pulling out my phone, I check it for the billionth time since leaving Breathless Whispers. Still no word from Ace, not that I was holding my breath that he'd reach out to me. Between the two of us, I'm the one who has more explaining to do. If I could muster up the courage to call, I might actually get the answer to the bazillion questions racing through my mind at warp speed.

God, what if he thinks I'm a horrible person? A cheater? A whore? Will he give me the chance to explain? Believe that I only ever got off that one time, and it turns out it was with him? My mind plays all these questions, and more, on overload, yet I'm too afraid to reach out.

At the familiar *ding*, I'm pulled out of my panic zone and step out of the elevator onto my floor. Turning right, my footing falters when my eyes land on the one person I need most right now, the one person who can tell me if we're going to get the ending we deserve.

The ending I want us to have, the ending I want—*with him.*

Ace.

Turning towards me at the sound of my feet, our eyes clash—his eyes assessing yet smiling, mine no doubt unsure and reluctant. I freeze mid-step, my body going into some kind of reactive mode from the uncertainty of where things lie between us. Feet suddenly heavy as if encased in cement, unable to inch or step closer if I wanted to, I'm simply stuck. My heart palpitations are so strong, he must be able to see the organ itself trying to break free from the confines of my chest. My hands shake like leaves, my breathing is shallow, my mouth is desert dry.

But then I see it. I feel it. *Hope.*

With one look, that familiar feeling of Jell-O that only he elicits makes its way to my legs. And when I really look at him, that's when I see it. That familiar smirk pulling at his mouth, his damn dimple out on the loose again, here to taunt me, to make me want to climb him so I can lick it and give it the greeting it deserves for being so bloody sexy.

But I don't climb him, and neither of us speaks.

Like in an old Western movie, we stand facing each other, preparing for the gunfight about to happen on the seventh floor of my high-rise, waiting the other out. Who'll be the first to draw? Who'll be the first to broach the subject weighing on both our minds? I'm dying to speak, but I'm tongue-tied.

I'm caught up in not only the situation, but in him, his presence, the way he's looking at me. He's striking; I can't take my eyes off him. His inky hair is mussed up like he's been pulling at it for hours. His emerald eyes have a little glint in them, highlighted—of course—by those glasses that only make him hotter. His lips look especially kissable right now and I want them all over my body. Cocking my head, I let my eyes drop, taking him in from toes to nose, like he's done to me so many times. Ace Ryan offers the promise of being one hell of a sexy thrill ride and if I could right now, then I would definitely hop on. My eyes continue to roam up and down, down and up, hopefully silently conveying how badly I want him, how badly I am hoping that he wants me too—*still.*

"Ellie." My head snaps back to his face. There's a surprising edge to his voice, but relief floods me, seeing a playful grin.

"Ace," I murmur tentatively.

"And…*action,*" he calls.

Without hesitation or forethought, it's as if we both know what to do at the mark. Breaking the mould weighing me down, my feet are released and follow my heart and mind to Ace, who's striding towards me. Meeting in the middle, our bodies collide at full tilt, our mouths connecting with a jet-fuelled fire that's inextinguishable, our hands roaming to touch and grip each other everywhere and anywhere we can. Pulling back, rubbing his thumb along my cheek, Ace looks at me with an intensity I feel to the bottom of my soul.

"I can't believe it was you," he says, and I close my eyes, working to keep the tears at bay. Placing gentle kisses over my lips, he whispers, "Don't cry, baby."

"I'm sorry." I barely let my words escape, a feeling of enormous guilt consuming me for keeping this a secret from him.

Opening my eyes, we stare, communicating so much without words. Then: "Kiss me, Ellie. That's all I need right now. I only want you." He tugs me even closer, if that were possible. Ace and I stand, kissing one another like long-lost lovers uniting after the most painful of absences. I delight in every moment, my body relaxing with the comforting thought that everything is going work out as it should after all.

Ace pulls at my bottom lip, a move I feel between my legs. "We need to talk, E."

"Talking is overrated," I whisper. Then I sigh, exasperated. "But I know. We do. I have a good excuse, though, Ace," I say, moving past him to unlock the door to my apartment.

"I have no doubts you do, sweetheart. I trust you. I'm the luckiest son of a bitch and I know it. I'm grabbing onto you and I'm never letting go. Now relax, everything will be all right," Ace says gently, as he shuts and locks my apartment door behind us. After toeing off our shoes, he guides me to the couch and sits close beside me, resting his arm over my shoulder while our legs touch, side-by-side. Wanting to be closer, I move to straddle him instead.

"Hi," I say softly, staring at his chest to avoid his eyes for a moment.

"Hi. You ready to talk?" he asks, tilting my head up to meet his eyes as he drops a sweet kiss on my nose.

"Hold. I'll be right back," I say, jumping off him and heading to the kitchen to get us two shot glasses and the tequila. "Okay." I take a deep breath walking back into the living room. I pour and take a shot before mounting him again and offering him his own. Amused, he takes the drink.

"All set now, are we?" he chuckles.

"Yeah, I think so. It's a little weird talking about this with you when you're, you know..." I nod my head towards him.

"No, I don't know," Ace says, pulling me tighter to his chest. "Tell me."

"When you're Jake, but also *you*. I've told you some crazy stories, and I'm a bit embarrassed right now thinking of all the things I said to you when you were Jake and I was Chanel," I admit, feeling my face turning hot.

"Ellie. Don't be. It's me. We can talk about anything, besides those stories were sexy as fuck. Do you know how hard you made me? Shit, woman. And to come to learn that you're 'Chanel'? My little dirty girl…" he laughs, running his hands over my bum and giving my cheeks a little squeeze. "Now, tell me the story of how you ended up there from the beginning, then we can get back to the tales you tell best," he says, laughing, while pulling me in for a soothing hug and another one of those sweet kisses I love. This time, it's my lips that reap the reward.

After another shot or two, lots of tears, and a few laughs, I get through telling Ace everything; I spill the beans about the last eight months, starting back at the very beginning. From my knee, to my mom's situation with the sperm donor, to applying for the job with Egg Yolk Man, to the Conrads, and to Courtney and me trying to find a sexy handle and coming up with names like "Rideanne" and "Kitten." I tell him about Destiny, about my training, about Greta, about some of the different callers I've experienced and finally finish the story with tonight's adventures: where I ended my career as a Phone Sex Superhero with my favourite regular—Jake.

And the whole time, Ace is there holding me close, wiping my tears, teasing me a little. But most of all, he shows acceptance of my choices for the reasons I had to make them, as well as understanding and support for my decisions.

"Do you have any questions?" I ask, once we've been silent for a few minutes, his hand running through my long hair.

"Yeah, but not right now, though. Because right now, I'm too fucking hard with the idea that all this time you've been my fantasy and reality, wrapped up in the perfect package that is *you,* Ellie Hughes," he says, palming my breasts over my pink cotton V-necked shirt, the telltale sign of his erection nudging my bottom. "You amaze and captivate me. I've fallen in love with you, Ellie. I need you, baby."

"I love you too, Ace. So very much. Thank you for giving me the chance to explain," I wipe away more escaping tears, "and thank you for explaining Jake's intentions." I kiss his jaw. "You sure there isn't anything else you want to know right now?"

"No, E. I don't need to know everything tonight about why you work—no, *worked*—there. But you aren't working there ever again, though. You know this, right?" He pulls me off his chest to look at me, his tone taking on a more serious edge.

I smile. "Yes, Caveman. I quit tonight. A few days early, mind you, but yes. I'm done. My Phone Sex Superhero days are gone."

"Thank fuck," he says, kissing my forehead, then dragging his mouth along my cheek, before moving to cover my mouth with his. Stopping all too soon, he looks at me again—this time adoringly—and shakes his head. "I still can't believe it's been you all this time, dirty girl," he laughs, and I swat his chest.

God, I love him. He really is an amazing man.

Oh, and I take it back. I'm glad Courtney's gone for the weekend, especially because of what happens next.

Chapter 51

Ace

SCREWED.

Done for.

Finished.

Finito.

Fucked.

Completely fucked, and I love it.

I love her.

And I told her.

And fuck me, she loves me too.

Ellie Raine Hughes.

Chanel69.

The best distraction to ever come my way…loves me.

That knowledge alone is enough to make my dick hard for eons. Sitting here with her on my lap after she told me everything about taking the job at Breathless Whispers, her knee, her mom, the scholarship—everything—I'm even more in love with this woman, if it were possible. Her tenacity and unwillingness to give up on her dreams is admirable, even if I don't love the idea of her having had to work in the sex trade to get there. And the need to finally claim her as mine is thundering through my system.

"I'm thinking we need to live out a few of those fantasies you told me, now that we're face-to-face. I've got some dialogue for you: 'I can't wait to slip inside you'. To feel you, touch you, and best of all, to watch as you finally take my cock, over and over again. Maybe we could replay that masturbation sequence too? That shit brought me to my knees, picturing you doing that to yourself," I whisper in her ear, my voice husky from the memory. She squirms on my lap, and I know my words are getting to her just as much. "Are you wet for me, Ellie? Am I going to feel how hot I make you when I touch you…here?" I ask, sliding my palm along her thigh before snaking my hand to the front where I can feel her heat. She's wearing a pair of those sexy black tights we both love so much. Unable to control the urge to take her, I flip us, causing Ellie to yelp in surprise at the sudden position change, with her now lying on the couch underneath me.

"Ace!"

"Fuck, I love these bloody tights," I bite out, trailing my face down to her centre while my hands move along her toned legs.

"You smell like you're wet and ready, baby. I can't wait to slip my cock inside you. To feel you clinging to my dick with this sweet pussy of yours." I rub my hand along the inseam of her pants, pressing my palm into her pussy.

"Jesus," she bites her lip. Her walnut-coloured eyes dilate with lust when I slip my hand down the front of her tights, rubbing against her core.

"So wet," I share, after I start running two fingers along her pussy lips, coating myself with her excitement, loving the feeling of her juices as they cover my fingers. Slowly removing my hand, I hear her whimper at the loss, a sound I love. I love the pout that graces her lips. Knowing she misses my touch is empowering and sends a bloody zing right to my chest.

"You want my cock, E? You ready to feel me, greedy girl?" I ask, smirking at her reaction. Taking the glistening fingers, I rub them along my lips before bringing them to my nose. "Your smell is exquisite, baby." Her eyes go wide as they trail the path my fingers make from my nose to my lips where my tongue darts out to join the party, licking them clean. "Mmm, perfection." I move my hand back down for more. *Always wanting more of her.*

Lifting her shirt, I run my other hand over her taut stomach. Her skin is flawless, like her. Moving both hands now, I grip her waist, holding her in place as I trail my tongue and cheek along her sides and stomach, the need to be close to her overwhelming.

"Love you, baby," I say, my mouth running back up to the material covering her amazing rack. Pulling at the large cups of her black lacy bra, I release one breast then the other. Wrapping my mouth around one nipple I suck and nip at it before moving on to the next, giving it the same treatment.

"I love you too, Ace. Oh shit, that feels like heaven." Ellie continues to moan while I'm hard at work, sucking one tight peak then the other. She arches into my touch, feeding me more of her sweet tits. Taking both into my hands, I move my stubbled chin along the soft skin of her cleavage, leaving a trail of flushed skin in the wake of my kisses and sliding tongue as they move over each of her pert nipples again and again. Her tits are fucking perfect. She writhes beneath me, while she pulls me closer to where she wants me most.

"Touch me, please, Ace. Now. I need to feel you," she squirms, and it's music to my cock. "Ace!" she shouts in surprise, when I pull her up off the couch, tug her shirt back down, then sling her over my shoulder.

"We need a bed for all the things I'm planning to do to you," I smack her ass, "my dirty Chanel." Then rubbing the same spot, I tell her: "I can't wait to taste and see all of you, my sweet, sweet Ellie." Shaking my head, I can't help but laugh at what a contradiction my girl turned out to be.

"You're my little vixen, aren't you, E? Let's go act out some stories."

She giggles, as I carry her down the hall to her room.

Chapter 52

Ellie

KICKING THE DOOR shut, Ace stops in the middle of my room, lowering me at an excruciatingly slow pace down the front of him, allowing me the privilege of feeling every hard dip, plane, dive and bulge that exists on him.

Wrapping his hand in my hair, he tilts my head ever so slightly and kisses me with everything he's got, once again leaving me breathless. Groaning into my mouth, Ace dances his tongue into mine while his hands move to the hem of my shirt, my arms immediately cooperating as he tugs the shirt up and over my head.

"I can't fucking wait to touch you, beautiful. Let's get the rest of these cock-blocking clothes off of you, now. I want to see what's all mine," he grits out, his grass-coloured eyes alive and intense with desire. Unable to control myself, I jump up, wrapping my legs around his front, thankful he's there to catch me. He lifts me up higher with his hands gripping my ass, connecting us as closely as two people can be, and I kiss him again with everything I have. It feels incredible finally having this; everything out in the open, no secrets lingering in the dark waiting to surface anymore. And the fact that I'm straddling parts of Jake mixed in with Ace astounds me. The idea that they are the same person overwhelms me, knowing it's true.

"I just can't believe it was you, Ace. It was so weird, I felt this connection with Jake. Like I knew it was you or something," I whisper, resting my forehead on his shoulder, an overwhelming feeling taking root again.

"I know exactly how you feel, baby. It's crazy, but it's true," he says, and I tighten my hold around his neck before bringing our lips together, fusing them together in a soul-searing kiss.

"Make me yours now, Ace," I plead, a second before my back hits the mattress.

"Great minds, E," he says, and I giggle. "Now, let's get this off."

"God, yes," I say, leaning forward so he can finally remove my lace bra. And remove it he does; without a worry, he tosses it behind him.

"Fucking beautiful. These tits are going to be the death of me," he says, fondling both with his big hands. "They are in direct competition with that sweet pussy of yours; each needing so much attention, my insatiable girl. How ever will I decide?" He raises a brow, and I melt at his playfulness.

Stepping back, Ace starts to remove his T-shirt—featuring Tony Montana from *Scarface*—his eyes never leaving mine as he strips off the blue material in that sexy, nonchalant way guys do it, over their heads from the back.

Grin in place, I wipe my face to check for drool as his lust-filled eyes smile down at me, knowing exactly what he's doing to me. Ace's chiseled body never ceases to make me turn into a completely non-verbal mess of take-me-right-now, the way his tanned skin highlights his cut abs, wide shoulders, and the sexiest set of traps I have ever seen. I have big plans to lick those in the near future. *Damn.* I bite my lip, taking him in.

"When you look at me like that, it makes me crazy for you, E," he says, running his hand along my cheek.

Moving into his touch, I meet his gaze and elicit my own challenge: "Show me how crazy."

"Get over here," he says, pulling my legs so I'm hovering at the edge of the bed. Right where he wants me, right where I want to be. Placing each of my legs to rest over his shoulders, Ace runs his finger along my slit, the squelching sound of my desire for him flagrant.

"Love that sound. Always wet for me, huh, Ellie? I fucking love it. Makes my cock so goddamn hard knowing that's for me," he says, adjusting himself in his jeans.

"Yes, it's all for you. Please touch me, Ace." I move my hips forward, hinting at what I need, my voice shaky with desire and the asshole laughs before finally giving me what I want.

"Fuck. You taste like *more,*" he says, after he's licked me from bottom to top, over and over, teasing my sensitive skin with his coarse hair as it moves from my inner thighs back to my pussy for the *more* that he mentioned. "Could eat you all day long." Ace moves his mouth to suck on my pulsing clit. Swirling his tongue over the sensitive bud, he inserts his tongue into me, giving me tiny ministrations over and over again, driving me crazy. I'm a withering mess under his onslaught. My breathing is heavy and my body takes on a floating feeling as he inserts first one finger, then another, into play and I know I'm not going to last.

"Please, Ace. I want you inside me, want your cock, I can't, I'm not—"

"Easy, baby, I've got what you need." But instead of slipping inside me, giving us both what we've been waiting for, he…*pauses*? And removes his hand completely.

"No. Now. Now. Put it in," I try to reach for his hand.

"Soon." He runs his finger along my thigh, trying to bring me back down.

"Are you trying to kill me? Please, I want you to come inside me."

"Oh, I plan on it. With nothing between us, Ellie. Ever."

"Oh fuck, that's hot. Let's do that. Let's do that right now. Please," I groan, frustrated. The fact that I'm begging isn't lost on me, either.

Moving my hand to Ace's pant button, my mission to rid him of them as he hovers above me, he swats my fingers playfully away, clearly entertained with his little game.

"Take your pants off! Why are you wearing pants at a time like this?" I shout, frustrated.

Jerking out of my hold, he moves to stand at the foot of the bed. Grinning, the bastard finally makes a show of removing his jeans and black boxers.

A-fucking-men! His magnificent cock seems to be as excited as I am as it bobs up and down for joy, its girth making my mouth salivate. I notice a pulsing vein and it soon becomes my future target. It's a perfect cock, really, and I know it's ready for my touch. "I want you in my mouth," I tell him, while staring at his cock in awe.

"Jesus, Ellie. Make up your mind."

"Well, I do," I shrug.

"Eyes up here, Ellie," he teases, and I look up. "Before I give us what we both want, I need to know something," he says, moving his hand up and down his huge, hard shaft, and I'm so jealous. I want it to be my hand.

"Anything, I'll tell you anything." I spring up on the bed in front of him trying to reach for him. Well…*his cock*. I groan in frustration when he dekes around me, pushing me back onto the bed with his weight as he covers my naked body with his own.

"Tell me first, before I give you my cock," Ace says, starting to nudge his smooth tip between my lips, teasing me with how good I know he'll feel once he's inside me. "Who were you thinking of when you told me all those naughty stories? When you'd make up the scenes, Ellie? Who did you imagine doing them with?" Ace asks again, reaching around with one hand to dig his fingers into the cheek of my ass, while lowering his head to rest on my chest. Waiting. Challenging.

"Please, Ace," I plead, knowing he already knows the answer.

"I want to hear it from your lips, E. Tell me," he grunts, hovering over me now, his cock sinking in a little more, where I want it most. "Fuuuck. You're so tight. I want to be all the way in, baby. All it takes is one simple answer. Come on, I know you wanna tell me," he teases, taking my nipple between his teeth, his hard length shifting in an inch more.

"You." It's barely audible.

"Thank Christ. I thought I was going to have to spank that pussy to get it out of you. That's what I needed to hear, baby." He breathes into my neck as he finally thrusts all the way inside me, my pussy immediately clamping down around him, hugging him like a long-lost relative. "You feel perfect." He kisses my neck, then goes down to my nipples, where he sucks on each one again, causing me to moan with pleasure.

"Ahhh. God," is all I can mutter as I adjust to him. He's filling me in the most perfect way. He feels incredible, as he moves deeper and deeper inside me, his cock hitting every sweet spot along the way. He spreads my legs wide, and pulls my ankles up near his ears, bringing him in deeper. My knee protests but I ignore it.

"Say it again, Ellie. Please," he begs, the drag and pull of his hard cock making it hard to focus, but I give him what he wants.

"You, Ace. Only and always you," I say, pulling his face to mine, searing his lips to mine.

"Thank you, E." He kisses my nose before flipping us. "Ride my cock. I want to see you take my cock in and out of that gorgeous body while I watch," he growls. Moving his hands to my ass, he stares intensely while I lower myself onto his erection. Once settled, I begin rocking my hips, making small circles, as I slip his cock in and out of my body. He's moaning and muttering words of encouragement, telling me how good I feel. His hands land on my ass cheeks once again, trying to quicken the pace, moving me up and down, mimicking my own moves.

"I'm fucking close. I'm going to come soon, Ellie," he says, eyes vigilant on where we're connected. "Look how perfectly we fit. You feel incredible, Ellie. I could stay like this with you forever, seeing my cock slipping in and out of your warmth. Fuck, my cock looks good with you coated all over it."

I bite my lip and quicken the pace, bottoming myself out over and over again while I ride his cock. Ace's hand makes its way between us to my clit, the friction of his fingers rubbing matching the pulsing rhythm of my pussy and I splinter above him. Colours dance behind my eyes like a kaleidoscope dream, and Ace pulls me down into him as tremors wrack us, and he shoots his release into my welcoming body.

Holding me tight to his chest, he whispers promises and words of adoration that are music to my ears. After a few beats, he pats my bum.

"That was hot. Give me ten minutes and we can role-play that it's my birthday," Ace says, before adding: "Oh, and about that gold Leia bikini..."

Chapter 53

Ellie

"PINEWOOD STUDIOS, THIS is Ellie," I say into the phone in my office, which is located on the third floor of Toronto's most prestigious film studio.

I'm one of three tenant service managers here, and I love it. I enjoy getting to tour the studio with potential clients, talking up how fantastic everything we have to offer is. Best of all, I love working to convince bigwigs to film here in Toronto, to use one of our many stages, including—our *pièce de résistance*—the Mega Stage, a 46,000 square foot soundproof stage, a rarity today.

I was actually headhunted by the CEO himself, Frank Strata, after he read the excerpts from my thesis in *The Canadian Journal of Film Studies*. I started working here a few weeks after graduation. Frank has also taken me under his wing, he's helping me to make the right connections, and doors are opening that will surely help me in my end game. There is huge potential to grow here at Pinewood, and I'm excited to see where this path will take me.

I've also been working on writing the screenplay for Cherry's memoir—"Call Me: My Life as a Phone Sex Superhero," a screenplay Frank has offered to help me shop around once it's complete. So be sure to keep an eye out, it just might be coming to a big screen near you.

"Well, has our naughty professor heard yet?" I smile at Courtney's third call, along with the twenty or so text messages this morning.

"No, Court. Not yet, it's only ten in the morning."

"Well, come on, I mean the Oscars announce their shit at like six a.m. What, is TIFF too fancy to get up early?"

"I think those pregnancy hormones are eating up your patience," I laugh. Not long after Jax and Courtney returned from their weekend getaway celebration, they discovered she was pregnant. At almost six months along, she's sporting a pretty cute bump, and I'm beyond excited to be an auntie. Although it wasn't planned, everyone is thrilled, including both sets of parents. "How is our little 'shroomie, anyway?"

"Huge. I swear they've made a mistake and it's twins. But Jax says I'm glowing and perfect, so as long as he keeps boinking me, I'll be happy, even if two pop out."

"TMI, Court. TMI."

"Whatever. Anyway when will Ace hear? I'm seriously wearing a hole in my carpet waiting for the news."

"I know, me too. I think he's shut off his phone. I've texted him too much. I keep willing them to call him, but, of course, my voodoo is lacking."

"Ugh. Okay, well, text me as soon as you hear. I have to pee again."

"You know I will. Just like I've promised the last million phone calls," I laugh.

"Blah, blah, sorry I care," she huffs, before hanging up.

After another few hours of returning calls, replying to emails, and checking my cell phone non-stop, I decide it's time to grab some lunch. I'm just about to call Piper, my coworker, to see if she's ready to go, when my cell rings.

Fumbling for it on my desk, I answer on the third ring.

"Ace, oh my God. It's you, *finally!!* Tell me you've heard," I greet my sexy man.

"Yeah, it's me, sweetheart." My heart skips a beat hearing his deep chuckle, a sound I've come to love. "I've got some news, E. You'd better sit down."

Stepping back, I pull up my leather roller chair and sit. Taking a deep breath, I close my eyes, my hands trembling and my heart beating at a jackhammer's pace.

"Okay, lay it on me." I open my eyes and cross everything: legs, fingers, arms—and even my eyes—for good measure.

"We're in, baby. I made it!" Ace shouts excitedly through the phone, and instantly I feel myself welling up. After all of his hard work and dedication, Ace Ryan's documentary *Sex for Sale* has been selected and will be presented at The Toronto International Film Festival this September.

"Congratulations! I knew you'd do it. Oh, Ace, I'm so proud of you," I sniffle.

"Don't cry, Ellie."

"I know, I'm just so happy for you. For TIFF and for everything this film has done already. Shutting down two seedy operations, getting local MP's to consider new legislation. I'm just…wow, I'm so proud of you. And I love you so much, *Doctor* Ryan. You're an amazing man."

"I love getting to share this with you, E. I'm glad I make you proud. I can't wait to take you shopping to celebrate…maybe live out that change room scene while you dress shop?" he utters, his voice throaty and laced with promise.

"But first, I'm taking you out tonight, mister. We're going to celebrate in style."

Ace's deep laugh meets my ears. "Nice non-committal answer, Ellie. But I know you. You're probably thinking about how hot it will be, too. Maybe to tide us over until our shopping adventure, we could add a little Jake and Chanel into the celebratory mix tonight? Maybe we can talk on our cell phones again?" he asks, his voice low and sexy. He's such a bugger.

Ever since the whole Chanel/Jake thing came to light, Ace has enjoyed pretending on several occasions that Jake can still access Miss Chanel69 when the mood should strike. The man is lucky I love him.

Since Courtney has moved in with Jax, I took over the apartment from her parents, deciding it was a good investment, and they sold it to me for a steal. Ace and I bounce back and forth between his place and mine. On one of the nights where we couldn't swing staying together, Ace had dropped me off at my apartment following our date. I was lying in bed reading when my cell phone started vibrating on my nightstand. Seeing it was Ace calling, I picked up immediately, asking if everything was okay. But rather than hearing Ace's voice, I heard Jake's familiar gruff voice and laughed. Well, until I heard the things Jake was telling me. Needless to say I busted out Chanel69 and gave it back as good as I was getting it. I swear, we've had some of the hottest phone sex since we've started allowing Jake and Chanel to visit and make appearances from time to time.

"If you're a gentleman tonight, Doctor Ryan, I'm sure I can convince Chanel to come out and play."

"I love you, Ellie, but quit calling me 'Doctor'. Pick you up at seven? I'm almost done here. Tell me again why I agreed to teach for the Summer Institute?" he moans about his agreeing to teach two summer film courses being offered at U of T. While he complains, the perfect way to kick off our celebratory evening pops into my head. *Ace is going to love it.*

"Because you're an amazing teacher, *Doctor* Ryan." I say, knowing it drives him crazy.

"E!"

"See you later. Love you."

“Love you too. Can’t wait to see you.”

“Me too, my big shot TIFF star.” With that I hang up, as I hear him begin to growl at my comment.

Looking at my watch, I notice that I’ve got just enough time to stop at the store for a few props. Logging into the computer, I book myself off using some lieu time and make my way out of the office for an early weekend.

Chapter 54

Ace

STILL REELING FROM the news that my documentary will be seen by thousands, the knock at my office door surprises me. It's then I realize that it's almost five-thirty p.m., and the last of the people who were here in the department with me today left over an hour ago. Assuming it's Reg, the custodian, I open the door. "Sorry, Reg, I'm almo—" I say, but instead of seeing Reg, my eyes land on Ellie.

In a trench coat, in August?

"Oh, thank goodness you're here, Coach Ryan. It's my paper for gym glass. I can't remember all the food groups," she says, rushing past me, that fruit-and-candy smell that is all her tickles my nose as it wafts through the air behind her.

Shutting the door, I turn to offer her a smile and ask what the hell she's talking about, but seeing her, my smile drops immediately, and a grin full of white-hot lust takes its place.

"Jesus, Ellie."

She's taken off the coat. A simple cheerleader uniform is all that registers. Well, that and a whole bunch of exposed Ellie skin, as it's clearly a few sizes too small. *Fuck me!*

"Oh, Coach Ryan, please say you'll help me?" she winks, before jumping up and down, her spectacular tits bouncing along for the ride. Her tiny cheerleader top rides up, exposing what I know to be the softest skin I've ever had the pleasure of getting to know. I can't look away. All I can do is nod, lick my lips, and smile.

"Well, will you help me, Coach? Pleeease?" Ellie whispers over her shoulder, a satisfied smirk tugging at the corner of her sexy mouth when she catches me ogling her exposed ass while she reaches for something on my desk in her barely-there skirt. "Oh, see? You've got what I need, right here." She pulls a pamphlet off my blotter, turns back towards me, and sits on top of my desk. Meeting my heated stare with her own, Ellie scoots back, separates her legs, and places her feet up on both sides of the desk, creating a view that is unparalleled: her open for my taking.

"I'm one lucky son-of-a-bitch. Jesus, E. Look at you, all pretty and pink," I say, moving closer, but not before rushing back to lock the door.

"Oh, I sure hope you're looking, I like when I catch you looking at me, Coach Ryan. Always have, always will," she giggles over the pamphlet, before going back to pretending she's reading it. "See? Everything I needed is right here." Moving closer, I take the paper from her hands and toss it on the floor behind me.

"Everything you need is right *here,*" I say, taking her hand in mine and placing our joined hands on my heart. "My love," I whisper over her lips while sliding her other hand down to my raging hard-on. "This right here, the pleasure I'll always give to you."

She cocks her head to the side, a lazy smile breaking out under my touch—at my words.

"You and those words of yours. But it's sexy-time now. You can share your sweet thoughts after you play with me." She squeezes my cock. "My, Coach Ryan, what a big, hard dick you have for me. Are you going to fuck me with that whopping cock of yours while I'm perched on your desk? 'Cause if not, I'm going to have to take matters into my own hands." She licks her lips, before removing her palm from my chest and sliding it under her panties. My eyes trail the movement as her hand feels its way around my favourite spot in the world.

"Let me taste you, my bad girl." I lean in, sighing near her ear. Watching her is driving me wild with lust and desire.

Ellie tugs at the back of my head, the move forcing me to shift my focus back onto her face, and my eyes collide with her mischievous-looking ones, curious to see what she's up to. I attempt to open my mouth, when suddenly she removes her hand from her folds, takes her finger and traces my bottom lip with her juices, immediately shutting me up. Growling at the bold move, my tongue immediately follows the trail.

"You always taste so good, that perfect balance of sweet and salty. I hunger for you. More," I groan, before stepping even closer between her legs, my own fingers taking over massaging her soaked pussy. "You're fucking hot. Always so ready for me. How about you lift that shirt up so I can suck on those pretty tits, and see all of you?"

"Fuuck, yes," she mews, and I pick up the pace, my fingers fucking her while my mouth pulls at her taut nipples. Ellie's hands find my belt and within seconds, my cock is in her grip. She's stroking me with determination, matching the rhythm my fingers make on her sweet spot. Our breaths hitching, I continue to fuck her with three fingers, while she jacks me off.

"Fuck, I need to be inside you."

I spread her legs apart a bit farther before lifting both of her arms and wrapping them around my neck. Instantly, she pulls me in close, and kisses me. "I love you, Ace. So very much."

"God, I adore and love you, E. But right now, I'm going out of my goddamn mind. You here like this, this has been one of my biggest fantasies, thank you. Now I need you to hold on, Ellie. I'm about to fuck the hell out of you, my naughty girl."

Looking up at me from under her long eyelashes, her beautiful golden-brown eyes meet mine, reflecting back all the love I feel for her.

Grinning, she kisses me softly before grabbing my cock and lining it up to her welcoming entrance. "It's about time you fucked me in this office, Coach Ryan. Now give it to me hard. You aren't the only one with fantasies."

Sliding into Ellie's warmth is almost my undoing. Her pussy contracts as I slip in deeper and deeper, taking her to the hilt. My cock twitches as her juices cover me, her sweet heat welcoming me back again, welcoming me home as she accommodates my size, the feel of her walls stretching is enough to make me shoot my load alone. "You feel so fucking good, E," I huff, moving my hips forward and back again, her pussy milking my dick with each movement. Looking down, seeing her open on my desk, giving me this, is fucking with my head. I'm not going to last. She's soaked, and my cock is glistening with her wetness, the sight giving me a feral need to fuck her senseless.

Arching her back, Ellie moves her arms behind her to support my increased pace. She's panting and I revel in the feeling of her breath as it reaches my chest. Her spectacular tits bounce with every thrust and move I make. The friction of her walls hugging my hard shaft over and over is going to be the death of me. Leaning in closer, I rub her nipples with my chest, the skin-to-skin connection eliciting a deep moan from both of us. *Christ, she feels like heaven.*

"Oh shit, Ace, that feels so good," Ellie cries out. Shifting my head down, I take first one nipple then the other into my mouth, sucking on and swirling my tongue around each hard tip, offering tiny nips of pain to match the pleasure as I suck on each tit. My hands sliding up around her shoulders, I look into her eyes, channeling my inner Jake, remembering a scene from when Ellie first told me this scenario, the way I need this fantasy to end.

"I want you to suck my huge cock while I sit in my chair pulling your hair, Ellie. Would you like that?"

Looking at me, a twinkle of recognition obvious in her eyes, my little vixen plays right back: "Do you want me to suck you dry, Coach? Do you want to feel my wet mouth all over that big cock?" she asks, popping the 'k' sound. She pushes against my chest, and I step away, hating the loss of her tight cunt.

"Fuck, yes. I need your mouth," I grit, as she moves to her knees in the middle of my office, her hands going straight for my ass as she slips me into her hot mouth. Pulling me out, she looks up at me while she kisses around my tip, running her tongue in a circular motion, lapping up her juices and mine. "My cock looks good in your mouth, Ellie. Yeah, fuck, take it all."

I breath out as she slides her teeth ever so gently along the outside of my cock, stopping to lap her tongue over her favourite vein, the one that pulses only for her. She takes me all the way down, slipping me in and out, gripping my cock in her hand to work in tandem with her mouth. With a solid rhythm in place, Ellie moves her other hand between my legs and starts playing with my balls. Within seconds, my spine is tingling and I'm ready to combust, but the need to be inside Ellie has me moving her back up to my desk once again.

"Sit up on the desk, Ms. Hughes," I order and she complies instantly, leaning back on the desk. "I can't finish like that, I miss this tight pussy too much, want it to pump me dry," I say, positioning myself in front of Ellie and sliding my cock back where it belongs.

"Yes, oh God yes! I want that. Give it to me, Ace. Fuck me hard," she pleads, and I comply with pleasure. I fuck us both into oblivion.

Once sated and back down to planet Earth again, I decide it's time to ask Ellie one of the questions I've been wanting to know for some time now.

"E, baby. Can you look at me?" I ask, chuckling at seeing her face still smashed into my chest.

"Mmm hmm." She looks at me through-satisfied eyes, a lazy smile curling up the corners her lips.

"Move in with me?" I ask. "I need you with me all the time. I think it would be pretty kick-ass. Let me be the Han to your Leia, and love you with all my *Force*. Allow me to be The Crazy 88 and Gogo Yubari to your O-Ren Ishii, and let me have your back, fight for you, and be by your side, always." I kiss her forehead, and she laughs while a lone tear escapes.

"Ace, that was incredibly corny, but wonderfully kick-ass at the same time. Are you sure?" She looks down, uncertainty lacing her voice.

"Never been more." I run my finger along her cheek. "I'm madly in love with you, Ellie Raine Hughes. You are totally kick-ass. And together, we are the most kick-ass."

"Well, when you put it like that, I agree. We really are a kick-ass team. Yes. Yes, I'd love to. Oh my God, Ace!" She hugs me tight. "This is going to be amazing."

"I love you." I kiss her nose.

"To quote my girl, Leia: 'I know'." She bursts out laughing. "I love you too, Ace. So very much.

"Thank you for giving me you, Ellie. You'll always have all of me."

"Aww, see? You really do have a kick-ass way with words, when you want," she says, laughing again, and my chest swells, knowing that this girl is mine.

"*Totally* kick-ass," I say.

One "yes" down, and one to go.

Chanel was my fantasy, but Ellie's my reality.

My leading lady.

My trifecta.

The End

(Roll credits).

Acknowledgements

I have the best people in my life. There is no way I could do this without any of you. I'm thanking in ABC order, because that's the way I roll, and every one of you is important. Blessed, I am, yes. To the following people: love you all!

Amanda—Lobby, I love you. Thank you for being you with this book. Ace needed you to advocate for him. I could not have done this one without you. Keep pushing me, always. Your feedback is so valuable, and the time you give my stories is always appreciated more than I can express.

Cassia—Thank you for being such a great friend and support, I love you, lady. Thank you again for proofreading, you always find something! LOL

Dad—You're simply awesome. Thank you for always being so proud and supportive of me, your daughter who writes smut. Just remember you CANNOT read these books.

Deanna—Again, thank you for the feedback and for pushing me with this one. I love you hard, lady!

Doris—Thank you again for reading over my stories. Your keen eye is so very much appreciated. I hope you'll continue to stick with me!

Jade—Gah!!! Thank you for allowing me to manipulate you into being a beta reader! Your feedback was perfect and so bang on. I loved getting to pick your brain. Thank you for your honesty, and best of all your friendship. I cherish it. xoxo

Jen (ESM)—Here we sit editing book #4, and I'm still in awe of you. You push, but give a little too, when I need to test the Panda's boundaries. I love doing this with you, and could not do it without you. Thank you for being the best editor, the most patient Panda, and above all my ESM. I love you, and cannot wait to continue this journey right alongside you.

Jenny—Thank you for being supportive and such an amazing friend. I love you.

JJ—Thank you for taking the time and being such a great beta reader. I appreciate all the support and love you've given me.

Karl & Max—My amazing hubby and son, there is no way I could so this without you. All I can say is thank you for being everything that you already are, and supporting me on this crazy adventure. You two are my most favourite people of life and I love you both so much, even when I might ignore you a little. Karl, you're my ultimate partner-in-crime, and I cannot do this without you by my side. You really are my superhero, and you both are my world.

Kymmie—Again my friend, you ground me and keep me calm. Thank you for not letting me get inside my own head for too long. I value our friendship and your opinion so much. Ace thanks you for not letting him get away with some girlie behaviour early on. LOL xo

Mom—I owe you so much. I can't seem to find the right words this time. Thank you seems too little, but you need to know how lucky I am to have you in my corner rooting for me, reading and rereading, looking for mistakes, giving me words of encouragement, and—best of all—telling me how proud you are of me. I love doing this with you, Mom, and I totally could not do it without you. I love you.

Laurie—Thank you for always being so excited to read, over and over again. Thank you for being my kind of crazy and helping to work the shit out that gets caught in my head. I could not do this without you!

Lissy—Thank you for being such a wonderful friend and support. I simply adore you, my Twinnie!

Lia—Thank you, once again, for being an amazing beta reader and friend. I'm so thankful for your support and feedback. Your excitement for this one made me excited! Xox

Paige—I really don't have sufficient words to describe how important you are to this process. Your willingness to hear me out and offer advice is greatly appreciated. You are amazing and I cannot thank you enough for giving me such valuable feedback. I adore you!

Radha—My Brownie, thank you for always encouraging me and making sure I keep going. This is still all your fault!

River—Thank you for listening, and offering me your advice and opinions. I value getting to work through this crazy with your help. I love you hard.

Toni—Thank you for always finding the silly mistakes that most would miss, thank you for loving Ellie and Ace, but, most of all, thank you for being such a great friend. You are the best whore I know! x

Gilly's Gems—Again, I cannot thank you guys enough. I continue to be so lucky to have you all by my side. Your support and eye candy make this the most fun. I adore each of you and love hanging out with you in our little group. Your friendship means the world. Please know I am eternally grateful, and I hope to meet you all in person one day. Xox

Ashley at Book Cover by Ashbee Designs—OMG! This cover was all you and I love it! You are amazing! Thank you for being so awesome to work with. You always know exactly what I will love. I appreciate the time and patience you have with me. I look forward to many more covers together.

Between the Sheets Promotions—Thank you again for arranging an amazing blog tour, you ladies are incredible to work with.

Thank you to all the amazing bloggers for all you do. I could not do this without your support, and I appreciate you taking a chance on me. If ever I can help you in return, please contact me. Once again, you continue to make this adventure even better.

About the Author

I'm a wife, mother, and a crazy Canadian, living in Ontario with the loves of my life—my amazing hubby and sweetest little boy. I'm admittedly addicted to: my friends, red wine, and laughter. Also, I'm a devoted lover of alpha males and hot sex, all coupled with the perfect side of angst topped off with an epic happily ever after.

Follow Me Here

Website:

authorgillianjones.wordpress.com

Facebook Author Page:

facebook.com/pages/Gillian-Jones-Author/1493072067635651

Facebook:

facebook.com/gillian.jonesauthor

Twitter:

twitter.com/gillianJ_author

Goodreads:

goodreads.com/author/show/7144405.Gillian_Jones

Join my group Gilly's Gems:

facebook.com/groups/617265411707215/

We talk books, eye candy, and everything in between.

Books by Gillian Jones

My Mind's Eye
(Pub Fiction Book 1)

On The Rocks
(Pub Fiction Book 2)

One Last Shot
(Pub Fiction Book 3)

Made in the USA
Charleston, SC
23 September 2016